You'll Never Know. . .

You'll Never Know. . .

Jeanne Whitmee

ROBERT HALE · LONDON

© Jeanne Whitmee 2008
First published in Great Britain 2008

ISBN 978-0-7090-8587-4

Robert Hale Limited
Clerkenwell House
Clerkenwell Green
London EC1R 0HT

www.halebooks.com

2 4 6 8 10 9 7 5 3 1

Typeset in 10½/13pt Palatino
by Derek Doyle & Associates, Shaw Heath
Printed and bound in Great Britain
by Biddles Limited, King's Lynn

CHAPTER ONE

HAZEL
September 1943

The train journey from York to Valemouth seemed interminable. Hazel had been travelling since early morning and had dozed on and off ever since Euston. The sandwiches she had packed seemed like a half forgotten memory and hunger and fatigue made her light headed. Her half-awake dreams were punctuated by the remorseless clatter and rhythm of the train. *Helluvva mess – helluvva mess* they seemed to mock over and over. At last she opened her eyes and straightened her back, forcing herself awake as she stared out of the window into the gathering dusk. It was no use. The past refused to go away. She knew it would go with her no matter how far she travelled. A hell of a mess it certainly was, she told herself. How could she have made such a complete hash of her life?

She had been just twenty-one when she got her first teaching post at Grant Street Elementary School in the little Yorkshire town of Mekeley Moor. Fresh out of college she felt she had the world at her feet. Was that really only three and a half years ago? It seemed a lifetime away. The war had been in its early and most critical months and like so many 'safe towns' Mekeley Moor was overflowing with evacuees, mainly from the industrial northern towns. In her youthful naïvety Hazel had believed the people who said it would all be over in a few months. Arrival at Mekeley Moor soon made her see the reality of the situation.

The first weeks were frantically busy. Thrown into the deep end

5

with a class of twice the normal size, she rose to the challenge with trepidation. But in spite of sharing a classroom with another class, children three to a desk, she threw herself into her work and once she had got used to the mixed northern accents and the children had accustomed themselves to her southern one, she built up a good rapport with them. She got along well with her colleagues and she liked the kindly northern folk, admiring the way they opened their homes and their hearts to the evacuated children as well as to her.

Apart from the sudden increase in the population the war hardly touched Mekeley Moor. Life went on much as always with a market twice a week and a cattle market on Saturdays. After a few months a lot of the evacuees were taken home again and life at school became easier and less crowded. Hazel had managed to rent a tiny cottage on the outskirts of the town. It was two and a half miles from the school but she bought a bicycle and happily pedalled her way to and from work each day.

The spring of 1940 was sunny and pleasantly warm. The cycle ride into town each day was a pleasure – until the afternoon when the chain snapped and she found herself standing outside in the road with the unwelcome prospect of pushing her bike the two and a half miles home. She had stayed on after school to prepare a lesson for the following day, so all of her colleagues had left some time ago. Hazel sighed resignedly and prepared for the long trek home. She'd been walking for five minutes or so when a car drew up alongside her.

'Are you in trouble – is it a puncture?'

She looked round; surprised to see that Gerald Mayfield, the headmaster was speaking to her through the window of his smart little Austin car.

'Worse than that, I'm afraid,' she said. 'The chain's broken. I'll have to take it to a garage or somewhere.'

'Jim Smith at the pub does cycle repairs,' he told her. 'Just over there, look. I daresay he'd have it ready for you tomorrow.'

'Really? Thanks. I'll go and ask.'

To Hazel's relief Jim, the elderly potman at the Fox and Grapes was happy to mend her cycle and promised to have it ready for her the following afternoon. When she came back out into the sunshine again she was surprised to see that Gerald Mayfield was still there, waiting at the kerb in his car.

'OK?' he asked.

She nodded. 'Yes. He says he'll have it ready for me for tomorrow.'

'That's good. Hop in.' He leaned across and opened the passenger side door. 'I'll run you home. Too far to walk all the way in the heat.'

'Oh, I couldn't . . .'

He laughed. 'Of course you could. I go your way anyway, so you might as well.'

Hazel felt slightly uncomfortable, sitting beside the headmaster she had barely spoken to since her interview. He was a good looking man whom she guessed to be in his late thirties. He was over six feet tall with smooth dark hair and brown eyes. He was always smartly dressed and well groomed but for some reason was regarded by the children with apprehension. *Maybe it's his size,* Hazel speculated as they drove. *Or perhaps his deep voice.* Truth to tell she was slightly in awe of him herself. After a few minutes he turned to look at her, one eyebrow slightly raised.

'All right?'

'Yes – fine. Thanks for the lift.'

He nodded. 'Just tell me where you want me to drop you. I'd better pick you up in the morning too.'

'Oh no!' She blushed and shook her head vigorously. 'I mean, it's all right, I'll be fine. The walk will do me good.'

It was the following lunchtime when he stopped her in the corridor at school.

'Did you get your bicycle back?'

'I'm picking it up after school. Thanks for telling me where to take it.'

He smiled and she noticed that the rather forbidding dark eyes were actually capable of sparkling. 'It occurred to me last night that we – you and I, I mean, haven't really had a chance to talk since you joined us. What with the influx of evacuees – trying to shoehorn everyone in and reorganize there hasn't been a chance.'

To her dismay she felt herself colour. 'No – I suppose not.'

'Have you eaten?'

'I – yes. I brought sandwiches.'

'Come into my office and I'll make you a cup of coffee.'

Unable to think of an excuse not to go Hazel swallowed hard and followed him into his office. As well as a desk there was an armchair and pleasant chintz curtains at the window which over-looked the playground. The place had a woman's touch about it. Hazel had heard from the other teachers that Gerald Mayfield's wife had died six years ago, giving birth to their only child, a still-born baby girl. She had wondered at the time why he had never remarried and assumed he was too grief-stricken. On a small table in one corner there was an electric kettle. He switched it on and glanced at her.

'Milk and sugar?'

'Thanks.'

'Do sit down.' He indicated the armchair but Hazel took the hard chair opposite his desk. When he noticed he laughed. 'It's all right. I'm not going to interrogate you – Hazel, isn't it?' She nodded. 'It's what I said, just an informal chat. I like to get to know my staff properly and we haven't had the chance, what with one thing and another.'

Hazel stayed where she was on her hard chair beside the desk. Somehow the idea of lounging in an armchair in the head's office felt ill-mannered and disrespectful, but over the coffee she found Gerald Mayfield easy to talk to and she gradually felt herself begin-ning to relax. He asked about her family and her education, expressing concern when she told him that her parents had died in a rail crash when she was six and that her grandmother had brought her up. He was interested in her convent school education and the south coast town where she had grown up.

'Valemouth, eh?' He leaned back on his chair. 'I remember going there for a holiday with my parents once when I was a boy. There's a lovely sandy beach there.'

She nodded. 'There was. It's all covered in beach defences now, I'm afraid. Concrete tank traps and barbed wire entanglements.'

He sighed. 'How sad. A whole generation of children will grow up not knowing the delights of paddling in the sea and making sandcastles.'

Her eyes widened. 'Oh, but surely the war will be over before long?'

He gave her a wry smile. 'If only I could share your optimism.

They'll be calling up my age group soon, too. My days are numbered her at Mekeley Moor.'

'Really? Oh dear.'

'You sound as though you'll miss me.' He laughed, his eyes sparkling again as he saw her blush. 'I expect they'll bring some old greybeard out of retirement to take my place. You'll be able to wind him round your little finger.'

'Oh! I don't think so.'

He leaned forward towards her. 'You're a very serious young lady, aren't you? What do you like to do in your leisure time?'

'Well – I like music and art. I like to dabble with painting – though I'm not very good,' she added hastily. 'And I like to walk – 'specially around this glorious countryside.'

'Right. So you don't sit in that cottage of yours embroidering doilies and listening to the wireless?'

She bridled. 'Not at all!'

'Good.' He stood up and she got the distinct impression that it was time for her to leave. As he opened the door for her he said casually, 'Come walking with me next Sunday if you like. I'm planning to go across to Fountains Abbey.'

Taken aback, she stared at him, her mouth slightly open. He laughed.

'Oh dear. Is it such a terrifying prospect?'

'No! It's very kind of you. It's just—'

'You need only say no if you'd rather not. I thought you might enjoy it. I'm not planning to walk all the way. I'll take the car as far as Knaresborough and walk the rest.'

As she cycled home that afternoon she could hardly believe that she'd actually agreed to accompany her headmaster on a walking trip next Sunday. That kind of thing just doesn't happen, she told herself. Then she remembered that he'd said he would soon be called up. People did all sorts of things in wartime that they'd never dream of doing normally. All the same, she decided not to mention it to any of her colleagues. She was a new girl, after all, and they might think her too forward.

The Sunday walking trips soon became a regular thing. Hazel found Gerald Mayfield was quite a different person when they were together at weekends. He had a fund of knowledge about the Yorkshire Dales and took her to places she would never have found on her own. Right through summer they spent their Sundays together. Hazel gradually grew fond of the man whom she came to think of as an older brother. He was fun to be with. He was kind and considerate and he made her laugh. He taught her things about the countryside and nature she had never known before. Then, one Sunday as he delivered her back to the cottage, he broke the dreaded news that his call-up papers had arrived.

'I'm to get a commission in the Ordnance Corps,' he said. 'I'll be Captain G.E. Mayfield. How does that sound?'

She shook her head. 'Horrible.'

He smiled wryly. 'Well, it's no surprise. We knew it was coming, didn't we?'

'I kept on hoping the war might be over before it could happen.'

'Oh, Hazel, you can't be that naïve. This year has been disastrous. We suffered that humiliating defeat at Dunkirk; Hitler marched into Paris, Mussolini has thrown in his lot with Germany – all in the month of June! And there's still no sign of America helping us out. Face it, Hazel, we're in the soup.'

'When do you have to go?' she asked in a small voice.

'A week on Monday.'

She gasped. 'That soon?'

'That soon, I'm afraid.'

'Who's going to take over?'

'Gladys Brompton is the most senior teacher at Grant Street. She'll stand in until a replacement can be found,' he told her.

Suddenly the enormous lump in her throat erupted into tears. 'Oh – oh, *Gerald*!'

'Hey! Come on.' He put his arms round her. 'Can't have this. You can write to me if you like – send me all the news.'

'Of course I will. But I'm going to miss you so much. I'll miss our walks.' She hid her face against his shoulder.

'I'm not taking the Yorkshire Moors with me,' he joked. 'You can still go walking.'

'You – know what I mean.' She hiccuped. 'It – it won't be the same without you.'

'Do you really mean that?' Suddenly and without any warning

his lips were on hers and he was kissing her with a passion and intensity that shocked her. 'Oh, Hazel, my little Hazel, I'll miss you too,' he whispered against her cheek. 'More than you can possibly guess.'

She raised her face to look up at him and he kissed her again. 'I love you,' he said raggedly. 'But of course you know that, don't you? Women always know. I daresay you knew it before I did.'

She opened her mouth to deny it but before she could utter a word his lips covered hers again. Deep inside she was a mass of confusion. She had absolutely no idea that he felt this way. She was fond of him, of course, but he was so much older. And love! What was love? She had never loved anyone except her grandmother and that was entirely different. Perhaps what she felt for Gerald was love – grown-up love. She had nothing to compare it with.

He was looking down at her. 'You love me too, don't you?' he said. 'Please say that you do.' He drew her close – so close that she could feel the drumming of his heart. 'Oh Hazel, do you have any idea how much I want you.'

Her own heart began to beat faster but when she felt his fingers at the buttons of her blouse she drew back instinctively. He stopped at once. 'Darling, I'm sorry.'

She shook her head. 'No. I don't – I'm not—'

'I don't mean to frighten you. I wouldn't dream of rushing you. It's just that there's so little time.' He took her face between his hands. 'If you want me to go away, just say. I'll go at once.'

'No, no.' She shook her head. 'You'll be gone all too soon. It's unexpected – so . . .'

For a long moment he looked at her until something inside her melted at the pleading look in his eyes. Reaching up she drew his head down to hers and lifting his hand she laid it against her breast. She heard him catch his breath sharply.

'Hazel. Oh, Hazel, my darling.'

Her heart was pounding now, so hard that she thought she might faint. 'I've never . . .' she began. 'I don't think . . .'

'I know. I won't hurt you,' he whispered. 'I promise nothing will happen . . .'

'I know. I know.'

Upstairs in the little bedroom under the eaves he made love to her with as much restraint as he could. Afterwards he fell into a dead sleep whilst she lay wide awake, listening to the summer-evening sounds coming in at the open window. Everything seemed enhanced and slightly surreal, like a dream; insects buzzing gently in the ivy growing round the dormer, birds rustling in the thatch; the babbling of water running over the stones in the nearby beck. The small square of sky she could see framed by the window seemed impossibly blue.

She tried to examine her feelings. She had allowed – no, *encouraged* a man to make love to her; something she had been brought up to believe was wrong outside of marriage, yet she didn't feel wicked or sinful. Gerald had wanted her so much and he would be going away soon – going away to God alone knew what? By the end of the war who knew what would have happened or where either of them would be? Surely it could not be wrong to give him some small comfort? But had she wanted him as much as he had wanted her? She supposed she must have done. Otherwise she would not have let it happen. Had she enjoyed it? She bit her lip, hoping he hadn't noticed her sigh of relief when it was over. How could something called making love be so excruciatingly uncomfortable?

When Gerald wakened he talked. It was as though a floodgate had been opened. He told Hazel about his wife; how they had been married for only a year and a half and how devastated he had been at the heartbreaking tragedy of her death along with that of his baby daughter. Since it happened he hadn't looked at another woman or even thought of forming a new relationship. He'd been unable to imagine that he ever would, until Hazel had come to Mekeley Moor. He told her that for him it had been love at first sight. His first glimpse of her had hit him like a lightning strike and he had known in that moment that he wanted to be with her for always. He took her hand and raised it to his lips, looking into her eyes.

'If these were ordinary times I'd wait,' he said. 'Go through the courtship process in the customary way. But we have only a few days and I can't leave anything to chance. We'll get married, Hazel. I'll get a special licence on my first leave. Until then we're engaged, aren't we?'

She nodded helplessly. How was she to know that the coming

months would turn her life completely upside down and prove to her that she was making the worst – the greatest mistake of her life?

CHAPTER TWO

LILLIAN

Lillian had just reached the bottom of the stairs when the little brass bell that stood on her mother's bedside table tinkled again. With a resigned sigh she turned to retrace her steps. In the first floor bedroom with the blinds half drawn Laura Mason sat up in bed, the corners of her mouth turned down petulantly.

'Do you really have to go out this evening, Lillian?' she asked. 'I'm not feeling at all well.'

'It's only a film, Mummy. I did ask you last week if you'd mind. Hilda said she'd come in and keep you company.'

Laura sighed. 'That woman never stops talking. She makes my head ache.'

'It's only for a couple of hours,' Lillian said. 'I'll be back before you know it.'

'What's so special about the wretched film anyway?' Laura snapped. 'Why can't you just listen to the wireless like you usually do?'

'I've wanted to see it for so long, Mummy. It's Ingrid Bergman in *For Whom the Bell Tolls*.'

'I didn't know you were interested in campanology.'

'It's about the Spanish Civil War.'

'Haven't we got enough to worry about with the war we're in now?' Laura began to pluck at the sheet. 'Oh! My bed's all wrinkled and uncomfortable.'

'Let me help you out and I'll make it for you.'

'No! You know perfectly well that when I stand up I feel faint. Heaven knows I've told you enough times but all you ever seem to think about is your own pleasure. Oh, don't stand there looking useless. Just go if you're so determined to. We can't have you late for the cinema, can we?' she added sarcastically.

Lillian was on the point of giving in when there was a ring at the front doorbell downstairs. 'That'll be Hilda,' she said. 'I'll go and let her in.' As she ran down the stairs she heard Laura muttering in her wake,

'That's right. Don't keep her on the doorstep. Never mind how uncomfortable I am. *I'm* only your sick mother.'

Hilda Brown was the Masons' 'daily'. She was a motherly soul in her fifties who had brought up a large family and worked hard all her life.

'Phew! It's raining cats and dogs out there,' she said breathlessly as she took off her headscarf and raincoat. She nodded towards the stairs and lowered her voice. 'How's her ladyship this evening?'

Lillian sighed. 'I feel I shouldn't be going really,' she said. 'She says she doesn't feel very well. I know she doesn't want me to go.'

Hilda sniffed. 'No, well, she wouldn't would she? You're too soft for your own good, my girl. She's got you just where she wants you. It's time a young woman like you started having some fun out of life instead of being stuck here, waiting on her hand and foot.'

'I don't mind really,' Lillian said. 'Daddy's death hit her so hard.'

'I daresay it hit you hard too,' Hilda said bluntly. 'And it'll go on hitting you as long as you let her have all her own way.' She took in Lillian's worried expression and chuckled good-naturedly. 'Oh, go on, girl.' She gave her a friendly push. 'Get your coat on and clear off. And stop worrying. I'll handle her all right.'

Lillian lost herself in the film. She hardly ever managed to get away from The Laurels except to do the weekly shopping and pick up her mother's prescriptions from the chemist. Going to the cinema was a special occasion that had taken days of planning. She'd even treated herself to a tub of ice cream in the interval, spooning it up guiltily in the half-light during the organ interlude. At the end of the programme, as she stood for the national anthem, she spotted a face she thought she recognized in the row in front. As the auditorium began to empty she found herself standing side by side with the girl. Turning her head, she plucked up her courage and said,

'Excuse me for asking, but are you Hazel Dean?'

The other girl turned in surprise then a smile lit her face. 'Yes. Oh! It's Lillian, isn't it? Lillian Mason?'

Lillian flushed with surprise. 'You remember me?'

'Of course I remember you,' Hazel said. 'We used to be such pals at St Margaret's. What are you doing these days?'

Lillian shrugged. 'Oh, you know; this and that. I thought you went up to Yorkshire to teach.'

'I did but after Nana died I decided to come and work back here.' Hazel stumbled as someone pushed past her. She took Lillian's arm. 'Let's get out of here and go somewhere for a coffee,' she suggested. 'There's a nice quiet café opposite the cinema.'

Lillian hesitated. 'Oh – I shouldn't really.'

Hazel looked at her. 'Are you married – children at home?'

Lillian shook her head. 'No, nothing like that. It's Mummy. She's bedridden.'

'Oh, I'm sorry. Is someone with her?'

'Well, yes.'

'Come on, then. It's not very late and we must catch up. Half an hour won't hurt, will it? Do say yes.'

Lillian nodded, her face flushed with delight at the thought of her company actually being wanted. 'I suppose half an hour would-n't hurt,' she said. 'Mrs Brown is with her. She's our cleaning lady and she's a kind soul.'

The Bay Tree Café stayed open to catch the last house at the cinema. There were wheelbacked chairs and tables with red checked tablecloths. As Hazel had predicted, it was quiet. Lillian and Hazel took a table in the corner and ordered two coffees.

'So, tell me what happened to you after you left school,' Hazel asked.

Lillian shrugged. 'Nothing really. Sister Magdalene was furious with me for leaving right after school cert. She wanted me to stay on like you and go on to teacher training college.'

'But didn't you fancy it?'

'I did, very much as a matter of fact, but Mummy and Daddy needed me at home,' Lillian explained. 'They were both in poor health; Daddy with his asthma and Mummy with her nerves.' She looked at Hazel. 'I used to keep house and look after them. It wasn't too bad then. We used to go out together sometimes, to the theatre or the cinema, but that was when Daddy was alive.'

'You lost him. What happened?'

'I expect your grandmother will have told you about the daylight hit and run raids we had here. The Canadian Air Force requisitioned all the big hotels. The town was full of Canadian airmen for a while and the Germans must have known. The bombers used to fly in low over the cliffs, drop their bombs and fly out again before our fighters could even get off the ground. It was horrible. Sometimes they machinegunned people in the streets too.'

Hazel nodded. 'Yes. I heard. It must have been horrible.'

'One day, about eighteen months ago, Daddy got caught up in one of these daylight raids when he went to pick up his pension. He was killed instantly.'

Hazel reached across the table to cover Lillian's hand with her own. 'Oh, Lillian, I'm so sorry.'

'After that Mummy took to her bed. She hasn't been up and about since.'

'That must be hard for you. What does the doctor say?'

'He said at first that it was grief – that she would gradually get over it, but if anything she's getting worse. He's told her that physically there's nothing wrong with her and that staying in bed will make her weak and even more depressed but she says he doesn't know what he's talking about.'

Hazel was looking at her incredulously. 'So you're her nurse. And you've never actually had a job since leaving school?'

Lillian sighed. 'To be honest with you, Hazel, I've never really had a life,' she said. 'I don't complain. There are lots of people worse off than me. It's just that sometimes . . .' She broke off and forced a smile. 'But what about you? I thought you'd have been married by now. You were always the prettiest girl in the school.'

Hazel laughed. 'What an exaggeration! No, I love my teaching career. I was sort of engaged,' she added with a sideways look at her friend. 'He was called up – the RAOC – Ordnance Corps you know. He was sent abroad and – well, you know how it is. It just sort of fizzled out.'

'What a shame. And there's been no one since?'

Hazel shrugged noncommittally. 'No one – well, not really.'

'So – now you're back in Valemouth.'

'Yes. When Nana died there were so many loose ends to tie up. She didn't leave a will, you see and I was her only relative. I knew

I'd have to come home and sort things out properly and I was ready for a change anyway. I should have given a term's notice at Mekeley Moor but they agreed to release me under the circumstances. I've got a job at Peele Road Elementary School. I went there when I first started school.'

'Me too! That's nice.'

'It's a challenge,' Hazel said. 'I'm teaching year nines and that's something new for me.'

'That must be . . .' Lillian glanced at her watch. 'Oh, good heavens! Look at the time. It's almost eleven o'clock. I must go.' She grabbed her coat and bag and stood up.

'Let's meet again,' Hazel said. 'We mustn't lose touch with each other now that we've met up again.'

'No, of course not. It would be nice to meet.'

'OK. Where – and when?'

Lillian looked flustered. 'Oh – I don't know. It's so difficult for me to get away. I do go shopping on Friday afternoons though.'

'Fine. Let's meet here next Friday then. After school, say a quarter past four?'

'That would be lovely.'

They walked out into the street and found that it had started to rain again. Lillian turned up the collar of her coat. 'My bus stop is over there,' she said. 'If I make a dash for it I might catch that one that's just stopped. I'll see you next Friday.'

'Next Friday. Look forward to it!' Hazel put her umbrella up and waved as Lillian sprinted across the road to catch the bus. Fancy meeting her again after all these years, she reflected. Poor girl. What a life – or lack of it.

Lillian was full of anxiety as she put her key in the lock. Mummy was going to be so angry that she'd stayed out so late. Hilda Brown met her in the hall.

'Don't look so worried,' she said. 'Your ma's asleep; dropped off a good hour ago.' She chuckled. 'Not that she didn't fight it, mind – wanted to be awake so she could give you a good wiggin' for stoppin' out late!'

'I'm so sorry, Hilda.' Lillian was struggling out of her wet raincoat. 'I met an old school friend I hadn't seen for years and we went for coffee. I lost track of the time.'

'Good for you!' Hilda reached for her coat. 'Tell her you got in just after half-ten,' she instructed. 'And make sure you stick to your story, girl. I'll back you up. Time you stood up for yourself. G'night then love. See you in the morning.'

Lillian made herself a cup of cocoa and took it up to bed with her. She looked in on her mother and found her fast asleep, her mouth open and snoring gently. She wondered whether she'd have the courage to lie as Hilda had suggested, knowing at the same time that if she didn't Mummy would harangue her all tomorrow for her late homecoming.

Hazel let herself into the little house in Broadway Lane. She'd lived in the house with her grandmother since she was six but somehow now that Nana was absent it had a totally different feel. It was almost as though the house had died too. When Nana was here it had always felt warm and cosy, smelling of newly baked bread and furniture polish. Now, it was just musty from closed windows and melancholy with all the nostalgic memories that gathered in every shadowy corner.

As she took off her coat in the hall she reminded herself that as soon as school broke up for the Christmas holidays she would spring clean – maybe change things round a little. The house was officially hers now, though somehow she didn't feel entitled to it. She felt she never would.

The kitchen had always been the heart of the house. It had an old fashioned cooking-range where Nana used to produce her wonderful cakes and bread, and a big dresser with willow-pattern plates. A round table in the centre of the room was covered by a red fringed chenille cloth. Hazel never lit the range now, which was why the house felt cold. She used the hissing geyser in the bathroom for hot water and cooked on the gas cooker in the scullery, where she now made herself a milky drink.

Sipping it in bed she thought about her chance meeting with Lillian. Poor girl. How could her parents have been so selfish as to make her devote her youth to them? The thought made her wonder about Nana. Had she felt lonely here all on her own? Would she have appreciated seeing her granddaughter more over the past years? Her letters had always been newsy and cheerful. She had never even mentioned the illness which had finally defeated her.

Hazel felt the tears well up in her eyes. Dearest Nana. She had devoted her life to bringing up her only granddaughter and what had she given her in return? Reaching out she switched off her bedside light and tried to settle for the night.

But sleep refused to come. In answer to Lillian's question she had said she'd been 'sort of engaged'. Before he left Gerald had given her his signet ring.

'I know it's miles too big for your little fingers but just keep it close to you,' he said. 'As soon as I get my first leave I'll buy you a proper one – a wedding ring as well.'

Odd that he'd never actually asked her to marry him. He'd just taken it for granted. And to her shame she'd gone along with it. She remembered the day he'd left. Handsome in his officer's uniform he'd toured every classroom to say goodbye to the children. They had stared at him, open-mouthed with awe at the tall figure in unfamiliar khaki. Some of the female teachers had had difficulty holding back tears.

The passionate letters he'd written to her filled her with misgivings. Now that he'd gone she felt nothing but relief – relief and guilt. Why hadn't she somehow found the courage to tell him she didn't love him? But how did you say that to a man about to go off and fight for his country? She promised herself that she would tell him – write him a carefully worded letter – soon – before that fateful first leave.

As it happened he was sent abroad shortly after his call-up. No embarkation leave – no warning; just a heavily censored letter giving her the briefest of details. Her feelings had swung backwards and forwards between relief, guilt and fear. She might not love him but she was fond of him. What if he were to be killed? She would feel in a strange way as though it was her fault.

No one at school knew about her relationship with Gerald except Gladys Brompton in whom, for some reason he had confided. The moment that Gladys took over as temporary head Hazel had felt her hostility like a wall of ice. Her whole manner was one of resentment and dislike. Whenever she could find fault with what Hazel was doing, she would, seeming to take great pleasure in putting her down, often in front of colleagues. This went on for several weeks until one afternoon as she was leaving for home, Miss Jameson, the elderly reception teacher caught her up and cycled alongside her.

'I just wanted to say, my dear, that we've all noticed Miss Brompton's manner towards you,' she said. 'And believe me we're all on your side. I think the way she treats you is quite outrageous – almost tantamount to bullying.'

Hazel smiled. 'Thank you. I appreciate your support,' she said.

'Can you think of any reason for her behaviour?'

Hazel shook her head. 'I suppose my face just doesn't fit,' she said. In truth she knew the reason for Miss Brompton's attitude perfectly well. The older woman clearly did not approve of Gerald's feelings towards her, probably because she nursed a secret passion for him herself. She didn't mention to Joan Jameson that she'd already decided to look for another job. She was scanning the pages of *The Times Educational Supplement* weekly and had already sent off for a couple of application forms.

All next morning Lillian found herself running up and downstairs like a demented yo-yo. First Laura complained that her breakfast tea was cold and demanded a fresh pot. Then she insisted that Lillian had bought a different brand of marmalade and that it was inferior. Later there were gritty grounds in her coffee cup and the milk was 'off'. In the kitchen Hilda raised her eyes to the ceiling.

'You'll have to put your foot down, girl,' she said. 'Look at you. You're nothing but skin and bone from all that running up and down. At this rate she'll outlive you!'

'I'm all right, really,' Lillian insisted. 'She's not well.'

'Not well my backside! She's bored! That's all that's wrong with her,' Hilda said. 'She should get her carcass out of that bed and start living a proper life again.' She rolled up her sleeves. 'I'll go and tell her so if you like, too!'

'*No!*' Lillian held up her hand in protest. 'She'll give you the sack and then where will I be?'

'She can't sack me,' Hilda said. 'It's you I work for, not her. She's opted out of life and everything to do with it and it's time someone pointed it out to her.'

Lillian busied herself with her mother's lunch tray. 'Well, it won't be either of us. Even the doctor's given up.'

Hilda shook her head. 'Well, it can't go on, that's all I can say,' she said as she rammed her hat on to her head in front of the kitchen mirror. 'Somehow, some day someone's got to tell her straight.'

On Friday afternoon Lillian was ready to leave for the weekly shopping expedition right after lunch. She'd made a careful list and went first to the grocer's where she would leave an order to be delivered the following day. After that she went along to the greengrocer's. It had been reported in the papers that lemons could be available this year in time for Shrove Tuesday. Lillian did not intend to miss them. She hadn't even seen a lemon since the war began. Mummy would be so pleased to have real lemon juice with her pancakes this year. At last, with all her shopping done, she made her way to the Bay Tree Café, looking forward to meeting her friend for a cup of tea.

Hazel was already there when she arrived, sitting at a table near the window so that she could see her friend coming. As she spotted Lillian walking down the street towards the café she reflected that the other girl looked older than her twenty-five years. She was far too thin and her dark hair, which she wore in a loose knot on the back of her neck, looked dull and lifeless. The brown eyes that Hazel remembered as shining with life and enthusiasm at school now appeared clouded and preoccupied. She wondered if Mrs Mason knew or cared what she was doing to her daughter.

As she opened the door of the café and saw her friend Lillian's eyes lit up. 'Hazel! I hope I haven't kept you waiting.'

'No. I was early.' Hazel pulled out a chair. 'Come and sit down. You look exhausted.'

Lillian put her basket on a vacant chair and sat down with obvious relief. 'Thank goodness the weather is better,' she said, pulling off her gloves. 'It seems to have been raining for weeks.'

Hazel signalled to the waitress to bring the tea she had already ordered. 'They've got cakes today. I've ordered some. Is that all right?'

'Lovely.'

As Hazel poured the tea Lillian asked. 'Are you enjoying teaching at Peele Street?'

Hazel nodded. 'I am now that I've got used to the age group,' she said. 'You know what year nine children are like at elementary school – they're the ones who didn't pass the scholarship. Most of them are resigned to being in some dead-end job and most of them have reached the stage where they resent having to come to school at all and most of the parents just want them to leave as soon as they can and start contributing to the family income. For one or two of them it's a real tragedy.'

'How do you mean?' Lillian helped herself to a slice of fruitcake.

'There's no second chance for the ones with potential,' Hazel said. 'Just because for some reason they didn't achieve the necessary marks on the day they're doomed to a full stop as far as their education is concerned. There's always night school later, of course, but how many of them will have the energy or the motivation to go – let alone the encouragement from their parents?'

'I suppose we were lucky,' Lillian remarked. 'Our parents could afford to send us to St Margaret's.' She smiled wryly. 'Not that it made much difference to me.' She looked at Hazel. 'I have tried though. I read as much as I can. And listen to all the documentary programmes on the wireless.'

'It's not too late for you to go to night school, you know,' Hazel told her. 'You could enrol at the WEA classes. They're for adults who . . .' She stopped as she saw Lillian shaking her head.

'Mummy hates me going out in the evenings,' she said. 'She'd never agree to anything regular.'

Like Hilda, Hazel thought it was high time Lillian started putting her foot down, but she refrained from saying so. 'That's a shame. I thought we might make a regular date,' she said. 'Go to the pictures or the theatre once a week.'

Lillian's face was wistful. 'I'd love that. I suppose you could always come round to The Laurels,' she said without conviction.

Hazel put her hand over Lillian's. 'Look, it's none of my business, but you are entitled to a life,' she said. When Lillian didn't reply she asked, 'How old is your mother?'

'Sixty-five,' Lillian told her. 'My parents were getting on when they had me.'

'But that's not your fault, Lillian. She could live for years yet – ten or even twenty. Maybe she'd be better off in a nursing home.'

'No. The doctor says there's nothing physically wrong with her,' Lillian said. 'It's just depression.'

'Not helped by lying in bed making your life a misery.' Hazel clapped a hand over her mouth. 'Oh, I'm sorry. I didn't mean that the way it sounded. It's none of my business really. I'm just concerned for you.'

Lillian nodded. 'It's all right. The truth is, Hazel, I don't really know what I'd do without her. I've never worked; never been trained for anything. If I didn't take care of Mummy what would I do?'

Hazel's heart sank. She was quite shocked at Lillian's predicament. It was almost as though the girl had become institutionalized. She patted Lillian's shoulder. 'Take no notice of me,' she said. 'What do I know about anything? Have another cup of tea and let's talk about something else.'

'You were saying about the children in your class who will miss out on an education,' Lillian reminded said. 'Were you thinking of anyone in particular?'

'As a matter of fact, I was,' Hazel told her. 'There's this one girl, Ruby Sears. She's an evacuee, from London, the East End. She's really bright but always dog tired. I get the impression that the people she's billeted with exploit her. They've got a greengrocer's shop and I happen to know she gets up early to work in the shop and then works again after school. Yet somehow she always manages to do the homework I give her. I wish you could see her. She's such a little waif; small for her age and undernourished-looking.'

'What can you do, though? And if she's so tired why do you give her homework? She'll have to leave at fourteen anyway, won't she?'

Hazel looked thoughtful. 'I've been thinking about that,' she said. 'The local girls' high school was too overcrowded to give a lot of kids the chance they deserved, but things are a bit easier now. If I could prove that Ruby is bright enough I might persuade them to give her a place. She'd have to pass an entrance exam, which is why I'm giving her homework.' She sighed. 'The problem is that when she reaches fourteen her mother will probably want to whisk her back to London.'

CHAPTER THREE

RUBY

'I'll take five pounds of potatoes, please,' Hazel said, holding out the canvas shopping-bag so that Mr Jones could tip the weighed potatoes in. Since the outbreak of war shoppers had grown used to there being no paper bags or carriers and Hazel noticed that the potatoes were thickly encrusted with soil which meant that she was getting short weight. Normally she would have remarked on the fact, but today she was here on a mission so she kept quiet.

'I wonder if I might have a word with you or your wife, Mr Jones,' she said as she handed over her money.

'Warrabaht?' Edgar Jones was a small wiry man with pale-blue eyes and a ferret-like expression. His long thin nose seemed to have a permanent dewdrop attached to its end. He sniffed and it disappeared momentarily. 'Social call, is it?' he asked with a hint of sarcasm.

'Not really. I want to speak to you about Ruby. I'm her teacher.'

'Oh yeah? What's she been up to now – lazy little cow.'

Hazel felt her colour rise as well as her hackles. 'Ruby hasn't been up to anything,' she said. 'And she's far from lazy in my experience.'

'That so, is it? Well, you'd better speak to the wife.' He went to a door at the rear of the shop and bellowed up the stairs, '*Myrtle!* You're wanted down 'ere. Some woman from the school.'

When she appeared Mrs Jones was the very opposite of her husband. She wore a grubby print overall that seemed to be bursting at the seams in a vain attempt to contain her bulging figure. Her hair was cut short and clipped back on one side and Hazel couldn't help noticing that she had a dark line of hair on her upper lip which made her look faintly menacing. She glowered at Hazel, looking her up and down.

'Yeah?' she said challengingly.

'Is there somewhere we could talk privately?' Hazel asked.

Mrs Jones exchanged a glance with her husband. 'You can come in the back kitchen if you want.' Without further ado she led the way through the door at the back.

The kitchen boasted a rickety table covered in oilcloth, and two chairs. There was cracked linoleum on the floor and the walls were painted a muddy brown. There was an all-pervading odour of rotting vegetables coming from the crates of waste piled against the back door.

Mrs Jones turned to look at Hazel. 'This do yer?'

'It's about Ruby,' Hazel began. 'She's very bright and I think it's a great pity she didn't get a place at the high school. She missed so narrowly. I wondered how you and Mr Jones would feel about me putting her name forward for one of the vacancies to come up shortly.'

Mrs Jones sniffed. 'What it got ter do wi' us?'

'You are her guardians at the moment. I'll write to her mother, of course, but I'll need her address.'

The other woman gave a short bark of laughter. 'Huh! You'll be lucky!' she said. 'That gel hasn't had a word from her ma since she's been with us. Probably not before neither 's far as I know. Not one penny piece 'ave Ed and me 'ad for her keep or her clothes. An' her growing like twitch an' all. So if you think we're gonna fork out for fancy uniforms on the pittance the government pays us you got another think coming, missis! We got two young'uns of our own to think of.'

'I see.' Hazel was taken aback. She had no idea that Ruby's mother had abandoned her. 'Nevertheless, I would like to try,' she said. 'So if you can give me the address I'll write to her.'

'Nuthin' to do wi' me. You'd better ask her.' Before Hazel could protest Mrs Jones opened the door and bellowed up the stairs in much the same manner as her husband.

'*Ruby*! Come down 'ere. Someone wants to see yer. And make haste. You're needed in the shop so's Father can have his tea.' She looked at Hazel. 'Her head's always full of that 'omework you give her,' she said. 'It's not right, y'know, fillin' her head with false 'opes. She ain't never goin' to no posh high school. Them places ain't for the likes of 'er!' She turned and began to stump back up the stairs.

A moment later Ruby appeared. She was small for her thirteen years and very thin. She had a pinched look. Her dark-brown hair was unbecomingly hacked off, Hazel guessed by Myrtle Jones, and held in place with a grip. The small oval face was dominated by her huge dark eyes; eyes which always looked guarded and apprehensive.

'It's all right, Ruby,' Hazel said reassuringly. 'You're not in any trouble. I want to talk to you about something.' She pointed to the chairs. 'Shall we sit down?'

'Yes, miss.' Ruby sat down on the edge of one of the chairs and looked at her teacher uneasily.

'You've worked hard since you've been in my class,' Hazel began. 'When you sat the scholarship examination eighteen months ago you had very high marks. The trouble was that the high school didn't have enough places at that time because of all the evacuated girls who had already been allotted places. But now that so many have gone home things are easier.' She looked enquiringly at the girl. 'Would you like me to put your name forward for a place?'

Ruby's colour rose. 'Isn't it too late?' she asked.

'You'd be more than a year behind,' Hazel conceded, 'but that's why I've been giving you homework. I'm confident that you're more than capable of catching up. You'd have to sit an entrance exam, but I'm sure you'd pass without any trouble.'

Ruby looked at Hazel with huge disbelieving eyes. 'Thank you, miss, but wouldn't it mean I'd have to stay on at school after I'm fourteen?'

'Well, yes, of course. You'd go on to take your school certificate. And you could go on to college to study . . . well, whatever you wanted. You . . .' She stopped as she saw Ruby shaking her head.

'I've got to leave after my birthday, miss,' she said. 'I've got to work so's I can pay for my keep, my clothes and everything.'

Hazel swallowed hard. 'But surely your parents – your mother and father . . .'

'I've never had no father,' Ruby said. 'And Mum – well, I don't know where she is no more.'

'Hasn't she been to visit you, Ruby?' The child shook her head. 'But she writes to you, doesn't she?'

'I've never heard from her since I first came here.'

'When was that?'

Ruby pursed her lips and looked up at the ceiling. '1939, I think it was; when the war started.'

'So you were only nine when you last saw her?'

'Yes.'

'Hasn't anyone tried to get in touch with her, Ruby?'

'Someone tried but there was so much bombing where we lived in Hackney. No one really knows whether Mum's even still alive.' She glanced at the half-open door and lowered her voice. 'If it wasn't for Mr and Mrs Jones they'd have put me in a children's home by now,' she said.

Hazel was appalled. While Ruby had been speaking she had been taking in the child's appearance. Her shoes were worn and down at heel and the once white ankle socks were grey and had holes in the heels. Her skirt and jumper were pathetically inadequate for her pre-pubescent body and she looked undernourished. Hazel had noticed that she was poorly dressed at school but this was the first time she had realized just how desperate the child's circumstances were. Privately she thought that Ruby would probably have been better off in a children's home.

'Will you give me your mother's address?' she asked. 'I'll try to get in touch with her for you.'

'Even if you find her she won't let me stay on at school,' Ruby said. 'But thank you for thinking of me, miss,' she added shyly.

Hazel took a notebook and pencil out of her handbag. 'That's all right, Ruby. Now if you just tell me the address. It's Hackney, you said?'

Ruby had just finished giving Hazel the address when Myrtle Jones was heard thumping down the uncarpeted stairs again. She burst into the kitchen and glared at Ruby.

'What d'you think you're doin' sitting about in 'ere when there's work to be done?' she demanded. 'Just get in that shop this minute, miss.' She held the door open and Ruby scuttled through it, getting a cuff round the ear from Myrtle to help her on her way. Hazel was shocked.

'I'm sure it's not necessary to treat her like that, Mrs Jones,' she said. 'I asked Ruby to sit down so that I could talk to her.'

'More fool you then!' The woman stood in the doorway, her hands on her hips. 'Fillin' her head with a load of rubbish about posh schools! You want your brains testin' if you ask me. Who the hell d'you think's gonna foot the bill? Not muggins 'ere, I can tell you. We've looked after that girl for nigh on four years. The best of everything, she's 'ad and once she's left school she's gonna have to pay us back. There's a job waitin' for her right 'ere. And I'll thank you not to poke your nose into what don't concern you, miss what-ever-yer-name-is.'

As Ruby served in the shop she thought about Miss Dean and what she had suggested. She'd seen the girls from the high school around the town in their smart bottle-green uniforms and envied them. What wouldn't she give for the chance to be one of them. And to think that Miss Dean thought she was capable of passing an entrance exam to go there. She swallowed hard at the lump in her throat. Even if they ever found Mum she'd never agree to it. She'd always said she didn't believe in education – not for girls.

She thought back to the days before the war when she and Mum had lived in the flat above the baker's shop in Powers Street. Mum had worked at the Prince of Wales pub round the corner and Ruby had spent her evenings alone. Sometimes Mum would come home with a 'friend' and she'd be lifted out of bed and put to sleep on the sofa. Sometimes she'd bring someone home with her on a Saturday or Sunday and Ruby would be required to stay out in the street in all weathers till the man left and Mum said she could come in again.

She'd loved school right from her first day there and once she'd learned to read and could amuse herself with books from the school library the lonely evenings hadn't seemed quite so lonely. Then came the war and the frighteningly long train journey with all the other children down to Valemouth. Standing in the crowded church hall with their labels tied to their coats, the exhausted children had waited hopefully for someone to take them in. Ruby had been lucky. Tina and John Mitchell had picked her. They were quite a young couple who hadn't been married very long so they had no children of their own. They lived in a nice little house and for the first time in her life Ruby had her own bedroom and a garden to play in. Tina used to read her stories every night at bedtime and

John would give her piggybacks round the garden jogging her up and down like a horse until she laughed so much she almost fell off. That first Christmas of the war was the happiest Ruby had ever known. But soon after, John was called up to serve in the army and Tina decided to close up the house and go and live with her mum and dad again in Lancashire. Ruby could not go too. There was no room, Tina explained regretfully, so she had to be rebilleted.

The Jones family were quite a different story. The exact opposite to the attractive young couple she had grown to love. Right from the first they had treated her with resentment, seeming to grudge her every mouthful of food; every inch of space she occupied. Their own children, eight-year-old Tommy and nine-year-old Rene were spoiled and boisterous. They liked nothing better than to involve Ruby in rough games where she would be sure to get hurt, and were always playing 'jokes' on her, putting things in her bed – spiders and beetles – once even a dead mouse. They hid her school equipment, her pencil-box and her PT kit and they told tales about her – lies that they knew would get her into trouble, gloating as they witnessed her receiving a smacking. In desperation Ruby wrote to her mother as many of the other evacuees had done, begging to be taken home. Mum had never replied.

When she had been with the Jones family a year Mrs Jones told her she would have to work in the shop both before and after school.

'Your mum ain't sent no money for your keep,' she said with brutal frankness. 'We can't afford for you to be 'ere eatin' your 'ead off without gettin' somethin' in return. So if you don't wanna be carted off to the workhouse or some kids' 'ome you'd better start toein' the line.'

Ruby was not stupid. She knew that her rations, her clothing coupons and the government allowance were shared out by the rest of the family. Although Rene was a year younger than Ruby she was a bigger girl, so Ruby was given her outgrown clothes and shoes to wear.

She hated working in the shop. In winter her hands and feet were numb from the cold and soon became chapped and chilblained. Dirt from the potatoes and root vegetables stained her hands so that it was impossible to get them properly clean and her nails were permanently rimmed with black. Often there was no time for breakfast before school and she would feel faint with hunger before dinner-time.

She shared a room with Rene Jones who constantly baited her and mimicked her London accent, and was resentful because she did well at school and the teachers liked her. Ruby used to pray every night for her mother to appear and take her home or for Tina to come back and take her to live with her again. But her prayers were never answered. She wondered if Miss Dean would get any reply to her letter. She doubted it. If Mum hadn't been killed in the bombing her silence must mean that she didn't want her any more.

Hazel could not get Ruby out of her mind. Long after she had switched off the light that night she lay awake, thinking about the child. Of course there must be hundreds like her, deprived of a chance in life, their lives blighted because of the war. So many had been killed in the blitz. Just being alive must be considered lucky in these troubled times. She thought about the children at Mekeley Moor and suddenly she was transported back to the little village school and the happiness she had known there over the last months.

Gladys Brompton held sway for over a year as acting head-mistress after Gerald left and clearly revelled in her position. They had one or two temporary headmasters, usually retired men who would travel round the schools in the county, filling the gap until a permanent head could be found. Gladys did not approve of her regime being disrupted by someone who would only leave a few weeks later.

'I wish they'd leave us alone,' she said. 'They come here and undo all the good I've done, just to leave again a few weeks later.'

Everyone on the staff knew that Gladys coveted the post of permanent head herself and couldn't understand why she wasn't offered it.

It was almost two years before the staff heard that the post had been permanently filled at last, and they all heaved a sigh of relief that Gladys didn't get it. Everyone was slightly apprehensive, wondering what this new head teacher would be like, after all, as Mr Tebbut, the elderly games and woodwork teacher put it. 'Better the devil you know!'

When Peter Grainger arrived the first thing that struck them all was his youth. He could not have been more than thirty, if that, they speculated. They were to learn in due course that he had been badly wounded at Dunkirk and invalided out of the army.

Peter's presence was like a breath of refreshing spring air blowing through the place. He was so full of enthusiasm and had so many ideas. To begin with he decided to adopt a house system for the school. The children were divided up into four houses and captains and prefects were appointed. Also a system of 'points' was instituted. The children rose to the challenge with gusto, as did the teaching staff – all except Gladys Brompton.

'It's giving the children ideas above their station,' she was heard to mutter after the first staff meeting. 'Where does he think he is – *Eton*?' But as the only one against the plan she was out-voted.

Another of Peter's ideas was to form a school choir.

'I've listened to them singing in assembly,' he said. 'There are some very nice voices among them.' He looked at Hazel who always played the piano for assembly.

'What do you think?' he asked. 'Would you be willing to help me? We'll have to audition the children, but it will have to be done tactfully so that no one feels left out.' He smiled the attractive persuasive smile that lit up his grey eyes. 'I'm sure we can devise a suitable plan of some sort between us.'

Hazel had agreed enthusiastically. She'd always loved music and being involved in the forming of a school choir was an exciting prospect to her. 'I'm sure we can,' she said, returning his smile. Out of the corner of her eye she caught the fearsome look that Gladys Brompton shot her and ignored it. Gladys held no authority now. She could do or think what she liked.

Over the weeks that followed the children were invited to come forward if they wanted to be in the choir.

'It's no use if they don't want to do it,' Peter said. 'You can't expect enthusiasm from kids who are pressed into it.'

At first the children were invited to sing in small groups. Peter thought that asking them to sing solo would be too much of an ordeal for them. In groups of four or five it was easy to pick out the best voices. Eventually a choir was chosen and they began to practise together after school, Peter coaching and conducting and Hazel playing the piano. They collaborated on suitable pieces of music, getting together after school and going through Peter's extensive collection of music. To begin with Peter got the children to sing part songs and funny pieces with animal sounds to make them laugh and help them to relax before taking them on to more serious pieces. One evening after the children had been dismissed and while Hazel was packing away her music Peter said,

'Come and have a drink with me?'

She looked up in surprise. 'What – now?'

He laughed. 'It's only seven o'clock.'

'Oh, I know, it's just . . .' She laughed. 'Thanks, I'd like to.'

'As a matter of fact I've got an ulterior motive,' he said. 'I want to sound you out about something.'

In the Fox and Grapes he bought two halves of light ale and they sat together at a table by the fire. Hazel looked at him expectantly. 'OK, fire away. What do you want my opinion on?'

'I've been to see Mr Handley, the vicar,' he told her. 'I've done the hard sell bit regarding the school choir and I've persuaded him to give us our first gig.'

She laughed. 'Sorry, you've what?'

'I've suggested that he might like to have them sing at his Christmas carol concert.'

She looked at him. 'That's ambitious. Do you think they'll be up to it?'

'That's just the point. They'll have to be now, won't they? It's just the motivation they need. We're only just into October so we've got plenty of time. And of course it'll be a programme of carols they'll all be familiar with.'

'Well, it's a lovely idea if you think we can pull it off.'

'I do – as long as you're with me.' He looked at her enquiringly.

Smiling, she nodded. 'Of course I'm with you.'

From that night on they practised hard. The children loved it, especially when they knew they were to sing in public at St Mark's carol concert. Together Peter and Hazel chose the programme, consulting the vicar to make sure of his approval. They were to finish with 'The First Noel' and Peter taught them to sing the descant. They got hopelessly mixed up to begin with but in the end they became proficient and sounded quite impressive. It became Peter's and Hazel's habit each evening when choir practice was over to retire to the Fox and Grapes for a drink and to discuss the evening's progress. One evening they were just coming out of the lounge bar entrance when someone almost bumped into Peter in the blackout. It was Gladys Brompton.

'Oh! I'm so sorry. Do excuse – Oh! Mr Grainger – and *Miss Dean*!' The look she threw at them caused Peter to smother a smile.

'Good evening, Miss Brompton,' he said politely. When Gladys was out of earshot he looked at Hazel. 'What was the outraged look for?'

She shook her head. 'Gladys is teetotal, but apart from that I suppose she feels we shouldn't socialize out of school hours.' She sighed. 'I expect I'll get the rough side of her tongue in the morning.'

He stared at her. 'You're joking! Choir practice is out of school hours anyway. Just leave the old dragon to me. I'll make it right with her.'

Privately Hazel thought he was being over optimistic.

The following evening he said quietly, just before they began practice, 'I suggest we drive over to the next village this evening. I need to talk to you.'

Later they made the short drive to Addenham, parked Peter's car and walked the short distance to the Crown. Once settled he looked at her.

'I've been warned off you,' he said.

She shook her head. 'What do you mean, *warned off*? Who by?'

'The formidable Brompton,' he said with a lift of his eyebrow. 'She tells me that you are engaged to Gerald Mayfield, the previous head, now fighting gallantly for King and country.' He watched the telltale blush that spread up Hazel's neck to the roots of her hair. 'Ah. I take it she was telling the truth.'

'Even if it were true I'm doing nothing wrong,' Hazel said angrily. 'What right does she have to talk about me behind my back?'

'*Even if it were*?' He looked at her. 'Are you saying it *isn't* true then?'

Hazel passed a hand over her forehead. 'I suppose it is true – in a way.'

'In a way?' He looked puzzled. 'Either you are or you aren't.'

'It's all such a mess – a long and complicated story,' Hazel said. 'Believe me, you don't want to hear it.'

He leaned towards her. 'As a matter of fact I do – if you want to tell me, that is.'

Haltingly at first, she told him how she had formed a relationship with Gerald; a relationship initiated by him and one she had thought of as platonic until the evening when he had told her he had received his call-up papers – and that he loved her. 'He's such a good man;' she said. 'A sincere person.'

'But you don't love him,' Peter finished for her.

She nodded helplessly. 'I was shocked when he said he loved me. I tried to love him back but I'd never been in love before so I had nothing to compare it with. But in the end I knew that what I felt wasn't love. Not *that* kind of love.' She looked up, her eyes meeting his. 'But how could I tell him when he was about to join up? I expect you think it's weak, but I just went along with it.' She sighed. 'And now . . .'

'And now?' She felt his eyes on her.

'And now he's abroad, going through God knows what hell and I'm here – with . . .'

'With me – exactly. That's what's eating poor old Gladys. I rather got the impression that she's more than a bit keen on him herself.'

'I know. She was the only person he confided in. On the face of it I suppose it does look bad.'

'Why though? We're colleagues, doing a job, working together. If you ask me she's got rather a nasty mind.'

'I suppose we'd better not go for a drink after practice any more.' Hazel looked pensive.

'I don't see why.' He reached across and touched her arm. 'Hazel – what do you intend to do – about Mayfield, I mean? You can't let it go on, feeling as you do.'

'I know. I had thought I'd wait till he comes home on leave. But first they sent him to North Africa and now he's in Palermo. When he does get leave it's too far to come home.'

'Well, it's none of my business. It's up to you, but the longer you leave it, the harder it will be.' He drained his glass. 'As for not socializing, I don't see why we shouldn't. If Gladys mentions it again just tell her to mind her own business.'

'You must be joking!' She laughed in spite of herself, imagining Gladys's face if she told her any such thing. However, Peter's easy attitude made her feel more relaxed.

The carol concert was a great success. Everyone was impressed by the children's singing and afterwards there was a party in the church hall. Some of the mothers had managed to rustle up some mince pies and lemonade for the children. Miss Jameson brought along some of her home made elderberry wine and a Christmas cake that her sister had made for the raffle. The vicar and his wife provided some sherry and plenty of tea and coffee. The party was in full swing and everyone seemed to be enjoying themselves when Gladys Brompton sidled up to Hazel.

'You must be missing your fiancé,' she said pointedly. 'I had a letter from him just the other day.' She gave Hazel a triumphant smile. 'We correspond regularly, but I expect you knew that.'

'Of course,' Hazel said, though in fact she did not know. 'I'm sure he would have been proud of the children this evening.'

'And do you think he'd be proud of you?'

Hazel looked at Gladys. The sherry in the almost empty glass she was holding must have loosened her tongue. Her cheeks were pink and there was a telltale red patch on her neck that Hazel had learned from experience always heralded trouble. Gladys took a step closer and lowered her voice.

'The way you've been throwing yourself at Mr Grainger is nothing short of scandalous,' she said. 'I've half a mind to write and tell poor Gerald how he is being betrayed.'

Hazel felt her heartbeat quicken with anger. 'Mr Grainger and I have been working together with the choir as you very well know,' she said levelly. 'If you want to read anything into that then I'm sorry for you, Gladys. Your mind must be tragically twisted.'

Gladys drew in her breath with a hiss. 'I don't know how you can stand there and look me in the face,' she said. 'Out drinking in public houses with him all hours of the night, when that dear man is fighting for his country. Don't you think poor Gerald has had enough suffering in his life? If I were you I'd be ashamed of myself!'

'Just what are you implying?' Hazel demanded.

Neither of them was aware of the fact that as their discussion had grown more heated their voices had risen. People were beginning to cast curious glances in their direction.

'Ah, *there* you are. My two favourite members of staff!' Peter said, slipping an arm around each of them and drawing them towards the buffet table. 'Come along now. You both deserve a mince pie and in a minute they're going to raffle that scrumptious looking

Christmas cake. We can't miss that, now can we?'

Hazel slipped away quietly before the raffle was drawn. She was badly shaken by Gladys's remarks and wanted to get away. She was almost halfway home when a car drew up at the kerb beside her.

'Going my way, miss?' Peter was leaning out of the lowered window.

'I'm all right, thanks. We don't want to cause any more gossip, do we?'

'Can't see anyone else around, can you? Oh come on, you're surely not going to let Gladys's shrewish remarks upset you, are you? She'd quite clearly been at the vicar's sherry.'

'She threatened to write to Gerald,' Hazel told him. 'Apparently they correspond regularly.'

Peter took a long hard look at her. 'And is that a problem for you?'

'No! It's just—'

'Get in,' Peter said firmly, opening the door.

She obeyed him and when she was seated beside him in the car he said, 'You're really mixed up, aren't you? Want to talk about it?'

She shrugged. 'Nothing to talk about. It's wrong, Gerald and me. But it's my fault. I've always known it and now it looks as if everyone else knows it too. But what can I do about it?'

'Look, it's nearly Christmas,' Peter said. 'Everyone says that next year will be crucial. The war will soon be over. Why don't you just put it all out of your mind till after the holiday?' He looked at her. 'What are you doing, by the way?'

'Going home.'

'Where's home? You've never said.'

'Valemouth. It's a little seaside town in Dorset.'

'Your parents live there?'

'My grandmother. She brought me up. I've been with her since my parents were killed when I was six.' She smiled. 'Nana's wonderful. You'd love her.' She looked at him. 'What about you?'

He shrugged. 'I've no family left and all my friends are away in the services – like the noble Gerald. I suppose I'll stay here.'

She looked at him, realizing for the first time how much being out of the war meant to him. 'Come home to Valemouth with me,' she said suddenly.

He stared at her, then burst out laughing. 'Is this the girl who just said we mustn't cause any more gossip?'

'No one need know. Oh, do come. Nana would be thrilled.'

He pursed his lips. 'My petrol allowance wouldn't take us that far.'

'That's OK. I was going by train anyway.'

He looked at her, eyes shining like stars in the dimness of the car and suddenly his heart was light. 'All right, yes! Damn it, I'd love to come,' he said. 'Oh and by the way, guess who won the bloody cake. *I did*!' And then, to her surprise, he kissed her.

CHAPTER FOUR

Lillian was appalled one chilly morning in mid-November when she went downstairs to find the kitchen floor awash with water. She was still mopping up when Hilda arrived.

'Oh my dear Lord,' she exclaimed as she took off her hat. 'What the 'ell is all that?'

'It seems to be the boiler,' Lillian said. 'I don't know what Mummy's going to say when she can't have her bath.'

Hilda hung up her coat and hat. 'Never mind *Mummy*,' she said. 'The thing is where do we find a plumber? Most of 'em are in the army. They're like hens' teeth these days.'

'We usually have Mr Blakely,' Lillian said. 'He's too old for the army, but he's always busy. I'd better go and give him a ring right away.'

Mrs Blakely answered the telephone. She told Lillian that her husband was out on a job and wouldn't be home until that evening. She asked what the trouble was.

'I think our boiler has burst,' Lillian told her. 'It looks very much as though we'll be needing a new one.'

Mrs Blakely tutted sympathetically at the other end of the line. 'Oh dear, that is bad luck. New boilers are very hard to get hold of nowadays.'

Lillian heard another voice cut in and a muffled exchange at the other end, then Mrs Blakely said. 'My son is home on leave from the Navy at the moment. He's just told me that he thinks we have a second-hand boiler in the yard. Would you like him to come round and see if he can help?'

Relief hit Lillian like a wave. 'Oh would he really? That would be kind.'

'Not at all. Just remind me of your address and he'll be round in about half an hour.'

Hilda nodded encouragingly at Lillian. 'You've struck lucky there all right,' she said. 'Just keep your fingers crossed that this second-hand boiler will fit all right.'

Upstairs Lillian explained what had happened to her mother when she took in her breakfast tray.

'Are you telling me that I won't be able to have my bath this morning?' Laura asked.

'It might only be for today,' Lillian told her. 'Mr Blakely's son is coming round immediately.'

'Why not Mr Blakely himself?'

'He's out, working somewhere else.'

'That's not good enough. We've been good customers of his over the years. His wife should have telephoned him to drop what he was doing and come here at once.'

'Perhaps she couldn't,' Lillian said. 'Perhaps there isn't a telephone where he is. Anyhow, we're getting his son.'

'An amateur! What does *he* know about anything? I won't have an amateur in my house.'

'Mummy, he's on leave from the Navy. It's very good of him to come. If we send him away goodness knows how long we'll have to go without hot water.'

Laura sighed noisily. 'Oh! I suppose we've no choice but to let him come and botch things up then,' she said. 'But if the wretched thing blows up in the middle of the night and we're all burned to death in our beds I shall blame you!'

Lillian sighed resignedly. 'Yes, Mummy.' She laid the tray across her mother's lap. 'Is there anything else you want?'

'Not a lot of point *me* wanting anything, is there?'

Lillian left the room, closing the door quietly behind her. Really, Mummy could be quite impossible at times.

When she answered the doorbell some twenty minutes later Lillian found herself looking into the brightest smile she had ever seen. The young man standing on the doorstep had dark curly hair and eyes the colour of warm brown treacle. He held out his hand.

'Good morning. I'm Alan Blakely. I believe you've got a malfunctioning boiler.'

'That's putting it mildly.' Lillian shook his hand. 'It's very good of you to come out like this, especially when you're on leave.'

'Not at all.' Alan came in and wiped his boots carefully on the mat. 'As a matter of fact I was bored stiff at home with nothing to do. I'd started working with Dad before I was called up so it's nice to get my hand in again. I've brought the other boiler on the off-chance. It's on the back of the truck outside, but I'll have a look at yours first, shall I?'

Alan quickly confirmed that the ancient boiler was beyond repair. 'What would you like me to do?' he asked. 'I can work out how much it will cost if you like, then you can make up your mind.'

Hilda put the kettle on and Alan sat down at the kitchen table and did some sums on the back of an envelope which Lillian took upstairs to show to her mother. Laura was appalled.

'That's outrageous,' she said. 'Is he quite sure he can't mend the old one?'

'It's burst, Mummy. They're made of cast iron. There's nothing you can do once they burst.'

'Huh! So *he* tells you.'

'I'm sure he's honest.'

'Then I suppose we have no choice. These people know we're reliant on them and they push up the price,' Laura said. 'It's sheer extortion.'

'I thought it was quite reasonable,' Lillian ventured.

'You would!' Laura scoffed. 'What do you know about running a household?'

Lillian could have told her mother that she'd been running this particular house for the past eleven years but she held her tongue. 'There is a war on, Mummy.'

'So I've been told – *ad infinitum!*' Laura shifted her position restlessly. 'I suppose you'll have to tell him to go ahead.' As Lillian reached the door she added, 'I shall need you to heat some water and give me a blanket bath, Lillian. You know how I feel about cleanliness.'

Lillian sighed. 'Yes, Mummy.'

'And I mean this morning – now. Not any old time.'

Alan announced that the work of removing the old boiler and replacing it would take two days. 'Not the kind of job you can rush,' he said cheerfully. 'You know, I'm surprised that a house this size hasn't got central heating.'

'My mother has always considered it unhealthy,' Lillian told him.

He laughed. 'How can it be healthy to be cold?'

Lillian took a bowl of hot water upstairs along with soap, towel and sponge and gave her mother a blanket bath. Laura repaid her with a stream of complaints. The water was too hot, then too cold. She was using too much soap, then not enough. The towel was too rough. At last, attired in a clean nightdress, she allowed Lillian to tuck her up for a nap before lunch.

Downstairs Hilda had returned triumphantly from the shops with some fish, which she was unwrapping in the scullery.

'Look at that,' she said proudly. 'A lovely bit of haddock. I had to queue for ages but I managed to persuade the man into letting me have a couple of pounds, 'cause I thought *he*,' she jerked her head towards where Alan was working, 'might like to stop an' have a bite to eat with you.' Before Lillian could reply she put her head round the door. 'Care to stay and have a bite to eat, Mr Blakely? There's a nice bit of haddock and I'm making a few chips to go with it.'

Alan looked up with a smile. 'That'd be smashing. Thanks very much.'

Hilda laid the table in the kitchen for two and when she'd dished up the fish, crunchy in its golden batter and surrounded by crisp chips she put on her hat and coat.

'Well, I'll leave you to it,' she said with a wink to Lillian. 'There's some cold stewed apple and custard for pudding in the pantry. Enjoy your dinner,' she lowered her voice, 'and don't rush it neither. It'll be nice for you to have a bit of company for a change.'

When Lillian took up her mother's tray Laura looked askance at the food on the plate. '*Fried* fish? Hilda knows perfectly well that I like my fish steamed,' she said. 'I'll be in agony with indigestion for the rest of the day.'

'Well, I'm sorry, Mummy but that's all there is,' Lillian said, and hurried from the room before her mother could reply.

Sharing her lunch with Alan Blakely was a delight for Lillian. He told her about the places he had seen since he joined the Navy and of some of the hair-raising adventures he'd experienced: being dive-bombed by Japanese planes; narrowly missing a depth charge fired by a German submarine and picking up survivors from a scuttled Norwegian battleship. She learned about the camaraderie among his shipmates and the pride he felt in his ship. It made her feel almost as though she hadn't lived at all.

'I've done nothing with my life,' she told him wistfully. 'I left school early to take care of my parents and that's all I've ever done.' She cleared the empty plates and brought in the stewed apple and custard. As he started eating Alan looked at her thoughtfully.

'What do you do with your evenings?' he asked at last.

She shrugged. 'Listen to the wireless mostly.' She'd been about to add that her mother didn't like her to go out but stopped, realizing how feeble it sounded.

'Do you like the pictures?'

She nodded. 'Very much.'

'Would you go with me – say tomorrow evening when I've finished your boiler? Call it a celebration.' He grinned his warm, twinkling grin at her and she felt herself blush.

'That would be lovely,' she said. 'But I – I'm not sure.'

'My leave's over the day after tomorrow,' he told her. 'So it's a case of tomorrow or wait till my next leave.' He smiled at her. 'And I don't know about you but I'd rather not wait.'

Suddenly Lillian knew that she wanted to go to the cinema with Alan Blakely more than anything else in the world. 'All right,' she heard herself say. 'Tomorrow night will be fine, as long as Hilda will be free to sit with my mother.'

When she told Hilda next morning that Alan had asked her out the older woman was delighted.

'There!' she said triumphantly. 'I knew he would. I could tell he fancied you right from the word go by the way he looked at you. That's why I asked him to stay for his dinner.' She frowned at Lillian. 'I do hope you said yes.'

'I said I'd ask if you could sit with Mummy,' Lillian said.

'Well o'course I will.' Hilda raised her eyes to the ceiling. 'Have you told her?'

'Not yet.'

'Well, if you take my advice you'll be a bit careful what you tell her. If she thinks you're off out with a young man she'll try'n throw a spanner in the works.'

'She might not,' Lillian said without conviction.

Hilda shrugged. 'Well, don't say I didn't warn you.'

Hilda was right. At first Lillian simply told her mother she was going to the cinema.'

'With whom?'

It was the question she'd been dreading. 'With – a friend.'

'A friend – what friend? Doesn't she have a name?'

Lillian fought with her conscience, wondering if she could make up a hitherto unknown female friend. She knew she couldn't carry it off. 'As a matter of fact it's Alan Blakely,' she said with a vain attempt at nonchalance.

Laura stared at her. 'Am I hearing correctly? Are you telling me that you are to be accompanied to the cinema by the *plumber's son*?'

'Yes.'

'The man I am employing to fit a new boiler?'

'I told you – yes.'

'You are to do nothing of the kind, you stupid girl.'

Lillian stood her ground, looking her mother straight in the eye she said, 'I have asked Hilda to sit with you. I shall be home at about half past ten.'

Laura pulled herself upright in the bed. 'Did you hear me, child? I said you are *not to go with that man!*'

Still determined, Lillian stuck to her guns. 'I am not a child. I am twenty-five, Mummy; more than old enough to make my own decisions and I shall be going out this evening with Alan Blakely. Now, is there anything you want before I go?'

Laura's normally pale face was rose pink with shock and anger. 'How *dare* you speak to me like that?' she said. 'Where would you be without me? Where would you be without the love and support your father and I have given you over the years?'

'Probably in a well-paid job with a good education behind me,' Lillian said. 'I've given up a lot of my youth for you and Daddy. I have never grudged anything I've done for you but I think I am entitled to do as I please in my free time.'

Standing outside her mother's door Lillian shook. What had happened to her? How had she found the courage to speak up like that? It had been like standing aside and watching someone else. She couldn't get the sight of her mother's pink, startled face out of her mind.

Downstairs Hilda looked at her. 'Gawd, gel, what's up?' she said. 'You look like you've seen a ghost.'

'I have in a way,' Lillian told her. 'My own! Mummy said I wasn't to go out with Alan and I've just told her I've got a right to please myself.'

Hilda clamped a hand over her mouth and chuckled till her shoulders shook. 'Good for you, gel. About time too. Now, off you go and get ready and don't forget to put a bit of lipstick and powder on.'

'Do you think I should?'

''Course you should. And untie your hair. Let it fall loose. You've got pretty hair, pity not to make the most of it.'

The film was an Abbot and Costello comedy and Lillian laughed till her sides ached. She was aware of Alan looking at her and in a quiet part of the film he reached across and took her hand.

'You look so pretty when you laugh,' he whispered, giving her hand a squeeze. Lillian was glad of the dim light that hid her blushes. After the film he took her to a café where they had coffee and cakes. He told her that after the war, when he came out of the Navy he was hoping to go to university.

'I didn't know what I wanted when I left school,' he said. 'Just sort of drifted into working alongside Dad. But I realize now that I could have done better. I was at the grammar school – stayed on and passed my exams and everything. The teachers were always on at me to aim higher. When the war's over I might apply for a grant – maybe go to Oxford or somewhere.'

'I admire you for that,' Lillian said wistfully. 'I had to leave school before I wanted to. My friend stayed on and went to college. She's a teacher now. I would have liked the chance to do something like that.'

'It's not too late,' he told her, covering her hand with his. 'You shouldn't waste your life or your talents. Surely your mum wants you to get on?'

Lillian sighed. 'What she wants is to have me at home, taking care of her.'

Alan opened his mouth to say something, then thought better of it and closed it again. 'Well, you never know what's round the corner.'

She smiled at him. 'I've enjoyed this evening so much, Alan, she said. 'Thank you for asking me.'

'It's a pity this is my last night,' he said. 'Just my luck to meet someone like you and then not have time to get to know you better.'

She met his eyes shyly. 'I know. I'd rather hoped you might wear your uniform this evening. I'd love to see you in it.'

'Would you really?' He laughed. 'Tell you what, why don't you come to the station to see me off tomorrow? Mum never comes. She's superstitious. It'd be great to have you to wave me off.'

Her heart stirred with excitement. 'All right. What time?'

'I'll be catching the twelve o'clock train from Central Station,' he told her. 'Platform three.'

'I'll be there,' she promised.

She was there at a quarter to twelve. After buying a platform ticket she walked over the bridge and searched the crowd of servicemen and relatives thronging the platform for Alan. She spotted him coming out of the newspaper kiosk, sailor hat perched on the back of his curly head, slim in the close-fitting navy-blue uniform. Standing on tiptoe, she waved, then made her way towards him. His face lit up in the familiar smile when he saw her.

'You came then. I wondered if you might not get away.'

'I promised, didn't I? I always keep my promises.'

'Will you promise me something else?'

'If I can.'

He pushed a piece of paper into her hand. 'Write to me. It means such a lot, getting letters from home.' He gave her the cheeky sideways grin. ' 'Specially when they're from a special girl.'

'Am I a special girl?'

'To me you are.' His eyes searched hers. 'What do you say then – will you write?'

She nodded. 'Of course I will, Alan.'

The train steamed in and the crowd moved to the edge of the platform. He gave her one long look then suddenly his arms were round her. Pulling her to him he kissed her hard. 'You're a great girl, Lilly,' he said, his lips warm against her cheek. 'The best.' Then he hefted his duffel bag on to his shoulder and a moment later he was gone, swallowed up by the crowd.

Lillian walked home in a daze. She could still feel his lips on hers and hear his words. No one had ever called her 'Lilly' before and she made a vow there and then that no one else ever would.

Lillian's date with Hazel every Friday afternoon had become a regular thing, something she looked forward to. Ever since the evening when she had gone to the pictures with Alan, Mummy had been subdued, not even asking her where she had been if she was a few minutes late home, or whom she had seen whilst out. Hilda said the little outburst had made her think, and 'about time too'. But Lillian wondered anxiously if perhaps her mother was sickening for something. She felt slightly guilty, wondering if perhaps it might be her fault.

Laura had a monthly visit from Doctor Frazer who was also an old family friend, and on his next visit she had mentioned her mother's preoccupation to him, confiding her own small rebellion at the same time. He had merely shrugged.

'Laura must understand that you are a young woman with a life of your own,' he said. 'Perhaps she is indeed coming to realize that and it is beginning to stir her conscience.'

'There's nothing for her to worry about,' Lillian said.

The doctor shook his head. 'She might be afraid you'll get married and want to leave her,' he said, patting her arm. 'Leave her to me. I'll try to put her mind at rest.'

Lillian wondered how he would reassure her mother that that was unlikely to happen. Did he consider her beyond hope where marriage was concerned? Sometimes she thought so herself. Sometimes her life looked like a long dark tunnel with no light at the end of it; or at least it had until she met Alan.

She was first to arrive at the Bay Tree Café that Friday afternoon, but Hazel arrived only minutes later. She looked troubled. After the usual greeting and the ordering of tea Lillian asked her,

'Is everything all right? You look a bit worried.'

Hazel sighed. 'It's school,' she said. 'I keep remembering Mekeley Moor. They'll be getting ready for Christmas there now. We had a lovely school choir. They'll be rehearsing now for the carol concert.'

'And there's no choir at this school?'

Hazel shook her head. 'The class I teach couldn't care less about carol concerts. They don't care about anything much. It's a pretty soul destroying job, trying to teach them.'

'What about the little girl you were telling me about?' Lillian asked. 'Ruby, wasn't it?'

Hazel nodded. 'Poor little scrap. I wrote to her mother about getting her a place at the high school.' She looked at Lillian. 'Yes, you've guessed.'

'No reply?'

'Not so much as a line. Not that Ruby was disappointed. She expected as much. You should see that child's face, Lillian. She's barely fourteen and she's already resigned to a bleak future.'

'Is the still living with those awful people at the greengrocer's?'

'Yes. And they're hell bent on getting her to work – or should I say *slave* for them when she leaves school at Easter. According to them she owes them for the years her mother has sent no money for her upkeep.' Hazel began to pour the tea. 'I wish there was something I could do.' As she lifted her cup she looked at her friend properly for the first time. 'But what about you? You're looking remarkably cheerful I must say.' She smiled. 'What's happened to make your eyes shine like that?'

Lillian blushed. 'The boiler burst,' she said.

Hazel laughed. 'Well! You're always saying your life lacks excitement but I'd have thought—'

Lillian cut in quickly, 'Mr Blakely, our plumber was busy so his son came to repair it. He was on leave from the Navy.'

'Ah!' Hazel smiled. 'Now I'm beginning to get the picture.'

'His name is Alan. He asked me out,' Lillian said. 'We went to the pictures. He had to go back the next day but I went to the station to see him off and – and—'

'And now you're going to write to him,' Hazel finished for her. 'Oh Lillian I'm so pleased for you. Is he nice? Did you get on really well?'

'We went for coffee after the film and I don't think I've ever talked so much to anyone, except you. He's got the warmest brown eyes and the loveliest smile.' Lillian stopped, biting her lip. 'Listen to me! We hardly know each other. It's silly really.'

'Not a bit silly. People get to know each other quickly in wartime.'

A wistful look came into Hazel's eyes. 'I envy you.'

'Do you ever hear anything of your – fiancé?' Lillian asked.

Hazel lowered her eyes. 'Just before I left Mekeley. I heard that he'd been wounded – at Palermo.'

'Oh, Hazel, I'm sorry. Is it bad?'

Hazel shook her head. 'I don't know.' She looked at Lillian. 'What will you be doing for Christmas?' she asked, changing the subject.

Lillian pulled a face. 'The same as I always do, I suppose.'

'Does your mother never get up and come downstairs?'

'No.'

'Not even at Christmas?'

' 'Specially not at Christmas. She thinks the whole thing is outrageously exploited and commercialized. I've tried to tell her we should at least try to celebrate it in our own way, but she refuses.'

'That can't be much fun for you.'

Lillian lifted her shoulders. 'I'm used to it. What about you?'

'Much the same as you.' Hazel sighed. 'Last Christmas was lovely,' she said. 'Nana was still alive and I brought a – friend home with me. Nana hadn't met him before but they got along like a house on fire. The three of us had such a good time.'

Lillian couldn't fail to notice the sad look in Hazel's eyes. 'You said "him",' she ventured. 'Was he someone – special? You said there was no one.'

Hazel busied herself refilling their cups and passing Lillian the sugar. 'He was the replacement headmaster,' she said, her eyes on the teapot. 'Peter Grainger. He was the one who started the choir and he asked me to help. He did wonders for the school. The children loved him.'

'And you?' Lillian asked gently. 'Did you love him too?' She bit her lip. 'Oh, I'm sorry, Hazel. I don't mean to pry but it's obvious you're unhappy sometimes. Did something happen between you? Was that the reason you left Mekeley Moor?'

'Partly.' Hazel met her friend's eyes and sighed. 'He'd been wounded at Dunkirk,' she said. 'He hated being out of the war so early on. He felt he'd failed and he missed his comrades. But I believe that when he came to Mekeley his life took on a new purpose again.'

'Because of you?'

'Oh no!' Hazel shook her head. 'He loved the school and the children and he had such a way with them. He made such a difference. The teachers rose to the challenges he presented too – most of them, that is. He breathed new life into the place.' She looked at Lillian. 'And yes, eventually into me too.'

'And you invited him home with you last Christmas?'

'Yes. He had nowhere else to go. We had such a good time, the three of us. Nana really took to him. He took us to the pantomime, and for a long walk along the prom on Boxing Day.'

'So – what went wrong, Hazel?'

For a long moment Hazel stared into her teacup. 'When I said the other teachers took to him that wasn't quite accurate. There was one – Gladys Brompton, who deeply resented him. She'd been appointed acting head when Gerald left and I believe she expected to be asked to stay on in the job permanently, so when Peter arrived she was bitterly disappointed. He couldn't do anything right in her eyes and when he asked me to help him create and run the choir she was furious. She accused me of being unfaithful to Gerald.'

'What a cheek! What grounds did she have for that?'

'We used to go to the village pub after choir practice, to discuss any problems and wind down a little. Gladys saw us coming out one evening and she read more into it than there was. She was teetotal and strict chapel, besides which I think she had a secret passion for Gerald herself, even though she must have been at least ten years older. She even warned Peter off, telling him I was engaged to Gerald.'

'I can see that must have put you in a difficult position,' Lillian said.

'I told Peter all about the mistake I'd made, agreeing to become engaged to Gerald and the dilemma it had put me in,' Hazel said quietly. 'In a funny way it drew us together. After that we grew more and more attracted to each other.'

'So how did it end in your resignation?'

'As I told you, Gerald was wounded at Palermo. But in the meantime Gladys had found out that Peter had come home with me at Christmas. Apparently she'd been talking to his landlady and she mentioned that Peter had been to Valemouth with me for Christmas.

It was all perfectly innocent, with Nana as chaperon, but she assumed the worst. She took it upon herself to write and tell Gerald. He must have received the letter after he was wounded, when he was in the military hospital. He wrote to me, releasing me from our engagement; a rather sad, disillusioned letter. You can imagine how I felt.'

Lillian gasped. 'What a horrible interfering old busybody,' she said. 'I hope she was happy with what she'd done.'

'We had the most awful row,' Hazel told her. 'After that it was impossible for us both to stay. The school needed Peter more than it needed me. He loved the job and he did it so well. Anyway in the meantime Nana became ill. I came home during the summer holidays and when she died I wrote asking to be released immediately.'

'But surely you kept in touch – with Peter, I mean?'

Hazel shook her head. 'It was all spoilt between us. I felt guilty about Gerald. I think he did too. Before I left I told him it would be better if we didn't see each other again.'

'But that's so sad.' Lillian looked at her watch. 'Oh no! I can't believe how the time flies when I'm with you.' She began to gather her bags of shopping together. 'Sorry, Hazel. I've got to rush. See you next week?'

'Of course.' Hazel smiled. 'Same time, same place.'

Lillian paused to lay a hand on her friend's arm. 'Thank you for telling me about Peter,' she said. 'Do you miss him?' Hazel nodded, her eyes misty. 'Please try not to be unhappy.'

'I'll try,' Hazel said. 'And write a nice long newsy letter to that Alan of yours.'

Lillian's cheeks coloured. 'I will. Not that there's much to write about in my life.'

In the bus on the way home Hazel's thoughts were of her last days at Mekeley Moor. When she had received the letter from Gerald she had been almost incandescent with rage. He had enclosed Gladys's letter in which she accused Hazel of 'disgraceful behaviour' with the new headmaster; that she had been 'drinking in public houses with him till all hours' and that she had 'gone away for the Christmas holidays with him to a seaside town where I strongly suspect that they shared a hotel room.' Gerald had written that he did not blame Hazel for seeking other company and that she was not to worry because he suspected that Gladys's misplaced loyalty had caused her to exaggerate. Behaviour such as Gladys had described did not relate to the Hazel he had known and he could not believe it to be true. But on reflection he felt that it was unfair to hold her to a promise that under the circumstances might never be fulfilled.

Without waiting for her temper to cool she had rushed to the staff room and confronted Gladys, oblivious to the fact that other members of staff were present.

'How dare you go behind my back and blacken not only my name but that of your headmaster?' she demanded, holding out Gerald's letter.

Gladys had been unrepentant. 'All I can say is that if the cap fits, you must wear it,' she said, smiling smugly.

'*If the cap fits!*' Hazel had shouted, uncaring of the embarrassed faces of the other teachers. 'This particular cap is big enough to fit right down to the ankles! For your information I invited Mr Grainger to come home to Valemouth with me to my grandmother's home for Christmas, because he had nowhere else to celebrate it. How dare you suggest that we shared a hotel room?'

'I only have *your* word for it that you went to your grandmother's.' Gladys was clearly going to stand and fight her corner.

'You are a nasty-minded, bitter old maid,' Hazel said. 'Because of your utterly transparent infatuation for Gerald you're ready to destroy the character of any other woman who gets in your way. You are a sad, twisted old – old witch!'

Gladys's face coloured and her nostrils flared a little but she remained outwardly cool. 'Behaving like a fishwife is doing you no favours at all, Miss Dean,' she said.

'And your letter did Gerald no favours either,' Hazel countered. 'Does it matter at all to you that he received this – this catalogue of lies when he was lying wounded in a military hospital? Or are you too eaten up with your own bitter jealousy to care?'

The barb went home. Gladys gave a gasp and fumbled in her pocket for a handkerchief; then, clamping it to her mouth she rushed from the room stifling a sob. Hazel looked round at the collection of astonished faces.

'Sorry about that,' she said inadequately.

Miss Jameson broke the stunned silence, clattering the cups on the tea tray with shaking hands.

'Do let me make you a cup of tea, Miss Dean,' she said. 'I'll put plenty of sugar in. They say it's good for shock.'

CHAPTER FIVE

Christmas had never held much wonder for Ruby, but at least when she was little before the war Mum had tried to buy her a cheap toy and an orange for her stocking and provide some kind of special dinner. The Christmas she had spent with Tina and John Mitchell had been a revelation to her; the house pretty with decorations and a Christmas tree with coloured lights. There had been a log fire and Tina's delicious mince pies. There had even been roast chicken for dinner and crackers that went bang when you pulled them and had little gifts inside.

The contrast at the Joneses could not have been bleaker. Rene and Tommy always received plenty of gifts from their parents as well as from relatives. Rene took great delight in pointing out that Ruby had none, rubbing in the painful fact that her mother seemed to have forgotten she had a daughter, whilst Myrtle Jones clearly grudged Ruby the meagre slice of tough boiling fowl she tossed on to her plate at dinner-time.

This year however, it was different. Ruby did have a present. On the last day of term Miss Dean had asked her to stay behind after the class had been dismissed. She had handed her a small packet, wrapped in pretty pink paper.

'It's just a little something for you to open on Christmas Day,' she said. 'I hope you like it.'

Ruby hadn't known what to say. She had felt the warm colour spread from her cheeks to her forehead. 'Thank you, miss,' she'd whispered. 'But I – I haven't got anything for you.'

Miss Dean had smiled. 'Of course you haven't, Ruby,' she said. 'I didn't expect it. Have you heard from your mother?'

Ruby looked at the floor and shuffled her feet. The fact that her mother clearly didn't want her any more made her feel guilty and ashamed. What could she have done to be so worthless? 'I – I expect she forgot,' she muttered. 'Or perhaps the letter got lost in the post.'

'Yes, perhaps. Well, off you go now, Ruby. Have a nice Christmas and I'll see you next term.'

'Thank you, miss.' In truth Ruby couldn't wait for next term. She loved school and she fervently wished that Christmas was over. But the thought that next term was to be her last filled her with foreboding. The prospect of being with the Joneses and working in the shop with them all day and every day was something too horrible to contemplate.

On Christmas morning when Rene was taking the parcels out of the pillowcase at the end of her bed and counting them greedily, Ruby took the small pink package out from under her pillow and began to unwrap it. Rene glanced across the room.

'What you got there?'

'It's a present.'

'Who from?' Rene sounded deeply affronted.

'It's from Miss Dean. She gave it me on the day we broke up for the holidays.'

'Give it here.'

'No! It's mine.' Ruby pulled off the paper to reveal a pretty scarf crocheted from the softest wool in a pale shade of violet. Ruby blushed with pleasure. Rene was out of bed in a flash, snatching the scarf from her hands.

'She's got no right, giving you presents,' she said. 'Did she give the whole class one?'

'I don't know. No, I don't think so.' Ruby reached out for the scarf but Rene jumped up on a chair and held it high above her reach.

'You ain't 'avin' it. It ain't fair,' she said. 'You think you're everyone, don't you? Teacher's pet. Why should *you* have a present from *her*? What's so special about you? I'm gonna tell our mam. I bet she'll say you got to give it back.'

'Give it to me – please,' Ruby pleaded. 'It's mine. It was given to me. You're stealing it.'

'*Stealing* it, am I? I'm tellin' our mam you called me a thief,' Rene said spitefully. She was out of the door in a flash, calling out to her mother as she ran along the landing. Ruby sank back and pulled the covers over her head as tears started to trickle down her cheeks. Why did everyone hate her so? What had she ever done to be treated so cruelly? But to her surprise a few minutes later Myrtle Jones came into the bedroom, the scarf in her hand.

'Rene says Miss Dean gave you this,' she said. Ruby nodded. 'Well, you'd better have it back then,' Myrtle said. 'Our Rene never meant nothing. It was a misunderstanding, see? We'll say no more about it, specially not to Miss Dean, eh?' Myrtle didn't want the interfering schoolteacher coming round again making trouble. Wouldn't do to have the authorities sniffing round. The sooner this girl was their employee and no longer a billeted evacuee the better. Best to keep their heads down till after Easter.

Ruby took the scarf and held its softness against her cheek. It smelled of Miss Dean's perfume, a mixture of roses and violets. Ruby thought she was the kindest, the loveliest person she had ever known.

Each of the Jones children had been given a bicycle for Christmas, second hand of course; new bikes were almost impossible to come by. But Edgar had put on new tyres, painted and polished the cycles until they looked as good as new. After dinner Rene and Tommy went off for a bike ride with their father while Myrtle put her feet up on the settee.

'Better get on with the washing up, Ruby,' she instructed, picking up a magazine. 'Look sharp about it and make sure you shake them crumbs off the cloth outside, not on the floor. And when you're done you can make me a cup of tea.'

Hazel spent Christmas alone in the little house in Broadway Lane. She had hoped that Lillian and she could have spent the some of holiday together but clearly it was not something that Laura Mason would allow.

She had spent the week after school had broken up for the Christmas holiday giving the house the promised spring clean. She worked hard, getting up early each morning and working on until darkness closed in. By the end of the week when the freshly washed curtains were back at spotless windows; the paintwork cleaned and the furniture shining with polish she felt more at home. This was how Nana had loved the place to look. It was how it should be.

Opening the Christmas cards that came with the post on the

morning the day before Christmas Eve she was surprised to find one from Miss Jameson. With it was a short letter, written in the elderly teacher's characteristic style.

My dear Miss Dean

This is just to send you the season's greetings and to wish you a happy New Year. Let us all hope it will be the last year of this dreadful war.

You are very much missed at school by the children and staff. We had a supply teacher last term, an elderly gentleman who, although rather deaf, did well enough. After Christmas a new teacher will be joining us and I hope that as a result the children will be more settled. Mr Grainger coached the choir again this year and they gave a successful carol concert both here at school and at St Mark's.

You will no doubt be saddened to hear that Mr Mayfield tragically lost a leg as a result of his injuries at Palermo and has now been invalided out of the army. As his job as head here was to be kept open for him he will be rejoining us here as soon as he is fit enough. Mr Grainger will be leaving us at Easter, supposedly for a new post.

I hope this finds you well and in good spirits. All here are in good health apart from the usual winter ills and chills.

Everyone on the staff has asked me to convey their good wishes to you.

I remain, your sincere friend and colleague, Joan Jameson.

Hazel read the letter through twice, then folded it and put it in her pocket. Poor Gerald. That must have been what he meant when he had written that it would be best to release her 'under the circumstances'. She couldn't help feeling a pang of guilt. At least he had a job to come back to. As for Peter . . . while he was at Mekeley Moor she had always known she had the option of contacting him if she wished. Now his whereabouts would be a mystery to her. A cold feeling of finality swept through her. Should she write to him while she still had the chance? No. He had always known where she was yet he had made no effort to contact her. Clearly after the furore with Gladys Brompton he had seen her in a new light – as an unfaithful, promiscuous woman from whom he had had a lucky escape.

On Christmas Day she lit the fire in the little parlour and cooked herself the small joint of beef she had saved up her meat ration for. Afterwards she listened to the wireless for a while and then went to bed early, admitting to herself that, like Ruby, she would be glad when the new term started.

Laura Mason was at her most difficult on Christmas Day. Nothing was right for her. She ate hardly any of the meal Lillian had prepared, grumbling that the meat was overcooked, the vegetables undercooked, the gravy lumpy and the pudding dry. After lunch she complained that she was cold and insisted that Lillian light a fire in her room, which entailed carrying wood, paper and coal upstairs. The chimney had not been swept for some time and Lillian's attempts resulted in smoke filling the room, which threw Laura into a rage, insisting through much melodramatic coughing and spluttering that she was sure to finish up with pneumonia. At last she conceded that a cold bedroom was preferable to a smoke-filled one and Lillian was allowed to give up the struggle.

'Why don't you come downstairs to the drawing-room, Mummy?' she suggested. 'There's a nice fire in there and we could listen to the wireless together.'

Laura shook her head. 'You really have *no idea* how weak I am, do you Lillian?' she whined. 'So unless you intend to carry me down I think I will have to stay where I am; even though I shall probably freeze to death.'

She eventually agreed to let Lillian bring her a hot-water bottle and soon after it was tucked in beside her she fell mercifully asleep, allowing Lillian to creep downstairs and draw up an armchair to the fire. Once in the cosy solitude of the drawing room she took Alan's letter out of her pocket and read it for the hundredth time. It sounded as though they were to have a merry Christmas aboard the HMS *Redoubtable*. Their ship's cook was a genius, he said, though not as good as his mum of course. He wrote that he missed Lillian and that he wished they had been able to spend more time together to get to know one another better. *On my next leave I'll make sure we see plenty of each other*, he wrote. Lillian wondered wryly how this would be possible, but all the same she cherished the notion that it was what Alan wanted. He ended the letter by asking if she would send him a photograph. *To show the lads what a smashing girl I've got waiting for me at home.* This last sentence made her blush with delight. But she had no photograph to send him. The last one had been taken when she was still at school. Maybe she could have a professional one taken. She would ask Hazel the next time they met.

January came in with snow and ice and Lillian had a struggle keeping the house warm. Coal was in short supply and she was in a constant state of anxiety that they would run out before the coal merchant was able to deliver. So that her mother could have a fire in her room she had the chimney swept in her bedroom, removing Laura temporarily to her own room until she and Hilda could spring clean Laura's after the sweep had gone. Naturally Laura was full of complaints.

'Why couldn't you have had the chimney swept last summer?' she asked in the whining voice she had recently adopted. 'I suppose you think I enjoy being bundled about like a rag doll.' Hilda and Lillian exchanged weary glances as they tucked her into Lillian's bed.

'You'd like me out of the way for good no doubt,' Laura went on.

'No such luck,' Hilda muttered under her breath.

Laura looked at her sharply. '*What* did you say?'

'I said "Are you comfy, duck?" ' Hilda said without batting an eyelid.

Laura assumed a martyred expression. 'I'm comfortable enough, I suppose,' she said. 'And I do have a name, you know. I'm not a farmyard bird!'

'Tough old bird.' Hilda muttered.

'What?'

'I said I heard,' Hilda said.

'I do wish you wouldn't mumble so.' Laura punched her pillow into submission. 'I'll have my coffee now – that is if anyone can be bothered.'

Lillian kept the boiler going as best she could so that they could have hot water and spent most of her time in the kitchen so as not to light any more fires than necessary. Life was bleak. The only brightness on her horizon was the occasional letter she received from Alan. They were few and far between; posted whenever his ship was in port, but they were always full of news and his plans for what they would do when next they met. After she had defied her mother to meet him at the cinema that evening neither of them had mentioned him again. Laura certainly didn't know that Lillian and he corresponded.

She and Hazel continued to meet for their weekly chat over a cup of tea at the Bay Tree Café every Friday afternoon. Hazel was growing more and more unsettled in her job, as she told Lillian one afternoon in March.

'After Easter Ruby will no longer be with us,' she said. 'I hate to think what awaits the poor child. She's the only one of my pupils who actually enjoys learning. She's a joy to teach. It's such a shame she can't continue with her education.'

'Still no word from her mother?' Lillian asked.

Hazel shook her head. 'The woman has obviously given up on her,' she said. 'Ruby is afraid she might have been killed in the blitz but I can't help thinking that she would have been informed by now if that were the case. The child is going to have to make her own way in the world alone. My heart goes out to her.'

'I suppose you could always keep in touch with her,' Lillian suggested.

'Oh, I intend to,' Hazel assured her. 'I shall call round at the Jones's shop regularly and make sure she's all right.'

Hazel had told Lillian about Gerald's amputation and the fact that he was to be released from the army and return to Mekeley Moor; also that Peter was leaving the school to make way for his predecessor's return.

'Have you heard any more from your old school,' Lillian asked with a tentative glance at her friend. She knew it was a delicate subject and she suspected that there was more to it than Hazel had confided. She did not wish to appear inquisitive.

Hazel looked up. 'I replied to Miss Jameson's letter,' she said. 'I asked her to keep me informed. I thought I would write to Gerald on his return and wish him luck.'

'To *Gerald*?' Lillian bit her lip, checking her surprise. 'I mean – I thought you'd want to write to Peter – to – to wish him luck in *his* new job.'

Hazel smiled gently. 'To find out where he was going, you mean?'

Lillian blushed. 'Well – I did sort of get the impression that you and he – that you were quite fond of him.'

'I was – *am*,' Hazel admitted. 'But I think I killed anything he felt for me when I had that awful slanging match with Gladys.' She looked up. 'It was so awful, Lillian. I'm sure he must have thought I was some sort of slut – cheating on the man I was supposed to be engaged to.'

'But you told me you'd explained that it was all a mistake,' Lillian protested. 'You said it actually drew you closer.'

'I know.' Hazel picked up a spoon and began to make patterns in the sugar bowl. 'But you must admit that it sounds a bit lame. Maybe he half believed the things that Gladys said. Perhaps he had second thoughts. All I know is that when I suggested we stopped seeing each other he didn't argue. In fact he agreed all too readily.'

'And now, in a few weeks' time he'll be leaving and you'll have no idea where he is,' Lillian said. 'You mustn't let that happen.'

Hazel shrugged. 'Maybe it's for the best. After all, he's always known where I am and he hasn't written so I have to resign myself to the fact that it's over.'

The Easter holidays came and went. Back at school Hazel missed Ruby's bright little face at her desk in the front row. The rest of her class made no secret of the fact that they were only marking time till the end of the school year when they would be free to start earning a wage. Almost every day one of them would tell her of the promise of a job they had received – one girl behind the counter at Woolworth's, another as a filing clerk; a lazy but bright boy in a garage.

She thought often about Peter, wondering where he was and what he was doing. She had written to Gerald, wishing him well and had received his rather stilted reply, thanking her and saying that he was well and happy to be back in the job he loved and among good and loyal friends. She took this last phrase as implied criticism, but persuaded herself that she was being paranoid.

Then one morning in early June the door of her classroom burst open to admit a pink-faced Miss Jenkins, the headmistress's secretary.

'I'm so sorry to interrupt your lesson, Miss Dean,' she said, her voice shaking. 'But I'm sure you will all of you be thrilled to know that the Allies have opened up a second front. I've just heard it on the staff room wireless. It said that Allied troops have stormed ashore in Normandy.'

The class gave an involuntary cheer and Miss Jenkins turned to them, her hands clasped. 'Thank God!' she said emotionally. 'I do believe that this could be the beginning of the end.' As she turned Hazel saw that tears were running down her cheeks. 'Isn't it *wonderful*, Miss Dean?'

'It certainly is.' Hazel reached out to touch the older woman's shoulder. 'Thank you for telling us, Miss Jenkins.'

'I'm afraid it will mean more lives lost,' the secretary said quietly. 'I have a nephew who is with one of the airborne divisions. I hope and pray that he'll be safe.'

'I hope so too,' Hazel said.

Lillian's first thoughts on hearing the news were of Alan. Would he be affected by this new spectacular push forward?

Laura remained unimpressed. 'I just hope this means that this tiresome war will soon be over,' she said. 'Then we can all get back to normal.'

Lillian wondered what her mother considered as 'normal'. As far as she could see Laura had not been affected by the war at all.

But the excitement that kept the nation glued to its wireless sets day and night in the days that followed were soon to be disrupted by the news that Hitler's dreaded 'secret weapon' was no myth. The deadly V1 pilotless planes were unleashed on London during the days immediately following the Normandy landing. Hilda was full of the news when she arrived for work on the morning after the first attack on London.

'They say these things have got a red tail-light,' she said as she took off her coat. 'My sister's hubby's a lorry driver and he was in London when the first one came over! The light goes out and the engine stops and when that happens you know you're in for it.' She shook her head. 'It's a case of run for your lives. Those poor devils. As though they didn't suffer enough in the '41 blitz. I hope that blasted Hitler gets what's coming to him.'

Lillian poured Hilda's first cup of tea, strong and sweet as she liked it. 'It says in the paper that they are terribly expensive to make,' she said. 'The Germans had to devise something to make up for the fact that the Luftwaffe is so depleted.' She passed Hilda her mug of tea. 'But surely it can't last long,' she said. 'Our forces are doing so well. They've taken Cherbourg and Normandy. Rome has been liberated. They say Paris will be next.'

'Well I don't know nothin' about that,' Hilda said. 'They can do a hell of a lot of damage in the meantime. You mark my words, we'll be getting another load of evacuees before long or my name ain't Hilda Brown.'

As it happened Hilda's prophecy was right. The V1 flying bombs continued to rain on London over the month that followed and early in July another mass evacuation plan was drawn up. Valemouth was flooded with children, many with their mothers in tow.

Early one Monday morning in late July there was a knock on the door of The Laurels. Lillian answered it to find a man carrying a clipboard and wearing an armband emblazoned with the word BILLETING OFFICER'.

'Good morning. Can I help you?'

The man took a step back to look up at the windows. 'How many in your family, miss?'

'Just my mother and me.'

'Then I shall have to ask you to take in a family of evacuees.'

Lillian's heart sank. 'My mother is an invalid,' she said. 'I don't think . . .'

'You seem to have plenty of rooms if you don't mind me saying so.'

'Well – yes, we have.'

'Then I don't think a small family would cause much over-crowding.' He looked at her doubtful face. 'It might not be for long – it's on account of these buzz-bombs.'

'Yes, I know, but—'

'These poor people have nowhere to go. They've already spent a night camping out in St Anthony's church hall.'

'Oh dear, how dreadful.'

'So I'll put you down as a yes, shall I?' The man licked his pencil and lifted his clipboard.

'Wait! I'll have to check with my mother first.'

The man sighed resignedly. 'All right. I'll wait.'

Lillian went upstairs to Laura's bedroom and closed the door behind her. 'Mummy, there's a man downstairs who wants us to take in a family of evacuees.'

Laura stared at her. 'A *family*? Out of the question! Tell him to go away.'

'It's because of this new blitz,' Lillian explained. 'These poor people have nowhere to go.'

'That's not my problem,' Laura said. 'One hears such awful stories about evacuees; children with running sores, lice and goodness knows what else. We managed to avoid it last time. I don't see why we should open our home to a lot of ragamuffins now that the war is almost over.'

'I'm sure those stories were exaggerated, Mummy,' Lillian said. 'I'll look after them. I'll see you're not disturbed. Anyway the man says it might not be for long.'

Laura sighed explosively. 'You sound as though you actually *want* to lay yourself open to filth and disease! Well, on your own head be it. But don't let them anywhere near me. And don't let them put their filthy hands all over my furniture.'

Lillian descended to the front door where the billeting officer was waiting patiently. 'Yes,' she said. 'We'll take someone.'

The man made a triumphant note on his clipboard. 'A mother and her three children all right for you?' He looked at her expectantly.

'Oh!' Taken aback, Lillian nodded. 'Er – yes, I suppose so. When shall I expect them?'

'Later today.' He was already walking away. 'It's a Mrs Jean Kendall and her children.' He paused at the gate. 'And by the way, the youngest is a month-old baby.'

CHAPTER SIX

It was almost lunchtime when the front doorbell of The Laurels rang. Lillian went down the hall to answer it, a tiny doubt niggling at the back of her mind. Surely it was extremely unlikely but what if her mother was right and they were to play hosts to a family of unwashed slum dwellers? Lillian had already made up her mind to do her best to make them at home, whatever they were like. After all, they had been torn from their home and everything familiar. But Lillian knew all too well how difficult her mother could make life if all wasn't to her liking. She decided that she would just have to keep the evacuees well out of Laura's way. The prospect of the worry and the tension it promised to cause far outweighed her uncertainties about her new house guests' behaviour or state of hygiene. But it was all arranged now and there was nothing to be done about it.

Standing at the door she took a deep breath, adjusted her smile and opened it. Outside stood the most pathetic little group she had ever seen and at once her heart contracted. The young woman looked pale and thin, her fair hair hanging limp about her face. She held a tiny baby wrapped in a shawl in her arms and two small copper-haired children clung to her skirts, looking up at their mother anxiously.

'Hello,' Lillian said. 'You must be Mrs Kendall.'

The girl smiled. 'Jean, please,' she said.

'And who are these little people?' Lillian crouched down to the children. The little girl pushed a grubby thumb into her mouth and stared at Lillian with huge blue eyes.

'That's Katie,' Jean Kendall said. 'And the big boy is Jim, he's the eldest. And this,' She held out the sleeping baby. 'This is baby Patsy.'

Lillian stood up. 'Please come in,' she invited. 'You all look so tired. I expect you're hungry too.'

The little group straggled in after her and stood looking lost in the hall. Little Jim stared at the huge moose head that hung on the wall and his face crumpled.

'I don't like that cow,' he wailed. 'It's lookin' at me.'

Lillian followed his gaze. 'You know what, I don't like him either,' she said. 'I'll take him down. Don't worry.'

She had been busy all morning with Hilda's help, preparing and cleaning two of the rooms on the second floor that were never used. Together they made up the beds and put hot-water bottles in to air them. Up in the attic Lillian found her old cot that had been stowed away ever since she outgrew it. Hilda helped her to lug it down and put it up in the room to be occupied by Mrs Kendall. Searching the airing cupboard they had found some small sheets and blankets with which to make it up for the baby.

When she showed the rooms to Jean and her little family the girl was clearly touched.

'Oh, two whole rooms. It's lovely. It's very kind of you to go to all this trouble,' she said.

Lillian shook her head. 'Not at all. It's horrible for you to have to leave your home again. We'll all get along just fine, won't we, children?' Jim and Katie nodded uncertainly. 'My name is Lillian,' she told them. 'You can call me Auntie Lillian if you like.' The two children nodded solemnly.

'Well, I'll leave you to settle in and I'll make you some lunch,' Lillian said. 'Just come down when you're ready. I'll be in the kitchen.'

Lillian had no idea what kind of food the Kendall children were used to. In the end she decided to play safe and make chips, frying eggs to go with them. It was a good choice. The two children tucked in hungrily and Jean managed to eat hers while giving baby Patsy her feed. Lillian had never seen anyone breastfeed a baby before and at first she was embarrassed, but she soon saw how natural it was and how much satisfaction it seemed to give both mother and baby.

When she took her mother's tray up Laura was anxious to hear about the evacuees.

'Well – what are they like? I hope you've laid down some very firm ground rules,' she said. 'They are not to go into the drawing room at all – or the dining room for that matter. They can eat in the kitchen. Keep the children out in the garden as much as you can,' she went on. 'That way they won't get in the way.'

'I haven't laid down any rules,' Lillian said. 'They looked exhausted when they arrived. They spent all last night camping out in the church hall.'

Laura sniffed. 'Probably better than they're used to,' she said. 'At least the church hall has indoor sanitation.'

'Mummy! They're not savages,' Lillian said.

Laura looked up at her daughter's sharp tone. 'I don't think I said that they were,' she said. 'But the East End of London is renowned for its poor housing. I only meant—'

'Mrs Kendall and her children are from Woolwich,' Lillian interrupted. 'I think you should try not to generalize.'

'Oh really?' Laura's colour rose and she looked down at her plate. 'I don't think I can eat this, Lillian. You know how my digestion reacts to fried food.'

'All right then, leave it.' Lillian turned and left the room, leaving her mother staring in astonishment at the closed door.

After lunch Jean Kendall put all three children down for a nap and rejoined Lillian where she was washing up in the kitchen. She picked up a cloth and began to dry the dishes. She chatted as she worked, telling Lillian that her husband was in the Army.

'My Dave was in the territorials when the war broke out so he was called up right away,' she explained. 'Only nineteen, he was. We got married straight away. I was only eighteen and my mum and dad wanted us to wait but we persuaded them in the end.' She smiled reminiscently. 'I fell for our Jim when we was on our honeymoon,' she said with a smile. 'Not that it was much of a one; just a weekend in Margate. Then the others happened each time he came home on leave. Last time he was sent straight out to the desert – North Africa. After that he was sent straight out to Burma so he's never seen our little Patsy yet.'

'It must be hard for you,' Lillian said. 'What about your parents? I expect they help.'

Jean shook her head. 'Both killed in the blitz,' she said. 'The house got a direct hit. Me and the kids have been bombed out twice. I thought we was safe at last till these doodlebugs started.'

Lillian's shook her head. 'I'm so sorry. We're so lucky here. All we've had is a few daylight hit-and-run raids when the Canadians were here. My father was killed in one of those.'

'And your mum's an invalid?' Jean looked ceilingwards. 'Stays in her room all the time, does she?'

Lillian nodded. 'To be honest I don't think there's all that much wrong with her. Since Daddy was killed it's all in her mind.'

Jean shook her head. 'Can't be easy for you.' She raised an enquiring eyebrow. 'So – you're not married obviously. Boyfriend?'

Lillian smiled and nodded. 'Alan. He's in the Navy.'

'Mum like him, does she?'

Lillian flushed. 'She doesn't actually know about him,' she said. 'We haven't known each other very long.'

'Oh dear.' Jean looked long and hard at Lillian. Privately she thought it was time she took charge of her own life, but she didn't say so. It wasn't her place. After all, they'd only just met.

When Jim woke up he didn't know where he was at first. His sister was still fast asleep in the big bed beside him, her cheeks rosy and her thumb still firmly plugged into her mouth. Very carefully he got out of bed and pulled on his shorts and jersey; then he let himself out on to the landing and stood listening. It was very quiet. He remembered now how they'd arrived and the nice dinner the lady had made them. Egg and chips; his favourite. Then he remembered the horrible cow thing on the wall downstairs and shivered. It was a big house. You could get lost in a house this big. There could be monsters and all sorts hiding in the shadows. Where was Mum? Suddenly he wanted very much to see her.

He went down the stairs and found himself on another landing with a lot of doors. Which one was Mum behind, he wondered? Better try them all. The first room was empty, but when he opened the next one a voice spoke, making him jump.

'What are you doing in here, child?'

It was dim in the room because the curtains were partly drawn but Jim could make out a big bed and someone in it. The person was sitting up in the bed and wearing a pink knitted jacket thing. He took a step closer and saw that it was an old woman. She was a bit scary, but not as scary as the 'cow'.

'Hello,' he ventured. 'I'm Jim. What's your name?'

Laura was slightly taken aback. 'Never mind that, child,' she snapped. 'You are not supposed to be in here. Where is your mother?'

'Dunno,' Jim said. 'I woke up and I was lookin' for her.' His throat suddenly closed up and his eyes filled with tears which he blinked back. He was a big boy. Big boys didn't cry. 'I – I want my mum,' he said shakily.

'There, there now, it's all right. Don't get upset. Your mother is downstairs I expect.'

Jim swallowed hard and took a step closer. The old woman didn't sound so bad after all. A sudden notion struck him. 'Are you Auntie Lillian's mum?'

'My name is Mrs Mason,' Laura said stiffly. 'And yes, Lillian is my daughter.'

'Are you 'avin' a lie-in?' Jim asked.

'Not exactly.'

'A forty winks then? Katie'n'me had a forty winks. Katie's still asleep but I woke up. I'm older than Katie. I'm four – nearly five.'

'I see. Run along now – Jim, did you say your name is? I want to be on my own.'

Ignoring the request, Jim took another step towards the bed and said in a soft conspiratorial voice, ' 'Ere, did you know there's a cow downstairs?' he whispered. 'It's 'orrible. It *looks* at you.'

'A *cow*?'

'Yeah, but it's only its 'ead. Auntie Lillian said she'd take it away, 'cause I don't like it.'

'Ah – you must mean the moose head in the hall,' Laura said. 'It's not a cow, it's a moose. That's a big animal from a foreign country a long way away – across the sea. My father shot that one.'

'Cor!' Jim's eyes grew round. 'Has he got a gun then?'

'He did have. It's a long time ago now.'

'Did he let you have a go with it?'

In spite of herself Laura was beginning to smile. 'Oh no,' she said. 'Guns are not for little girls.'

'You're not a little girl though, are you?' Jim stood on tiptoe to peer at Laura closely. 'Your face is all wrinkly like a granny's. Are you a granny?'

Laura bridled and was about to remind him that personal remarks were rude when he added, 'My granny got killed by a bomb; my granddad too. It hit their house when they was asleep and knocked it all down. Our house got bombed down an' all – two times.'

'Oh dear.' Laura leaned towards him. 'Do you like toffees – Jim?'

'Coo, yeah!'

She reached out to her bedside table and opened a tin, holding it out to him. 'Here you are. You can take one for your sister too. I suppose your baby sister is too little for sweets.'

'Yeah,' Jim said peering into the tin. 'She just has Mum's chest.'

'Take two then, and then I think you had better go downstairs and find your mother.'

Jim took the two sweets and trotted obediently towards the door. When he reached it he stopped and turned to Laura with a puzzled frown. 'It's not night time. It's sunny outside,' he said. 'So why've you got the curtains drawed?' With a sudden burst of inspiration, he asked. 'Have you got the measles? When I had the measles I had to have the curtains drawed in the daytime.'

Laura smiled. 'No, I haven't got the measles, Jim. You can open the curtains if you like.'

He went to the window and pulled the curtains back. 'There you are,' he said with a bright grin. 'I can see you now. An' you can see me.'

Laura smiled. 'So I can. And haven't you got nice red hair?'

Jim fingered his mop of ginger curls doubtfully. 'Have I? Tell you what,' he said. 'You can be my new granny if you like.'

'Can I? Thank you, Jim.'

At that moment the door opened and Lillian's head came round it. 'Oh there you are, Jim,' she said. She glanced anxiously at her mother and saw to her amazement that Laura was smiling. 'Sorry, Mummy,' she said, taking Jim's hand. 'I expect he got lost. I'll bring you a cup of tea in a little while.'

Outside on the landing Jim looked up at her. 'Your mum's gonna be my new granny,' he said happily through a mouthful of toffee. 'I like her. She gave me a sweetie. One for Katie 'n' all.'

Hazel also had two evacuees billeted on her; Mary Grant, an elderly grandmother and her ten-year-old grandson, Harry. Mrs Grant was a tall, dignified woman who clearly doted on her daughter's only child. Hazel took Harry along to school with her the following morning and registered him, even though there was only one week left of the term.

'It will help him to settle in,' she told his grandmother. 'And he'll probably make some friends he can play with during the holidays.'

There was plenty of room at 4 Broadway Lane and Mrs Grant, who asked Hazel to call her Mary, insisted that she would cook and clean for Hazel while she was there.

'I'm no good at doing nothing,' she said. 'I moved in with Sally, my daughter when her hubby went off to the war. She works in a munitions factory and I keep house for her and look after young Harry here.'

Looking in the local paper Hazel saw that the town's annual Holidays At Home programme was being arranged. There was to be a week of entertainments, the highlight of which was to be a big picnic in the park. There were to be two bands; competitions and races for the children with prizes, and later in the evening there was to be dancing for the adults. Hazel showed the paper to Mary.

'Shall we go to the picnic?' she asked. 'Harry would like it, wouldn't he?'

Mary nodded. 'Sounds good,' she said. 'He seems to have made a few mates at school. He says he's going to the swimming-baths this afternoon with two of them.'

'It's a pity we can't go to the beach,' Hazel said. 'There has been talk of taking down the barbed wire so that we can go on the promenade again, but goodness knows when the beach defences will come down.'

It was Friday and Hazel asked Mary if she would like to accompany her to the Bay Tree Café for her usual afternoon tea meeting with Lillian. The older woman shook her head.

'No, you go and meet your friend, dear,' she said. 'I'll be all right here. I've got my knitting. It's a nice day. I might even work in the garden. It could do with weeding here and there.'

So Hazel went off to meet Lillian on her own as usual.

Lillian was full of her family of evacuees. 'Jean is such good company,' she said. 'I can't believe that she's two years younger than me and yet she has three children already. Her husband is in Burma.'

'Have you heard from Alan?' Hazel asked.

Lillian shook her head. 'Not for weeks now. I don't know what to think. I don't want it to be because he's stopped being interested in me, yet at the same time the alternative is—'

'I'm sure you'll hear soon,' Hazel put in quickly. 'Getting letters posted when they're at sea can't be easy.'

'What about you? Have you heard any news about – anybody?'

Hazel laughed. 'Anybody being Peter? No. I don't expect to. He will have left Yorkshire by now. He could be anywhere. I've resigned myself to the fact that I won't see him again.'

'Well, I think it's a shame,' Lillian said.

Hazel passed her friend the plate of cakes. 'So do I, but there's nothing to be done about it.' In an attempt to take the woeful look from Lillian's face she said, 'Have you seen the Holidays At Home programme in the local paper? It looks even better this year – a whole week of things to do.'

'I did see something, yes. There are posters up everywhere.'

'Shall we go to the picnic – and take our respective evacuee families?'

Lillian looked doubtful. 'I don't know. There's Mummy.'

'Surely she'd be all right for a couple of hours.'

Lillian shrugged. 'It needn't stop Jean taking the children though.'

'I'm sure she'd appreciate your help with them,' Hazel suggested. 'Three is quite a handful and you'd enjoy it. We could all go together – make a party of it.' Hazel suddenly had a thought. 'I wonder if Ruby would like to go too. It's being arranged for early-closing day so she should be free. I'll go round to the Joneses on my way home and ask her.' She looked at Lillian. 'Is that a date then?'

Lillian laughed. 'You're not twisting my arm by any chance, are you?'

'Well, you must admit that it needs a little twisting occasionally.'

On her way home Hazel stopped off at the Joneses' shop. She found Ruby working behind the counter. The girl looked tired and grubby and totally downcast, but she brightened up when she saw Hazel.

'Hello, Miss Dean! What can I get you?'

'I'll have a lettuce and a pound of tomatoes, please.' While Ruby was getting the salad items from behind the counter she said, 'I wondered if you'd like to come to the Holidays At Home picnic with us, Ruby. My friend and I both have evacuees staying with us and we thought we'd make a party of it. You'd be very welcome.'

Ruby's pale cheeks coloured. 'Oh, Miss Dean, I'd—'

'She's got no time for gadding off to no picnics.' The voice was Myrtle Jones's. She stood in the doorway of the back room, her face glowering with disapproval. 'Ruby's got her work to do, thank you very much,' she said, folding her arms.

'It's on early-closing day,' Hazel pointed out. 'You do close your shop on Wednesday afternoons, don't you, Mrs Jones?'

The woman nodded. 'We do,' she conceded. 'An' that's the only time we gets for doin' the 'ousework. Ruby's needed 'ere.'

Hazel glanced at Ruby. 'So what time off do you get, Ruby?' she asked. When the girl simply looked at her feet she said, 'You do know that you are obliged by law to give your staff adequate time off, don't you, Mrs Jones?'

Myrtle sniffed. 'She gets time off when it suits me,' she said. 'Not when it suits some – some—'

'Some what?' Hazel's eyes flashed with anger. 'Some upstart school teacher were you about to say?'

'Well – you said it. Not me!'

'Then perhaps it would be more appropriate for me to send round someone from the child protection team,' Hazel wasn't at all sure that there was such a body but she saw that the suggestion, bluff though it was had hit the mark. Seeing she had scored she pressed the point: 'Ruby was billeted on you,' she went on, 'to be in your care, not to be your slave.'

'Her mam never sent a penny piece to help with her keep . . .'

'I am well aware of that,' Hazel said. 'That is Ruby's misfortune, not her fault and I don't see why she should be punished for it. I'm sure she has more than repaid her debt to you by now.' She looked from one to the other. 'Now – I came round to ask her out on her afternoon off. I take it that will be all right?'

Myrtle flushed an unbecoming shade of puce. 'I s'pose so, if you insist,' she said grudgingly.

Hazel smiled at Ruby. 'That's settled then. I'll come and pick you up at twelve o'clock next Wednesday.' She picked up her purchases and turned to leave. 'Good afternoon, Mrs Jones,' she said. 'And thank you for your co-operation.'

When she was out of earshot Myrtle looked at Ruby with spite glistening in her eyes. 'I'd like to know what a teacher wants with a girl like you,' she said. 'Something funny there if you ask me!' She half turned to leave then over her shoulder she delivered her parting shot. 'You needn't think you're takin' no sandwiches to this picnic thing,' she said. 'And don't you dare pinch no fruit from the shop neither. If Miss High'n'Mighty wants you there she can bloody well feed you an' all.'

The Kendall children were excited when they heard about the picnic. Lillian and Jean were deep in discussion about what food they could rustle up to take when Jim suddenly asked,

'What about Granny?'

Everyone stopped talking to look at him. Jean smiled. 'What do you mean love?'

'Granny Upstairs,' he said. 'We gotta take her too.'

Jean looked at Lillian. 'Does she ever get up?' she asked.

Lillian shook her head. 'She complains of weakness. Anyway she's been in bed for so long that I doubt if she could walk very far.'

'Could we borrow a wheelchair from somewhere for her?'

Jim jumped up and down and clapped his hands. 'Yeah! I could push her.'

Lillian was shaking her head. 'I doubt if she'd agree to that,' she said. 'She never was very keen on crowds and I don't know what she'd make of the suggestion of a wheelchair.'

'We could at least ask her,' Jean said.

'I'll ask her,' Jim volunteered. 'Let me – *please* let me!'

Before they could stop him he had jumped up and was climbing the stairs. He burst into Laura's room where she was reading the local paper.

'Granny! We're gonna take you to the big picnic in the park,' he said. 'We're gonna get you a pushchair an' *I'm* gonna push you!'

Lillian, who'd been hard on his heels winced as she heard his words and waited for her mother's angry retort. To her surprise she heard Laura say,

'Are you, Jim? Well, what a nice surprise.'

'They said you wouldn't wanna go, but you do wanna go with us, don't you, Granny?' Jim said, his copper head on one side and a cheeky grin on his face.

'Of course I'd like to go with you,' Laura said. 'I'm looking forward to it already.'

With the soft-fruit season in full swing there were plenty of strawberries and raspberries around. There was also a glut of local salad vegetables so that when it came to packing a picnic there were no problems. Hazel and Lillian had help from Mary and Jean. They were all up early, working hard cutting and wrapping sandwiches. Mary had made cakes and some apple pies and by the time they had finished they had a veritable feast to take to the park.

Lillian had discovered her old pram in the attic covered in dust sheets and it was dragged downstairs, cleaned and polished for baby Patsy. Lillian had made a phone call to Doctor Frazer to ask if her mother was fit to be taken out for the day. He had agreed that it would do her a world of good and had even arranged the loan of a wheelchair for Laura from the local hospital. Lillian still couldn't quite believe that her mother would actually get out of bed and go to the picnic, but little Jim had no doubts at all. He seemed to have worked some kind of magic on her. She was out of bed before seven o'clock and ordering Lillian to press her best dress and summer coat and demanding to know the whereabouts of her straw hat decorated with daisies.

Hazel went along to the Joneses to pick Ruby up at twelve. The girl had done her best with her appearance but the print frock she wore was too short and tightly strained across her developing chest. She wore no socks and her feet were squeezed into much worn sandals at least two sizes too small for her. But she had washed her hair and scrubbed at her stained hands. When she saw Hazel her face lit up. It was all too plain that a day away from the Joneses and their shop was something she'd looked forward to.

The park gates were decorated with streamers and balloons and a large banner fixed to the archway above proclaimed, *Valemouth Holidays At Home 1944.* Jean pushed baby Patsy in Lillian's high coachbuilt pram. Jim insisted that he was going to push 'Granny Upstairs' in her wheelchair, even though he was barely tall enough to reach the handle. Lillian was allowed to help, discreetly steering the chair while Laura sat rigidly upright in it wearing her daisy-trimmed straw hat and looking about her with more interest than Lillian had seen her show for years. Ruby walked behind holding little Katie's hand whilst Hazel and Harry carried the picnic basket between them.

The atmosphere was one of carnival with the band playing and everyone in a buoyant mood. Ice cream was on sale again after being banned for most of the war. Jim and Katie had never tasted it before and their eyes filled with delight as they licked their cornets. There were fairground rides too, with prancing horses for the older children and little cars with hooters for the younger ones.

They found a shady spot under some trees and while Jean found a private corner in which to feed the baby, Lillian spread out the rug she had brought and the picnic cloth, helping Hazel to set out the sandwiches and treats they had worked so hard to prepare. Ruby's eyes were round at the sight of the spread. Hazel looked at her.

'Help yourself, Ruby,' she said. 'There's plenty for all of us.'

The girl hesitated. 'I haven't brought anything,' she said. 'Mrs Jones wouldn't let me.'

Hazel smiled. 'I wonder why that doesn't surprise me?' she said. 'But we've made plenty for everybody so just tuck in. Today's a holiday and I want us all to enjoy it.' She sat down beside Ruby to make sure the girl did not hang back. She watched her as she ate. 'Ruby – forgive me for asking, but do the Joneses pay you a proper wage?'

Ruby coloured. 'Well – I get pocket money,' she said.

'How much pocket money?'

Ruby looked at her. 'You won't tell anyone, will you? She asked fearfully. 'I'm not supposed to tell.'

'I won't tell anyone if you don't want me to.'

'Promise?'

'I promise.'

'I get half a crown.'

Hazel stared at the girl, her sandwich halfway to her mouth. '*Two shillings and sixpence*?' she said. 'A week! For working all day in the shop and doing the housework on your afternoon off?'

Ruby looked uncomfortable and Hazel quickly checked herself. 'I'm sorry, Ruby,' she said. 'This is supposed to be a holiday. I shouldn't have asked you.'

'It's all right, Miss Dean,' Ruby said. 'You're right. It's horrible at the Joneses. Rene and Tom make my life a misery and Mrs Jones does nothing to stop them. I wish my mum would come and get me. I wish . . .'

Hazel saw the tears well up in the girl's eyes and put an arm round her shoulders. 'You don't have to put up with it, you know,' she said. 'You could always apply for another job. Look in the local paper to see what's on offer. You're a bright girl.'

'Where would I live though?' Ruby asked. 'I've got nowhere to go.'

Hazel paused. 'I know. There are jobs where accommodation is offered – in hotels and so on. You'd be paid a proper wage too. It wouldn't be much but anything would be better than the slavery you're putting up with now.' She gave Ruby's thin shoulders a squeeze. 'And any time you want a friend to talk to you can come and see me.'

Ruby blinked hard. 'Thank you, Miss Dean.'

The afternoon was taken up with the children's races and competitions. The Kendall children were too young to take part, but young Harry won the sack race and the egg and spoon and received a toy Spitfire as his prize. All the children had ride after ride on the roundabouts until Jean called a halt, fearing that Jim and Katie might be sick.

As four o'clock approached the little ones began to look sleepy. It was clear that Laura had had enough too. Mary suggested that she would help Jean take Laura and the children back to The Laurels.

'You and Lillian have an hour to yourselves,' she suggested to Hazel. 'You've both worked so hard, arranging all this for us. Go for a walk by the lake or listen to the band. I'll see that everyone's all right. Harry can manage the basket by himself now that it's empty.'

The girls agreed and watched as the little party made its way towards the park gates. Katie perched on top of the pram, heavy-eyed, thumb firmly wedged into her rosebud mouth. Tired out with his busy day, Jim submitted himself to the indignity of sitting on Laura's lap in the chair and being pushed home by Mary while Harry brought up the rear with the empty picnic basket. Ruby said her goodbyes too.

'I've had a lovely day. Thanks ever so much for inviting me, Miss Dean,' she said. 'And I'll remember what you said.'

The crowds were beginning to thin out and the air was redolent with the scent of bruised grass and hot engine oil. Hazel looked at Lillian.

'Well, I think we can safely say that today was a success.'

Lillian nodded. 'Yes, thanks to you. Sometimes I wonder what I did before you came back to Valemouth,' she said. 'You've made such a difference to my life.'

Hazel laughed. 'I think young Jim has woven some kind of spell around your mother,' she said. 'He seems to be able to twist her round his little finger.'

Lillian looked thoughtful. 'I overheard her talking to Jean when we were eating our lunch,' she said. 'She told her she had always wanted a son – that when she was expecting me she had prayed and prayed for a little boy. She said having a daughter had been the biggest disappointment of her life.'

Hazel saw how much the overheard remark had hurt Lillian and felt a pang of pity. 'I'm sure she didn't mean it,' she said. 'You've been such a wonderful daughter to her. She couldn't have had a better.'

Lillian nodded. 'Jean pointed out to her that a son would have been fighting in the war by now, or that if he'd married she would have lost him to his wife.'

'She was right.'

'I know.' Lillian looked at her. 'It didn't help though. I feel that my life has been wasted,' she said. 'That all I've ever done for Mummy has been no more than she feels I owe her. All these years she's been making me pay for not being a son.'

Hazel took her arm. 'I'm sure that if she knew you'd heard she'd be devastated.' She squeezed Lillian's arm. 'Come on, let's go and listen to the band. There are some free seats now and I could do with a sit down.'

They found two seats near the front of the enclosure and settled down to enjoy the music. The Valemouth Prize Brass Band had won accolades up and down the country before the war, but now the players consisted mostly of the very young or the elderly; musicians too old or too young for the services. However, they played well and even if their blue-and-silver braided uniforms did not fit quite as well as they might have done, at least they were smart and well pressed.

As the girls took their seats the band was playing a selection from *The Maid of the Mountains*. It came to an end and the audience clapped. The conductor turned to acknowledge the applause and Hazel gasped. He was smiling, bowing to right and left until suddenly his eyes found her astonished ones and his expression froze.

Lillian was looking at her friend in alarm. 'What is it, Hazel? Aren't you well? You've gone very white.'

But Hazel could not take her eyes off the man standing on the platform above them who was trying to make discreet signals to her.

At last she found her voice. 'It – it's Peter,' she said.

The man taking the part of master of ceremonies for the day stepped up on to the platform and took the microphone from its stand.

'Ladies and gentlemen. The band will now take a short intermission,' he announced. 'They will commence playing again at six o'clock and I would like to remind you that this evening there will be dancing to the Silver Wings RAF dance band from eight o'clock until midnight.'

Hazel hardly heard what he was saying. She was watching as Peter put away his baton and unbuttoned his uniform jacket. As the crowd began to disperse Lillian looked at her.

'What are you going to do?'

Hazel shook her head. She had lost sight of Peter now, lost him among the other musicians as they filed off the platform to the steps at the rear of the bandstand. 'What? Oh – maybe a walk by the lake,' she said vaguely.

The girls stood up and began to walk away but a moment later Hazel felt a hand on her shoulder and heard a familiar voice.

'Hazel!'

She turned. 'Peter! What a surprise.'

'Don't pretend you didn't recognize me. Were you actually going to leave without speaking to me?'

Lillian cleared her throat. 'I think I'll go now, Hazel,' she said. 'I shouldn't have left the others to see Mummy home anyway. I'll see you soon.'

'What? Oh, oh, yes – all right.' Hazel hardly saw her friend go. She felt as though she were in some kind of dream. Peter took her arm.

'Come on, let's go and get something to drink. We've got some catching up to do.'

Lillian walked home. She felt suddenly exhausted and it seemed a very long way. Fancy Hazel's friend Peter suddenly turning up like that. She couldn't help feeling a little envious but she pushed the feeling aside. It was just what Hazel needed. She obviously missed Peter and had a lot of regrets about the way they had parted. Now perhaps they'd have the chance they needed to straighten their feelings out.

She still hadn't heard from Alan. Was she foolish to have read so much into their short association? One visit to the cinema and a brief kiss on the station platform; that was all they'd had. He'd probably have forgotten what she looked like by now.

At home she found that Mary had kindly helped Laura to bed before she left with Harry. She went up to see if her mother needed anything and found her fretful.

'Lillian! There you are at last! Where have you been? Can you imagine how humiliating it was to have some complete stranger helping me to bed?'

'I'm sorry, Mummy. I'm here now. You had a nice day, didn't you?'

'If I did it was no thanks to you,' Laura grumbled. 'If it had been up to you I'd have been left here on my own all day. It was only that child who took pity on me.'

'I think you're a bit overtired, Mummy,' Lillian said, summoning all her patience. 'Shall I get you a hot drink?'

'Well, I'd have expected you to do that anyway. Why do you always have to be *told* to do everything? Even little Jim can anticipate my needs better than you can.'

As Lillian trailed wearily down the stairs the telephone began to ring. In the hall she picked up the receiver.

'Hello, Lillian Mason speaking.'

'Hello. It's Mrs Blakely here.'

'Mrs Blakely!' Lillian was at a loss to know why the plumber's wife would be ringing her. 'What can I do for you?'

'Oh my dear, I know you and he met only briefly, but he was very taken with you. He told me so,' the woman said breathlessly.

Lillian's heart gave a lurch. '*Alan*?'

'Yes. I'm sure he'd want you to know, dear, which is why I'm ringing you. His ship, HMS *Redoubtable* was torpedoed a week ago. We're praying as hard as we can but as far as they can tell there are no known survivors.'

CHAPTER SEVEN

In the tea tent Peter and Hazel sat opposite each other over a pot of tea at one of the spindly tables.

'I don't understand,' she said. 'What on earth are you doing here in Valemouth, conducting the local brass band? It's such a bizarre coincidence that I still can't quite believe it.'

He grinned at her across the table and her heart almost stopped. She'd almost forgotten that grin, half vulnerable, half confident; the one that could win him anything.

'It's not as bizarre as you think and it's certainly no coincidence.' He took a sip of his tea and sighed with satisfaction. 'God, I needed that. That uniform's so hot and scratchy, it almost killed me.' He put down the cup. 'I left Mekeley Moor at Easter. At least I left as Head. I stayed on with Gerald for the first two weeks of the summer term, just to help him settle in – his idea by the way, not mine. He was keen to keep the choir going and he wanted help with it. Well, then it was a case of where do I go from here? I've studied music and I've always wanted to teach it so I thought it might be worth trying for a Government grant – to get a post-grad teaching qualification in music.' He smiled. 'Luckily for me it came off. I start a one-year course at the London Academy in September. Meantime I saw some adverts for temporary conductors for various semi-pro bands in the music journal I take. I thought that might be fun, then I spotted an ad for the Valemouth Brass Band. They were short of a conductor for the "Hols at Home" season.' He grinned. 'The rest, as they say – is history.'

She looked at him. 'Are you saying that you took the job because. . . ?'

'Well what do *you* think? Of course I jumped at it, knowing

Valemouth was your home town. If you hadn't turned up during the week I was going to take a chance and come round to see you, though I wasn't even sure if you were still living at Broadway Lane, or what kind of reception I'd get.' He looked at her, his head on one side. 'Is my turning up like the proverbial bad penny, too horrible for words? You looked pretty shocked when you saw me.'

'No, of course it's not horrible.'

He ran a hand through his hair. 'Then bloody say something, can't you? Even if it's only *get lost*.'

Suddenly she felt the laughter bubbling up inside her. Reaching for his hand she said, 'Oh, Peter, it's so good to see you. I've missed you so much.'

'Phew! That's more like it! So if you missed me why didn't you write?'

'Why didn't you?'

He shrugged. 'I had the feeling you were mixed up – that you needed time to get your head sorted out. I even wondered whether you might still be having second thoughts about Gerald. I waited. I thought you might get in touch after you'd had some time away from us all – but you didn't.'

'I wasn't sure that you'd want me to. After that business with Gladys Brompton over her letter to Gerald I thought you'd think I was some kind of . . . of . . .'

'Of what?' His fingers closed round her hand and squeezed it, grinning impishly at her. 'That was a turn-up for the book all right, wasn't it? I wouldn't have missed it for the world. Everyone admired the way you let her have it. I don't think they thought you had it in you. Seriously though, Hazel, I think I'm a better judge of character than you think. You were always open about your relationship with Gerald. I got to know him a bit during the short time we worked together and we had some bloke to bloke talks. He felt bad about you. He felt he took advantage of your youth and inexperience. He did fall for you, it seems, in a pretty big way, but he could see afterwards that it was a mistake and very unfair on you.'

Hazel looked at him, her eyes wide. 'He said that?'

'Yes, he did. And a good deal more besides. He's a good chap, Hazel. He's been through a hell of a lot. I'm glad he's back in the place and the job he loves.'

'I had a letter from Joan Jameson last Christmas,' she told him.

'She filled me in on all the news.'

'I know.'

She stared at him. 'You – you *asked* her to write to me?'

He pursed his mouth. 'Mmm – well, let's say I sort of dropped the idea into her head and left the rest up to her.' He glanced at his watch. 'Oh God! Look at the time. I've got to get back to the stand.'

As they made their way out of the tent he took her arm. 'Hazel – will you come back this evening for the dancing? Meet me here at about half past eight?'

She looked up at him with shining eyes. 'I'd love that.'

'Me too. There's a lot more I want to say to you.' He was holding her arm, looking down at her when suddenly he drew her round to the side of the tent and pulled her close, his lips finding hers in a long, intense kiss. She found herself responding with all the pent up longing she'd tried so hard to stifle over the past months. As the kiss ended he tipped up her chin and looked into her eyes.

'I can't tell you how many times I've dreamed of doing that.'

She nodded. 'Me too.'

'I was beginning to think it would never be more than a dream. We've got so much time to make up.'

'I know.'

'Starting tonight. See you at half past eight?'

'See you at half past eight.'

'I'll wait for you near the bandstand.' A swift kiss on her forehead and he was gone, leaving her shaken – still half wondering if the whole thing had been a dream.

Hazel walked home to Broadway Lane in a daze, her feet hardly touching the ground. Seeing Peter again today was the last thing she'd expected. She could still hardly believe it. At home she bathed the grime of the day away and dressed in the only festive dress she owned, bought by Nana for her graduation ball in the summer of the year the war began. It was a classic style, blue silk with a swirling skirt, puffed sleeves and a tiny bodice with a heart-shaped neckline. And to her delight it still fitted her perfectly. From the back of her wardrobe she fished out the silver sandals and little evening bag that went with it. Mary looked on approvingly.

'At a guess I'd say that you've got a date with someone special,' she said with a smile.

Hazel returned her smile. 'Someone I haven't seen for months till today,' she told her. 'It was quite unexpected.'

'And more than welcome by the stars in your eyes.' Mary handed her a lacy black crochet shawl. 'Better take this,' she said. 'It might get chilly later on.' Her eyes twinkled. 'Even if you do have your love to keep you warm, as the song says.'

Hazel shook her head. 'I can't take this. It's lovely but it's yours.'

Mary smiled. 'It's for you. I always have a bit of knitting or crochet on the go, to keep my hands busy. I thought you might like it.'

Touched, Hazel held the soft wool against her cheek. 'Thank you. I shall treasure it.'

Everyone had read in the papers that the blackout was to be relaxed and in the park the trees around the bandstand were festooned with fairy lights, twinkling away among the branches as the dusk deepened. The enclosure had been cleared of chairs and a temporary wooden dance floor had been laid in sections. Hazel saw him at once, He'd changed into a dark suit and he looked handsome as he waited for her by the bandstand. He waved and came towards her as The Silver Wings RAF Dance Band struck up a popular tune. *You'll never know just how much I love you.* A vocalist in evening dress stepped up to the microphone at the front of the stage to sing. At once several couples took to the floor. Peter smiled at her.

'Shall we?'

'Let's.'

As they danced, Hazel's cheek pressed close to his, the words of the song seemed to take on a special significance.

You went away and my heart went with you.

Peter smiled down at her. 'And you did,' he whispered.

She smiled dreamily.

At The Laurels Jean and Lillian sat down together to share a supper of left-over sandwiches from the picnic and a pot of tea. The children were in bed and Laura was asleep at last. Ever since she had arrived home from the park she had complained non-stop. Her legs ached – her back ached – her head ached. She had indigestion, all due to the sandwiches Lillian had made. They had too much seasoning in them. Last but not least she insisted that she was suffering from sunstroke, even though everyone had taken care to keep her chair in the shade all day.

'Maybe it's all been too much for her,' Jean said, feeling sorry for Lillian, who looked exhausted. 'It was my idea. I should have asked you first.'

Lillian smiled. 'It was Jim's idea really,' she said. 'He adores Mummy. They seem to have built up a bond.'

Jean looked closely at Lillian. 'There's something wrong, isn't there, love?' she said gently. 'Is it to do with the phone call you had earlier?'

Although she bit her lip hard Lillian felt the tears welling up. Pulling a handkerchief from her pocket she dabbed at her eyes and swallowed hard. 'I'm sorry,' she snuffled through the hanky. 'This isn't like me. I don't normally do this kind of thing. It's just – just . . .'

'Just what?' Jean reached forward and laid a hand on her arm. 'Why don't you tell me – get it off your chest?'

'It's Alan,' Lillian said bleakly. 'His mother rang me. His ship was torpedoed a week ago. They say there are no – no known survivors.' The sobs began in earnest and Jean got up and went to put an arm around her shoulders.

'Oh, poor Lillian,' she said. 'You should have said something before.'

'I – I hardy knew him really,' Lillian said. 'You must think me really silly.'

'Of course I don't,' Jean said. 'It's a dread we've all had to live with all through the war; the telegram, the knock on the door. You met him and you fell for him quickly. It happens all the time.'

'The thing is I'll never have the chance to know him better now, will I?'

'You might,' Jean said. 'When it happens at sea there's always confusion. When they say "no known survivors" it means just that. There's still hope he might be OK.'

Lillian dried her eyes and stuffed the sodden hanky back into her pocket. 'Better to face facts,' she said. 'A torpedo does a lot of damage. There's not much of a chance really, is there?'

'Well I believe in having faith,' Jean said firmly. 'I've had to have it for the past five years and it's carried me through.' She took both of Lillian's hands in hers and looked into her eyes. 'I will say this, though, even though it's none of my business. You've got to stand up to your mum. She leads you a right merry dance. She should be told that you have a life too. And human feelings.'

'I overheard what she said to you today,' Lillian told her. 'I've always been a big disappointment to her. I don't think she sees me as a woman at all; just the girl child she didn't want and she means to make me pay for it.'

'Now you're talking like a victim!' Jean said. 'You've got to stop seeing yourself like that. If you ask me I think your mother could easily get up and lead a normal life like anybody else.' She smiled. 'And before the kids and me leave here I'd like to see that happen.'

Lillian smiled. 'Thanks, Jean,' she said. 'It's been lovely having you and the children here. It looks as if the V1s are easing off now and I'm glad about that of course, but I'm really going to miss you when you go home.'

Peter walked Hazel home slowly in the moonlight, his arm around her waist.

As they turned into Broadway Lane he said, 'I've only got two more days here, then we're off to some place called Branchester – know it?'

Hazel nodded. 'It's a little market town, not all that far away,' she told him. 'Where will you stay?'

'I've got digs with the tuba player and his wife,' he told her. 'Sam and Margaret West. They're smashing people.

'So you'll be coming back to Valemouth each evening?'

'Yes, though I have to rely on public transport nowadays. Once I stopped being a headmaster I lost my petrol allowance, so I had to sell the old crate.'

'But it does mean that we won't have to say goodbye this weekend.'

He stopped walking and drew her round to face him. 'You want to go on seeing me, then?'

She laughed. 'After tonight? Are you joking? I'm not letting you go that easily.'

'Oh, Hazel, I can't tell you how good that sounds. I just didn't want to take anything for granted.' He drew her into the shelter of a tree, pulling her close and for a long time neither of them spoke till Hazel stirred in his arms. 'Peter, it must be terribly late. How are you getting home?'

'Who cares?' he said, his mouth against her hair. 'At a guess I'd say I'll probably float home on a cloud.'

'Ever the practical one.' She touched his cheek with her fingertips and felt the faint roughness of his early morning stubble. 'There's an old bike of Nana's in the garden shed,' she told him. 'You're welcome to borrow it.' She paused, looking up at him wistfully. 'I'd let you stay only I've got evacuees so the house is full.'

He leaned his forehead against hers and groaned. 'Oh, Hazel, *don't*,' he begged. 'The images you're creating in my head are enough to send a sane man round the bend!' He kissed her. 'OK, lead me to Nana's sit-up-and-beg machine,' he said. 'But I warn you, those evacuees don't realize the diabolical torture they're putting an innocent man through!'

Lillian and Hazel met as usual on Friday afternoon. Hazel talked about Peter all the time. Lillian thought she looked ten times prettier and more alive than she had since they had renewed their acquaintance. She couldn't help feeling a pang of envy, which she quickly put aside.

'So the band is off to Branchester next week,' Hazel was saying. 'But he's staying with a local couple so he'll be back each evening.' She looked up at her friend and registered for the first time how pale she was. There were lines of anguish etched around her eyes and mouth and she looked quite ill. Reaching out her hand she touched Lillian's arm.

'Oh, listen to me,' she said. 'Here I am going on and on about Peter and I haven't even asked how you are,' she said. 'Is everything all right? Your mother. . . ?'

'Mummy's her usual cantankerous self,' Lillian said. 'It's Alan. I had a call from his mother on Wednesday evening. His ship has been torpedoed and there are no known survivors.'

'*Oh!*' Hazel's hand flew to her mouth. 'Oh, my God! I'm so *sorry*, Lillian. Why didn't you say something to stop my inane chattering? You must have thought me so self-centred.'

Lillian was shaking her head. 'You weren't to know. No. I'm really happy for you. It's nice that someone has good news.'

'There don't seem to be so many V1s coming over either,' Hazel said. 'We'll soon be losing our house guests.'

Lillian's eyes filled with tears. 'I'm going to miss Jean and the children so much,' she said. 'Having them around has brought the house to life again. When they've gone home . . .'

'I know. I'll miss Mary and Harry too.' Hazel was concerned for her friend. She was clearly exhausted but, more than that, she was showing signs of severe depression. 'Look, Lillian, you need a break,' she said.

Lillian laughed. 'A break – me? How can *I* have a break?'

'You say the doctor visits your mother once a month. He must see how exhausted you are. Ask him to get her into hospital or a nursing home for a week so that you can get away for a few days. If you don't have one you're going to crack up.' When Lillian still looked unconvinced she said, 'Look, it's the summer holidays now and I could go with you if you like. We needn't go far – just along the coast – maybe to Highcliffe Cove. There are no beach defences there. We could even bathe.'

Lillian looked longingly at her. 'Oh – that would be wonderful,' she said. 'But I don't think for a moment that Mummy would agree to it.'

'What would she do if you were ill?' Hazel asked. 'She'd have no option then so don't give her one now. Just do it. I'll make all the arrangements.'

'But – what about Peter?'

Hazel laughed. 'You're determined to put obstacles in the way, aren't you? It will only be for a few days and he's busy all week anyway.' A thought suddenly occurred to her. 'Tell you what – why don't we try and take Ruby too? I don't think the poor child has ever had a holiday.' She grinned. 'If I can brave the wrath of the ferocious Myrtle Jones I'm sure you can find the courage to persuade your mother.'

As it happened Lillian didn't have to ask the doctor to find a bed in a nursing home for Laura. When Jean heard of Hazel's suggestion she had one of her own to add.

'Just you go ahead and make arrangements. I'll look after your ma for a few days,' she offered. 'If I can cope with three stroppy kids one old lady won't make no difference, and I'll have Hilda to help me, won't I?'

'And me!' Jim, who had been listening, jumped up and down excitedly. 'I can help too! I can take Granny Upstairs's dinners up and talk to her.'

Jean smiled at him and ruffled his curly head. 'That's right – talk the hind leg off a donkey, you can! But maybe you can get her to come downstairs for a while. We could sit outside in the sunshine or even go for a little walk.' She winked at Lillian. 'There's no knowing what magic we can work once we've got Granny to ourselves.'

Hazel walked round to the Joneses shop the next morning. As usual Ruby was behind the counter. She looked up with a smile when Hazel came in.

' 'Morning, Miss Dean.'

Hazel came straight to the point. 'Ruby, have you had your annual holiday this year?'

'Holiday?' Ruby shook her head, looking puzzled. 'No, miss.'

'Good, because my friend Lillian and I would like to take you with us to Highcliffe Cove for a few days, if it can be arranged.'

'Oh!' Ruby bit her lip. 'I don't know if . . .'

'It's all right, Ruby,' Hazel said. 'You're entitled by law to an annual holiday so it's just a case of whether you'd like to go with us or not?'

Ruby coloured. 'Oh, miss, I'd love to.'

'Then I'll arrange it with Mr and Mrs Jones.' Looking much more confident than she felt Hazel went to the door at the rear of the shop and called up the stairs. 'Mrs Jones! Can I have a word with you, please?'

Half an hour later Hazel left the shop with a smile of satisfaction on her face. The Joneses knew they could do no other than agree that, as their employee, Ruby was legally entitled to an annual holiday. It was just a question of arranging when it would be. Hazel had fought them before and won. And lurking at the back of Myrtle's mind was the dark threat of the mythical 'Child Protection Team'.

It was all arranged that Ruby would join Lillian and Hazel for a week at Highcliffe Cove in two weeks' time. Now all Hazel had to do was book their accommodation.

CHAPTER EIGHT

Standing at the top of the cliff path Ruby stared and stared down at the scene spread out beneath her. Sparkling blue water stretched as far as the eye could see, and directly below a little cove nestled in the shelter of tall cliffs. Golden sand caressed by frothy little wavelets beckoned invitingly. It was the first time she had ever seen the sea unencumbered by barbed-wire entanglements and concrete tank-traps, as it was at Valemouth.

'Oh!' she breathed. 'Ain't – isn't it lovely? But why aren't there any defences here?'

'I think it's because it's such a tiny cove,' Hazel said. 'Any attempted landing would need more space than this. It probably isn't even on the invasion maps.'

At Ocean View, the small guesthouse on the cliff top that Hazel had booked the three of them into, Ruby had a room all to herself. It was the first time ever that she hadn't had to share with anyone and to begin with it had seemed very strange.

The last few days at the Joneses had been nightmarish for her. Myrtle had found her even more chores to do to make up for the time she was to be absent. She'd had Ruby washing curtains, ironing piles of clothes, cleaning paintwork and scrubbing floors, even the one in the back kitchen that was ingrained with the dirt of decades. Myrtle had not been satisfied until she could see the pattern on the ancient linoleum, which no one could remember ever seeing before. It had taken four scrubbings and by the time Ruby had finished the hot water, Lifebuoy soap and soda had reduced her hands to red rawness. There had been no let-up when she was in her room at bedtime either. That was when Rene had started her taunting.

'Where's your 'oliday clothes then, Rubes?' she sneered. 'You ain't even got a bathin' costume. Gonna swimmin' in your knickers and vest, are you? A right sight you'll look and no mistake!' She laughed the coarse, shrill laugh that set Ruby's teeth on edge. 'Your darlin' Miss Dainty Dean an' her posh mate'll be downright ashamed of you – sorry they ever asked you to go with 'em when they sees what a mess you look.'

But all that was over now and she was here at Highcliffe Cove, about to spend her first morning on the beach. When they'd arrived the previous afternoon Miss Dean had helped her to unpack. She hadn't said anything but the look on her face was enough to show Ruby that her ex-teacher was surprised at the sparse contents of the two carrier bags that made up her luggage.

'Tell you what, Ruby,' she'd said. 'You're going to want to bathe or at least paddle so you'll need a swimsuit. Let's go out and see if we can find one, shall we?'

Ruby blushed. 'Oh, I couldn't, miss. I haven't got enough money and—'

'That's all right. We'll call it a birthday present.'

'But it ain't – *isn't* my birthday.'

'It will be though, won't it?' Miss Dean had looked at her. 'You've got to have one sometime. And by the way, you're not at school any more so you can call me Hazel and my friend's name is Lillian.'

Miss Dean – Hazel even had her book of clothing coupons with her and in a local draper's shop they found a lovely swimsuit made of bright red elasticized material that fitted her perfectly. Never in her life had she owned such a garment. She had it on now under her cotton frock and she couldn't wait to get down to the beach where she could take her frock off.

The sun shone down out of a cloudless blue sky and Hazel held her hand as they walked into the water. Ruby gasped as a sudden wave washed up as far as her tummy, but she soon grew used to it and found the water quite warm. Lillian didn't join them but lay on a rug on the beach. She looked pale and tired and Hazel explained when they were on their own that her young man, who was a sailor, had been lost at sea with his ship and that they were to let her rest quietly.

Hazel insisted that she would teach Ruby to swim and after two days she was confident enough to float on her back without Hazel's hand to support her. The following day she took her first tentative two strokes and after that there was no stopping her. She couldn't bear to come out of the water. She would have liked to stay in all day but Hazel laughingly pointed out that her teeth were chattering and that it was time she had something to eat.

It was so lovely being wrapped in a big towel and rubbed hard – 'to get the circulation going,' Hazel explained. Then sitting down, glowing all over, to eat a packed lunch with a drink of hot tea out of a Thermos flask.

One evening, halfway through the week, a man arrived at Ocean View just as they were finishing their evening meal. He was tall with fair hair and when he smiled at Ruby with his warm blue eyes and white teeth she was quite overwhelmed. Miss Dean introduced him to her just as though she was a grown up person.

'This is Mr Grainger – Peter. He was headmaster at the school in Yorkshire where I used to teach.'

Peter shook her hand and after a little while he and Hazel went off together. Lillian invited her to go for a walk.

'We haven't had a chance to talk, yet, have we, Ruby?' she said. 'We could walk along the cliff path and see if we can find some wild flowers if you like.'

As they walked Ruby glanced at Lillian. She'd only met her once before, at the Holidays At Home picnic. She'd met her mother too and had thought privately that the old lady looked a bit fierce. After they'd walked in silence for a few minutes she ventured to ask, 'Is your mother OK?'

Lillian looked surprised, then she remembered that Ruby had met Mummy at the picnic. 'She's fine, thank you, Ruby,' she said. 'It's hard for me to get away, but Jean from London, who is staying with me, is looking after her for a few days.'

'That's nice.' Ruby looked at her companion. 'I haven't seen my mum since I left London when the war started,' she said.

'You don't hear at all?'

'No. I've tried and so has everyone else. Miss Dean – Hazel – wrote to her to see if she'd let me go to the high school but . . . she never answered.' Ruby kicked at a stone and watched as it went over the edge of the cliff, gathering momentum as it travelled downwards. 'Sometimes I wonder if she might have been killed in the blitz.'

'Why don't you go up to London and see if you can find her?' Lillian suggested.

Ruby shrugged. 'I can't afford the train fare,' she said. 'I don't get paid very much.

They came to a bench and Lillian sat down and patted the bench beside her. 'What are you going to do with your life, Ruby?' she asked.

Ruby shrugged. 'Looks like I ain't – *haven't* got much choice.'

For a moment Lillian was silent. She knew the feeling all too well. Lying on the beach these last few days she'd done a lot of thinking. This girl might not think that they had anything in common, but they did. 'You know what I think?' she said. 'I think you sometimes have to take your life into your own hands.'

'How do you mean, miss – er – Lillian?'

'You only have one life. You can't afford to let other people live it for you,' Lillian went on. 'It's not right, so you have to sit down and ask yourself what you want out of it. And when you've decided you have to think of a way to achieve it.'

'But if you've got no home and no money,' Ruby said, 'and no family either, what then?'

Lillian sighed. 'Sometimes it's easier that way,' she said wistfully. 'All you really need is a chance to get out of the rut – but more important is the ability to recognize that chance when it comes along. Jean says you have to have faith. Maybe she has the answer, who knows?' She shivered. 'Ooh, it's getting chilly.' She stood up and held out her hand. 'Shall we start walking back?'

Ruby walked beside Lillian in silence, trying to digest what she'd been hearing. Much of it was double Dutch to her, except for one thing – asking yourself what you wanted from life. Well, she hadn't really given it much thought. All she was sure of was what she *didn't* want. She didn't want to spend any more time than she could help with the Joneses. And since she'd been here with Lillian and Hazel – since she'd had a brief insight into what life could be like her eyes had been opened. *A chance to get out of the rut*, Lillian had said. *And the ability to recognize that chance when it came along.* Well that's what she'd keep looking for from now on, she told herself.

Peter and Hazel went to the village pub and sat hand in hand at one of the rustic tables in the garden.

'I can't believe you cycled all the way over here on Nana's old bike,' Hazel said.

He shrugged. 'Well, I did oil it and pump up the tyres. I had a bit of a tinker with the brakes too, so it's almost as good as new. It's not all that far and I wanted to see you.'

'But what about your old war wound?'

Peter spluttered into his beer. 'God! You make me sound like a veteran of the Crimean War.' He laughed. 'Look, I'm not one for going on about the workings of my innards but maybe I should explain, once and for all. I lost a kidney through my injuries at Dunkirk, which might have made me a liability as far as His Majesty was concerned. But you can function perfectly well with just the one in everyday life.' He grinned. 'And it certainly doesn't stop you from riding a bike.' He twinkled at her over the rim of his glass. 'Or doing anything else energetic for that matter.'

'What about going back though?' Hazel asked. 'If I remember rightly Nana's bike doesn't have any lights.'

'Damn! Never thought of that,' he said. 'Guess I'll just have to stay the night.'

'I think there's a vacant room at the guest-house. I could ask the landlady if you like. Or if not maybe Ruby could come in with Lillian and me and you could have her room.'

He looked at her. 'You and Lillian are sharing?'

'Yes.'

'Damn!' He slapped his knee. 'Foiled again! Am I never going to get you to myself?'

Hazel laughed. 'Ocean View is a very respectable establishment,' she admonished. 'Letting you share my room would be the scandal of the century.'

Peter drained his glass and smiled at her. 'I'm teasing. I've already booked a room for the night with your landlady. She's very kindly offered to let me invade her kitchen and make my own breakfast so that I can make an early start in the morning. I'll probably be gone by the time you wake up.'

They walked back along the cliff path and when they came to the little bench vacated earlier by Ruby and Lillian he took her hand and pulled her towards it.

'Sit down a minute. There's something I want to say to you.'

They sat close together and Peter slipped an arm around her

shoulders and drew her close. 'Another couple of weeks and the new term will begin,' he said. 'You'll be back at school and I'll be off to London. Maybe we'll get to see each other on the occasional weekend.'

She turned her head to look up at him. 'I hope so.'

He smiled. 'The thing is, Hazel, I don't want it to fizzle out. I'm hoping that the old adage will be true in our case.'

'Old adage?'

'You know – absence makes the heart... and all that.'

Hazel laughed. 'The time will go so quickly. You'll see. And we'll manage more than the occasional weekend.'

He was silent for a moment then he asked her, 'Where do you see us going, Hazel?' Seeing her smile and anticipating the flippant remark that rose to her lips he frowned. 'No, I'm deadly serious. When I got my ticket so early in the war I felt such a failure. During my convalescence I went up to York to live with my father but every time I went out there'd be some old biddy standing in the bus queue making pointed remarks about me not being in uniform. I got called all sorts of names, from "conchie" to "coward" – and worse – much worse. It doesn't do a lot for your ego. I went off to a teacher training college in Wales in the end on Dad's advice and became a supply teacher. There was plenty of work in that field as you know and it was a living. My dad died while I was at college though; cancer. He'd known about it for some time but never told me. It was a very bad time for me coming as it did on top of everything else. But starting the school choir with you at Mekeley Moor opened a new door for me. It made me see what I really wanted. For the first time for ages I felt I could actually be a worthwhile person again – someone people could respect.' He cupped her chin and turned her face to his. 'You may not have realized it but you did that for me, Hazel. You helped me to turn the corner. But I wouldn't let myself hope for too much, especially when I heard about you and Gerald.'

'But I told you; that was—' He stopped her words with a kiss.

'A mistake. I know that now. But I've lost you once and I couldn't bear the thought of losing you again. I don't want you making another mistake. I want you to be sure. It's vitally important to me. Coming back to Valemouth was taking a chance as far as I was concerned. I had no way of knowing how you really felt about me, but I found I just couldn't let it go. If you don't feel as I do we can end it here and now, but I need to know – and I need you to be honest about it.'

'Oh, Peter.' She reached out to stroke his face 'I would never have guessed you'd been through so much. I've never seen you so – so solemn. You're always so cheerful and . . .'

'Devil-may-care? That's what everyone thinks,' he told her. 'It couldn't really be further from the truth; at least, about the things that really matter to me.' He looked into her eyes. 'And you matter to me; more than anything in the world. I'm sorry to drop this on you, darling, but I'm afraid it's a case of "speak now or forever hold your peace". Whatever you say, I'll respect it.'

She reached her hands round to the back of his neck and drew his head down to kiss him. 'I've only got one thing to say, Peter. I love you,' she whispered. 'You are the only man I've ever loved which is why I was prepared to give you up. I'd resigned myself to the fact that we'd never see each other again and meeting you again in the park that day was like a miracle. Surely we can survive a few months apart after all we've been through and . . .'

He put his fingers against her lips. 'There'll be no parting. We'll manage to see each other somehow and we'll get through the coming year, I promise. There's just one thing.'

'What?'

'Could you please say it again?'

'Say what?'

'You know what.'

The huge lump in her throat made speaking difficult but she managed to say the words he wanted to hear: 'I – love you, Peter. I always have,' she said shakily.

He pulled her close, so close that she could hardly breathe, kissing her till her head swam. 'I love you too,' he whispered between kisses. 'So very – *very* much.'

Dusk was turning to darkness by the time they arrived back at Ocean View. The sky was a vibrant electric blue and a sliver of moon hung above the sea. The air was full of summer scents; roses, lavender and honeysuckle. By the gate Peter drew her close again and kissed her.

'I'll be gone when you wake in the morning,' he said.

She nodded. 'All this is going to seem like a dream.'

'It's no dream,' he told her. 'I'll prove that to you next time we meet.'

The following day was the last of the holiday. Lillian and Ruby couldn't help feeling sad as they enjoyed the last of the sea air and sunshine, but Hazel could hardly keep the reminiscent smile from her lips. She'd risen early and managed to catch Peter before he set off on the long bike ride back to Valemouth. Lillian had wakened too and crept out of bed to look out of the window, seeing Hazel standing by the gate in her dressing-gown, kissing Peter one last time before he wobbled off on the ancient bicycle. Now, sitting on the beach beside her she looked at her friend.

'You're in love with him, aren't you?' Hazel nodded, hugging her knees and looking out to sea with starry eyes. 'He loves you too, anyone can see that.' Lillian laid a hand on her friend's arm. 'Hold on tightly to it, Hazel,' she said. 'You're so lucky to have got him back. It's the most precious thing you can have.'

Ruby watched them from where she was swimming back and forth in the shallows. Hazel looked like a woman in a dream. It must have been that young man who visited last night. She seemed to have forgotten all about her friends today, Ruby reflected wistfully.

It had been a lovely holiday; the best – the *only* one she'd ever had. Tomorrow it would be back to Valemouth and the Joneses. She hated the prospect. But the little talk she'd had with Lillian had given her new hope. She'd made up her mind that she was going to look for that chance to get out of the rut; learn how to recognize it. And once it came she would seize it with both hands. Maybe she hadn't been able to go to the high school but somehow she was going to make something of herself.

CHAPTER NINE

At the beginning of September the evacuees were beginning to drift back to London in little groups. Hazel's new term began again and Peter announced his intention of going up to London before the start of term to find a comfortable place to stay that was not too far from college. When Mary heard about it she had a suggestion to make.

'Time Harry and I went back,' she said. 'There don't seem to be so many buzz-bombs now and Harry is missing his mum. We've got a nice spare room. Peter could stay with us – for a start at least.'

And so it was arranged. Hazel went to the station and waved the three of them off, feeling quite bereft as she walked away. It was bad enough, saying goodbye to Peter but the house was going to feel very empty without Mary and Harry. Having Mary around had been almost like having Nana back again.

At The Laurels Jean had received bad news. Her husband, Lance Corporal. Dave Kendall, serving with the King's Royal Rifles in Burma had been taken prisoner by the Japanese. Being away from London the news had been delayed in reaching her but it seemed that he'd been part of a reconnaissance party that had been ambushed. Two of the soldiers in his party had been killed, the rest taken prisoner. Poor Jean was devastated.

'He's gone all through the war with hardly a scratch and now, after all this time . . .'

Lillian put her arms round her. 'It surely can't be long before he's released,' she said. 'Everyone says the war will be over in a few months' time.'

It was three weeks since she, Hazel and Ruby had spent their short holiday at Highcliffe Cove. On her return she had found that her mother seemed hardly to have missed her at all. Jean, or rather Jim, had persuaded her to come down and sit in the garden, watching him and Katie playing ball. Lillian was astounded to hear that she had even rocked the pram to pacify Patsy while Jean went indoors to make the tea.

'Well, it was such lovely weather,' Jean told her. 'I thought it would do her good to get a bit of sun on her face.'

'And she didn't complain?' Lillian asked. Jean laughed and shook her head.

'Never heard a squeak out of her – except when she laughed at the kids' antics.'

Laura certainly looked a lot better for the fresh air. Doctor Frazer was delighted with her when he made his next visit. He even decided to take her off her sleeping tablets. Now that she got up and spent part of each day out of doors she was sleeping like a baby.

Jean had begun to talk about going back to London and had even been along to the station to find out the times of trains when suddenly, in the second week of September, they heard on the radio that London was once again the target of a devastating new German weapon, a rocket officially named the V2. The first of these had landed at Chiswick in West London, doing grave damage. As usual Hilda was the one who gave them a first-, or rather, second-hand account of it a few days later, relayed by her lorry driver brother-in-law, Sid.

'This one is even worse than them buzz-bombs,' she said in a gloomy undertone. 'There's no warning, you see. This thing's got no lights and there's no engine noise. Just this horrible roaring noise and then – *wallop*! You've 'ad it! They reckon the blast wave can be felt for miles.'

Jean shuddered. 'Will it never end?' she said. 'Well, that settles it. If it's all right with you, Lillian, we'll have to stay on.'

'No need to ask,' Lillian assured her. 'I've been dreading you all going home anyway.'

When she and Hazel met on the following Friday afternoon Hazel was anxious about Peter.

'These new rockets don't seem to be aimed at the docks or railways,' she said. 'They seem to be indiscriminate. They could drop anywhere. This time it's an attack on civilians. I worry all the time about Peter. The college where he's studying was evacuated in 1940. They've only just returned to London.'

Lillian nodded. 'I know. It's awful – just when things seemed to be getting back to normal. It's very bad for morale.'

She arrived home soon after five o'clock to find Laura in the garden as usual with Jean and the children. Coming in to start making the children's tea Jean met her in the hall.

'There was a telephone call for you, Lillian,' she said. 'About half an hour ago. I said you'd ring back.'

'Oh? Who from?' Lillian was taking off her jacket and hanging it on the hallstand.

'It was a Mrs Blakely,' Jean said with a frown. 'At least I think that was the name.' She reached out her hand as Lillian grasped the banisters and sat down heavily on the bottom stair. '*Lillian*! Are you all right? You've gone as white as a sheet.'

'Y-Yes, I'm fine. 'W-what did she say?'

'Just that she had some news – wanted to tell you herself.' Her hand went suddenly to her mouth. 'Oh! That was *his* name wasn't it? I knew it rang a bell. It's your feller – Alan.'

'He's not really my . . .' Lillian caught her breath. 'I'd better ring her,' she said. She rose unsteadily to her feet and Jean hovered uncertainly. 'Well – I'll leave you to it – unless you want me to—'

'No, no, I'll be all right.'

'I'll be in the kitchen if you need me.' Jean disappeared through the door to the kitchen as Lillian gingerly lifted the receiver. When the operator answered she gave the Blakely's number and listened as it rang out, holding the receiver with both hands to try to stop shaking. Perhaps they'd gone out. Perhaps... A click at the other end made her jump.

'Blakely and son, plumbers. Can I help you?'

'Oh, Mrs Blakely, it's Lillian Mason. I believe you rang me earlier.'

'Oh, Lillian, my dear. I wanted to give you the news. Alan is safe, thank God.'

'Oh!' Lillian felt the hall swimming round her. She felt for a chair and sat down again. 'He – he's safe? You're sure?'

'Yes, thank God. It seems that five of them managed to climb into a boat. They drifted in it for almost two weeks. Thank God it was summer and not bad weather. A Norwegian fishing boat picked them up. Sadly one poor fellow had already died and the other four were in a bad way. To cut a long story short they eventually managed to get them to a hospital in Sweden and they're making a good recovery. They'll get them back to England as soon as they're well enough.'

Lillian's mouth was so dry she could hardly speak. 'How – how is he?' she managed to ask.

'As far as we can make out Alan was suffering mainly from exposure and dehydration,' Mrs Blakely said. 'Some of the other poor lads weren't so lucky. One has lost a leg and the other has bad burns.'

'Thank you so much for letting me know,' Lillian said.

'Not at all, dear. I know it's what he would want,' Mrs Blakely said. 'I can't tell you how much his father and I have prayed for news like this.' Lillian could hear the smile in her voice as she went on, 'His dad was dead against his leaving the business and going to university after the war, but I reckon he'll agree to anything our Alan wants now we know he's safe.'

When Lillian walked into the kitchen Jean looked at her anxiously. 'Are you all right?'

'Yes. Alan's alive,' Lillian said. 'He and four others were adrift in an open boat for two weeks but he's been picked up and now he's safe in hospital.' She spoke the words like an automaton and suddenly it was as though the truth of it sank in at last. Staring at Jean she burst into tears. 'One of them died,' she sobbed. 'And two others had been badly injured. But Alan – Alan is safe.'

Jean put her arms around her. 'Don't cry,' she said, her own voice thick with tears. 'You'll start me off in a minute. Just think, he's coming home. Soon you'll be seeing him again. Aren't you happy?'

Lillian looked at her. 'I hardly know him,' she said. 'He's probably forgotten what I look like by now.'

Jean laughed. 'Not on your nelly!' she said. 'Why do you think he made sure his mum kept you up with his news? I wouldn't mind betting that the thought of you has been the one thing that's kept him going.'

Lillian thought of the cheap little Polyfoto she'd had taken for him at the photographer's studio in town. Did he still have it, she wondered? And when they met again, would he have changed his mind about her after all he'd been through?

At their usual Friday meeting Lillian told Hazel her news. Hazel was delighted.

'Oh, Lillian, that's wonderful. Have you any idea when he'll be home?'

Lillian shook her head. 'None at all. Mrs Blakely didn't know. We'll just have to be patient.' She looked at Hazel. 'Am I being silly, expecting him to want to see me again after all he's been through?'

'Of course you're not being silly. He must be longing to see you.'

Lillian sighed and stirred her tea thoughtfully. 'I keep having this dream – that we meet again and I'm all excited, then, when he sees me, he walks right past – doesn't recognize me.'

'We all get dreams like that,' Hazel told her. 'It's just anxiety. Everything will be fine when the time comes, you'll see.'

'I hope you're right,' Lillian said. 'I do hope I'm not expecting too much – that I haven't read too much into what was just a casual acquaintance.' She looked at Hazel. 'Have you heard from Peter?'

'Yes. He's settled in nicely with Mary and her little family and it's not too far for him to travel each day. He says the course is going well. He's really enjoying it.'

'Did he mention these new rockets?'

Hazel shook her head. 'I get the impression that he's playing all that down.'

Lillian laughed. 'I think Londoners are marvellous,' she said. 'Nothing Hitler can throw at them will ever bring them down. Jean is a typical example. She's so brave. I don't know what I'm going to do when she and the children go home.'

'They certainly seem to have done your mother a power of good,' Hazel remarked.

Lillian looked thoughtful for a moment. 'Yes. I just wonder if she'll keep it up when they've gone. Little Jim is the apple of her eye. By the way he starts school next week at a little infants' school just round the corner. He won't be five until February but he's so bright that Jean thought it would do him good to be among other children his own age and luckily they had a vacancy.'

*

Jim adored his new grown up status as a 'schoolboy' and although he looked tired when Jean collected him the first few afternoons he quickly got into his stride. He was old enough to know that his father had been taken prisoner of war. He didn't say much and Jean wondered if he worried about it deep inside. She had hoped that starting school would take his mind off it and in a way she was right. At the end of the first week he was full of stories about the other children and their families.

'Michael Smith's dad is a prisoner just like mine,' he told his mother on the way home from school. 'He was a pilot in the RAF and his plane got shot down. Michael said he tried to escape once.' He looked up at Jean with huge eyes. 'Will my dad try and escape? I hope he doesn't. Michael's dad got caught. He was shot and locked up worse than before.' Jean was trying to think of a reassuring reply when Jim rummaged in his little school bag and produced a crumpled drawing.

He held it up. 'Look, Mum. I done this for Granny Upstairs. D'you think she'll like it? It's me and Katie and Patsy. It's for her to keep so's when we go home she'll remember what we look like.'

Jean hid a smile as she looked at the drawing of three sticklike people with sticking-up hair and big smiles. One, clearly meant to be Jim, was much bigger than the others and the smallest sat in a boxlike pram. 'It's lovely, she said. 'I'm sure Granny Upstairs will love it.'

'Mum – when we go home couldn't we take her with us?' Jim asked. 'She'll be lonely without me.'

'She'll still have Auntie Lillian,' Jean pointed out. 'Granny Upstairs is her mum and I don't think she'd want to lose her.'

'No.' Jim was thoughtful for a moment. 'We can come back and see her though, can't we?'

'If Auntie Lillian asks us, and she'll only do that if you're very good.'

The autumn term passed quickly. Peter managed to get back to Valemouth for only two weekends, arriving on Friday evening and returning on Sunday afternoon. The time was frustratingly inade-

quate but, as Peter said as they kissed goodbye on the station platform, it was better than nothing.

'The first term is almost over,' he reminded her. 'I'll be taking my
exam in late May and after that we can be together as much as we
want.' He held her away from him and looked down at her, the
familiar twinkle in his eyes. 'You'll have had enough of me long
before that.'

She shook her head, a lump in her throat. 'You know that's not
true,' she said, giving his shoulders a little shake. 'You're just fishing for compliments.'

As the train steamed in he held her close, kissing her one last
time and whispering in her ear. 'I love you, Hazel. Six more months,
that's all. After that I'm not letting you out of my sight, so you'd
better get used to the idea.'

As December came in the Joneses started to order their Christmas
stock. Trees were in short supply but Edgar took Ruby along with
him to the auction sale where he managed to get a supply of holly
and mistletoe. Ruby soon discovered the reason she'd been
invited to accompany Edgar. While he went along to pay for the
purchases she was required to load the handcart. By the time she
had finished her hands were pierced all over with holly prickles
and chapped with cold and wet. Edgar returned and looked the
cart over.

'Yeah,' he said grudgingly. 'That oughter do it.' He nodded
towards the pub across the road where all the market traders
seemed to be heading. 'Better get orf back to the shop with that little
lot now, Rube,' he said. 'Don't you 'ang about now, and tell Myrtle
I've got a bit more business to see to. I'll see 'er at teatime.'

As Ruby began to manipulate the heavy cart through the streets
it began to snow. The load kept slipping, tipping the cart sideways
and she had to keep stopping to rebalance the contents. A knot of
sadness gathered in her throat as she remembered the holiday she
had shared with Hazel and Lillian last summer and how happy she
had been. She'd been made to pay for it when she got home though.
To make up for the time off she had been made to work even harder.
In desperation she'd tried again to contact Mum, writing her a letter
to say how unhappy she was. But once again there had been no
reply.

When she eventually arrived back at the shop Myrtle looked at her askance. 'On yer own then?'

'Yes.' Ruby was so cold she could hardly speak and her fingers seemed to have become permanently bent to fit the cart handles. She held them out over the paraffin heater in the back kitchen in the hope of thawing the flexibility back.

'So where's Edgar?'

Ruby looked up. 'He said to tell you he had some business to see to,' she said, her teeth chattering.

Myrtle's face reddened. 'Business! This business didn't 'appen to be takin' place in the Dog and Duck by any chance, did it?'

Ruby shook her head. 'I don't know.' She longed for a hot drink and something to eat, but dare not ask.

'Don't know much, do you?' Myrtle snapped. 'And if it's dinner you're looking for, you're too late. You should've got a move on instead of 'anging about.' She looked through the window into the yard. 'What's the stock doin' out there? It'll be covered in snow in no time. Get out there and unload it into the shed. And when you're done you'd better get into the shop. I want to get down the grocer's before they close.' She went to the back door and opened it, letting in an icy blast. 'You really are a lazy little cow, Ruby Sears. No wonder your ma don't want nuthin' more to do with you!'

One Saturday a couple of weeks before Christmas Lillian went shopping with Jean to buy Christmas presents, leaving the children with Hazel, who had offered to have them for the afternoon. Lillian enjoyed the expedition enormously. There were a few more toys in the shops this year and they were able to get a toy train for Jim and a doll for Katie. For baby Patsy they found a little teddy and a rattle with a teething ring attached. Lillian bought her own presents; a lacy bedjacket for Laura, handkerchiefs for Jean and Hazel; a colouring book and crayons for Jim and a dolly's tea set for Katie. As she and Jean treated themselves to tea in the Cadena café Lillian glanced down her list and saw that she had added Alan's name at the bottom. Would he be home by then, she wondered? And if he was would he want to see her?

'Penny for them.' Jean said, looking at her with raised eyebrows.

Lillian smiled and shrugged. 'I was just thinking about Alan,' she said. 'I've put him on my present list but I haven't a clue what to get him. I don't even know whether he'll be home or not.'

'Get him something anyway,' Jean urged. 'You can give it to him when he does get home, whenever that is.'

Lillian hesitated. 'It could be embarrassing. He might not want to see me – and even if we do meet he might not have got me anything and then he'd be embarrassed.'

Jean laughed. 'You think too much. Just get him some little thing to show you were thinking of him. It doesn't have to be embarrassing.'

'But if he—'

'Stop it!' Jean put her hand on top of Lillian's. 'I'd bet my last sweet coupon that he's dying to see you again. Everything will be fine so stop worrying.'

Christmas morning at The Laurels was the happiest that Lillian could ever remember. Jim and Katie were so excited with the mysterious parcels they found at the end of their beds. They all assembled in the rarely used dining room where a fire had been lit specially for the occasion. Laura had even risen early and come downstairs in her dressing-gown to join them. She smiled indulgently at the sight of the children's excitement, and even little Patsy, who was now able to sit up a little, seemed to catch the infectious delight and grinned with toothless approval at her fluffy teddy bear.

After breakfast Laura went back to her room and Lillian went off to the kitchen, where she donned an apron and began cooking Christmas dinner for them all. She had managed to obtain a large capon from the butcher and had made her own stuffing from sausage meat, onions, and herbs from the garden. She had just slid the bird into the oven when the front doorbell rang. Knowing that Jean was busy bathing Patsy while the children played with their new toys she quickly rinsed her hands at the sink and went through the hall to answer it. She opened the door, then stood staring in shocked silence at the smiling man on the doorstep.

'Merry Christmas Lilly, my love!'

'*Alan!*' She felt her face grow hot and then cold as the blood drained from it. 'Alan,' she said again. 'You're home. I . . .' Before she could say another word he had stepped forward and gathered her into his arms.

'I've dreamed of doing this for months,' he said, kissing her. 'All that time at sea when I thought we'd all had it; all those weeks in the hospital, thinking of you was all that kept me going a lot of the time, Lilly – my Lilly.'

'Aren't you going to ask your young man to come in? You're letting in an awful lot of cold air.' Lillian turned to see Jean standing in the hall, a big smile on her face.

'Yes – yes of course.' She took Alan by the hand and drew him into the house. 'You must come and have a Christmas drink with us.'

In the kitchen they toasted each other in cooking sherry and Alan was introduced to Jean who, when she had finished her drink excused herself tactfully and went to play with the children.

Lillian and Alan looked at each other across the kitchen table, littered with vegetables and half-filled saucepans. Now that they were alone Lillian felt shy and slightly embarrassed.

'Excuse all this,' she said. 'And me. I must look a mess.' She raised a hand to tuck a stray strand of hair behind her ear.

'You look marvellous to me,' he said. 'Just right – the way I remember you, just like you looked in all my dreams.' He took a step towards her. 'I can't stop long now. I wish I could but Mum's cooking the fatted calf and all that. But later – just say when and I'll be round to take you out. We've got an awful lot of catching up to do, Lilly.'

As he slipped his arms around her she said breathlessly, 'I wasn't sure whether you'd want to see me again.'

He stared at her. 'Not want to see you?'

'After all, it was only one date.'

'One date was enough for me,' he told her, his lips against her cheek. 'I hope it was only the first of many, though.'

'We have to get to know one another,' she told him.

'I know, and I can't wait. I just know it's going to get better and better.'

She looked at the blue serge suit he was wearing, which seemed a little too large for him. 'You're not in uniform.'

He grinned. 'My uniform was in a bit of a mess when they fished me out of the drink. Some fish is probably wearing it now. When I go back off leave they'll give me a new one.' He pulled at the front of his jacket. 'Reckon I've got a bit of weight to make up to fill this out again, but I daresay Mum's got plans for that.'

Her eyes filled with tears. 'Oh, Alan. I thought you were – I thought you'd . . .'

He pulled her close. 'Had it? Not yours truly,' he said. 'Indestructible, that's my middle name.'

She remembered something. 'I've got you something.' She went to the dresser drawer where she'd hidden the present she'd bought him. 'It isn't much,' she said, holding it out to him. 'Merry Christmas.'

He unwrapped the wallet she'd bought and looked up in delight. 'Just what I wanted. I lost the old one. And look, it's even got a place for your photo.' He put his hand in his breast pocket and drew out the faded, dog-eared photograph of her, inserting it into the pocket with the clear window. Lillian was appalled.

'Look at the state it's in!' she said. 'Throw it away. I'll give you another one.'

He shook his head. 'No chance. This one's been through everything with me. It was about the only possession I managed to save. I'm never parting with it.' He slipped the wallet into his pocket and then fished in his jacket pocket. 'I nearly forgot. This is for you. Sorry I haven't wrapped it.'

Lillian looked in delight at the tiny hand-painted box shaped like a heart. 'Oh, Alan. It's lovely.'

'When you open it, it plays a tune.' He opened the lid to tinkling strains of 'Ave Maria'. 'When we were convalescing they used to let us out to look round the shops and I thought this was just what you'd like,' he told her. 'You'd love Sweden, Lilly. One day, after the war I'll take you there.' He looked at her expectantly. 'So – when can I see you?'

Lillian shook her head. 'I don't know – next week. Monday say?'

'Monday it is. I'll be round for you about seven; OK?'

She laughed, her cheeks pink and her eyes shining with happiness. 'Seven – OK.'

He tipped up her chin, holding her close and kissing her; a lingering kiss that left her breathless.

'*Lillian*! I've been ringing my bell for ages. Am I going to get any coffee this morning or not? *Oh*!' Laura stood in the kitchen doorway, her face flushed crimson with shock at the scene before her.

'*Lillian*!' she repeated. 'What is the meaning of this? Who is this man? And what on *earth* do you think you are doing?'

Lillian stepped backwards and took a deep breath. 'Mummy, this is Alan; Alan Blakely. He is in the Navy and his ship was torpedoed, but he's safe – and – and home for Christmas. Isn't it marvellous?' she added breathlessly.

'Well, *you* evidently find it so!' Laura looked Alan up and down as though he were some kind of rare specimen. 'Isn't this rather an inconvenient time to be calling, Mr Blakely?'

'I was just leaving,' Alan said with the ghost of a wink to Lillian.

'Good,' Laura said rudely. 'At least your shipwreck hasn't robbed you of *all* your manners.'

Red in the face, Lillian took Alan's hand. 'I'll see you out.' At the front door she looked at him. 'I'm sorry about that,' she said. 'My mother can be a little – a little . . .'

'Eccentric?' Alan laughed. 'Don't worry about it. See you on Monday, then.'

'Yes – on Monday. Happy Christmas.'

'Happy Christmas, darling.' He bent and kissed her again. 'And don't worry.'

Lillian walked slowly back to the kitchen, steeling herself for the storm she knew was about to break. Laura was waiting for her.

'Close the door, Lillian.' Lillian closed it. 'Now perhaps you would care to explain what possessed you; making a show of yourself – behaving like a common street woman – and with the plumber's son of all people.'

'I wasn't making a show of myself, Mummy. There was no one here but Alan and me.'

'Unless I am very much mistaken when I entered the room you were actually embracing him – *kissing* the man! I find it hard to believe that a daughter of mine could act in such a wantonly abandoned way!'

'Alan and I have been writing to each other for months,' Lillian told her. 'When his ship was torpedoed I thought he'd been killed. It's a miracle that he's come through it.'

Laura shrugged. 'I don't see that as a valid reason for you to behave like a vulgar harlot.'

Lillian's heart was beating fast. 'We intend to see more of each other,' she said. 'He's taking me out on Monday evening.'

Laura gave a little bark of incredulous laughter. 'Over my dead body! I haven't brought you up to consort with tradesmen's sons.'

'That is a ridiculous attitude. Alan has had a good education. He's planning to go to university when the war is over.'

'If you believe that you'll believe anything!' Laura turned to the door. 'If you take my advice you'll forget all about this man, Lillian,' she said. 'I'll have my coffee now and when you've got the lunch under way you can come up and run my bath.'

'I'm going out with Alan on Monday evening, Mummy,' Lillian said firmly. 'I'm not a child to be told what I can and cannot do.'

Just for a second Laura hesitated then she turned. 'We'll see about that,' she said.

Lillian stood in the kitchen doorway and watched her mother walk majestically through the hall and up the stairs. 'You needn't look so smug,' she said under her breath. This time she knew with all her heart and mind that she would stand her ground no matter what. This time she would not be browbeaten into submission. This time there would be no giving in.

Hazel cooked Christmas dinner for herself and Peter and afterwards they went for a walk down to the promenade. Some of the sea defences had been taken down and there were rumours that by next summer the beach would be open and clear for visitors again.

'Do you really think the war will be over soon?' Hazel asked, her hand tucked warmly into the crook of Peter's arm. He smiled down at her.

'Sure to be. Hitler can't possibly hang on much longer now.'

'I wonder where you'll be this time next year?' she mused.

'With you, I hope.' He stopped and turned her towards him. 'I'm going to try to get work in this part of the country,' he told her. 'I like it here. But if I can't will you come with me wherever I go?'

Hazel pulled the corners of her mouth down in an expression of mock uncertainly. 'Oooh, I don't know about that. I'd have to think very carefully,' she said teasingly.

He took her hand and drew her across to a beach shelter with a bench inside it. 'Look, I was going to save this for this evening but as I've brought the subject up . . .' He put his hand in his pocket and drew out a small box. 'This isn't a Christmas present, Hazel. It's a lot more serious than that.' He opened the box to reveal a ring with a gleaming sapphire at its centre, surrounded by sparkling diamonds. 'Hazel, will you marry me?'

She caught her breath. '*Peter*! It's beautiful.'

'So – will you?' He took the ring from its velvet nest and slipped it on to her finger. It fitted perfectly. 'There – look, that's a good omen.' There was a moment's silence and he looked at her expectantly. 'Well, aren't you going to say anything?'

'I – it's – I didn't expect—'

'*Bloody hell*! Is it yes or no?'

She laughed. 'Yes, yes, yes! Of course I'll marry you.'

'Thank goodness for that. I thought I was going to have to try and find a woman with the same size finger!' He drew her close and kissed her. 'You have no idea how happy you've made me, Hazel,' he whispered. 'But can we go home now. I'm bloody freezing and I could murder a turkey sandwich.'

They spent all evening sitting close together on the settee in front of the fire, dreaming and planning their future. At bedtime they went upstairs together. At the top of the stairs Peter turned to her.

'I hope you appreciate all the restraint I've shown over these past months.'

She was smiling. 'Of course I have. You've been very noble and gentlemanly.'

'But – at the risk of being thought conniving – now that we're promised to each other.. . . ?'

'Do you think you're the only one who's been making a sacrifice?' Taking his hand she drew him towards her own door. Inside the bedroom she looked at him, her face serious now. 'Peter, before we – now that we're engaged there's something I have to – something you should know.'

'Wait.' He took both her hands and together they sat down on the edge of the bed.

'You're going to tell me that you slept with Gerald,' he said very quietly.

She stared at him. 'You *knew*! He told you?'

He shook his head. 'No. Gerald would never do anything so ungallant. It's just the way he spoke about you. He might have thought I knew. If it's of any comfort to you he felt bad about it – thought that he took advantage of you. He regretted it. I guess you feel the same.'

She nodded. 'He was about to go away. I felt I couldn't—'

'No!' He put a finger against her lips. 'No explanations. It's in the past – it happened before we even met. Now it's just us; you and me and the future. I love you, Hazel and I always will; no matter what.'

CHAPTER TEN

Ruby's cold started on Boxing Day. She felt feverish and poorly, but when the shop opened again the following day Myrtle insisted that she was well enough to work.

'If Edgar and I skived off for every little sniffle we'd have no business left,' she said.

By New Year's Eve it was clear that the cold had turned to something worse. Every time Ruby coughed her chest felt as if it was being torn apart. It kept her awake at night. Rene, trying to sleep in the other bed was disturbed too and she was far from sympathetic.

'Oh shut up coughing, can't you?' she shouted as she pulled the covers over her head. '*Bark bark bark*! It's enough to drive anyone barmy.'

Ruby tried hard to suppress her cough without success but by the morning of the third day she was past caring. When Myrtle called her at half past six and received no reply she burst angrily into the room.

'Can't you hear me shoutin' me head off for you? Deaf now, are you?' She pulled back the covers from Ruby's face and started back. '*Oh!*'

Ruby lay in her bed oblivious to Myrtle's haranguing. She was burning hot and muttering deliriously, her eyes were glazed, her hair damp with sweat and her cheeks a bright, hot red. Myrtle called to her husband who looked at Ruby and shook his head.

'She looks proper bad to me,' he conceded. 'I reckon it's a case for the doctor.'

'The *doctor*!' Myrtle looked scandalized. 'What's that gonna cost?'

'I don't know but we don't want her dying on us, do we?'

'Dying? Don't be daft. It's just a cold,' Myrtle said. 'Surely a day off and a couple of Aspros'll put her right?'

'It's me who needs a day off,' Rene whined from the other bed. 'Kept me awake for nights on end with her cough cough coughing, she has.'

Myrtle rounded on her daughter. 'Just get up and get yourself dressed,' she said. 'You'll have to help in the shop today if Rube ain't well enough.'

'*Me*?' Rene protested. 'She's all right, just skiving, that's all, lazy cow. Give her a shove and make her get up. *I'm* not standin' in that shop freezin' to death all day, so there!'

'You'll do as you're told, miss!' Edgar shouted. 'Get up and less o' your sauce. Get down them stairs and get the kettle on if you want any breakfast. We'll be opening up in an hour.'

Rene dragged herself resentfully out of bed, grumbling all the time. 'Don't see why I should do *her* job, idle little slut. She's puttin' it on if you ask me.'

Edgar sent Tommy for the doctor who came as soon as his surgery was over. He listened to Ruby's chest and looked grave. 'I'm afraid it's pneumonia,' he said as he removed his stethoscope. 'I shall have to have her admitted to hospital.' He looked at Myrtle. 'How long has she been like this?'

'Not long – no time at all,' Myrtle blustered. 'We thought it was a bit of a cold. She seemed all right.'

The doctor shook his head. 'The poor child must have been feeling terrible for days,' he said. 'I'll send for an ambulance right away.'

When Hazel went into the shop for vegetables a few days later she missed her young friend. 'Where's Ruby today?' she asked Edgar.

He sniffed. ' 'orspital,' he said tersely.

'Hospital? You mean she's ill?'

'Well she wouldn't be there if she was 'ale and 'earty, would she?'

Hazel ignored the sarcasm. 'What's wrong with her?'

Edgar took out a grubby handkerchief and blew his nose. 'Nuthin' much,' he hedged. 'We're expectin' her out again any day.'

'Is she in St Mary's?'

He shrugged. 'If that's what it's called, yeah. Big place opposite the b'tanical gardens.'

Hazel went along to the hospital at visiting time that evening. There were a few oranges about now and she'd managed to get two, which she peeled and segmented. She'd also bought some chocolate and a couple of magazines. Enquiring at reception she found that Ruby was in the children's ward and had suffered a bad bout of pneumonia from which she was making a slow recovery.

'Are you a relative?'

Hazel shook her head. 'I used to be her teacher and I've tried to keep in touch. She was an evacuee but her mother seems to have vanished.'

'She was rather undernourished, poor child,' the ward sister told her. 'But she's responding well to care and treatment.'

Hazel barely recognized Ruby. She looked pale and heart-breakingly thin, but her eyes lit up when she saw Hazel walking towards her.

'Oh, Miss – er – Hazel!'

'I only heard you were ill today, Ruby,' Hazel pulled up a chair. 'I'd have come earlier if I'd known. How are you feeling?'

'Better,' Ruby said. 'They're ever so kind to me in here and the food is lovely. My cough is ever so much better.'

'So you'll soon be going home.'

Ruby's face fell. 'I suppose so.'

Hazel covered the thin little hand with her own. 'You're not looking forward to that though, are you, Ruby?' The girl shook her head. 'Listen, there are nice children's homes you can go to for convalescence,' Hazel said. 'Would you like me to ask the sister if you can go to one? You'd stay there till you were fit and strong again and able to cope.'

Ruby turned hopeful eyes on her. 'Oh, could I really?'

'Of course. I'll see what I can do. I'll make sure you don't go back to the Joneses until you're well enough.' She paused. 'Have they been to visit you by the way?' Ruby shook her head. 'Not even once?'

'I expect they were too busy.'

Hazel said nothing but inside she seethed with anger. If only there was something she could do to get Ruby out of this ghastly situation. She smiled and opened her bag.

'I've brought you some oranges and some chocolate, and I

thought you might like these magazines. I'll come and see you again tomorrow evening, Ruby. And I'll come every day until you are well again.' She leaned forward and kissed the girl's cheek. 'Just hurry up and get well soon.'

On the way out she stopped at the sister's office and asked about the convalescent home. 'The people she lives with are rather uncaring,' she explained. 'I think she really needs to be completely well before she goes back to them.'

'And she has no one else?' Sister asked.

'No one, I'm afraid.'

Sister smiled and nodded. 'Leave it with me. I'll do my best.'

Lillian saw Alan three times during his short Christmas leave. Each time her mother made a fuss but each time Lillian stood her ground.

'You'll be all right, Mummy,' she said on the last occasion they were to meet. 'Jean is here and so are the children, and I won't be late.'

'I don't know how your conscience can allow you to go off and abandon your responsibilities,' Laura complained.

'I'm not abandoning anything. This is Alan's last day and he wants me to go and have a meal with his parents this afternoon.'

Laura snorted. 'Whatever for?'

'He'd like us to get to know one another,' Lillian told her patiently.

'And why should you wish to socialize with a *plumber* and his wife?'

Lillian counted to ten under her breath. 'It has nothing to do with Alan's father's work,' she said. 'Anyway, I'll have to go or I'll be late.'

They went to a matinée at the cinema. Alan held her hand and afterwards they walked along the deserted seafront. It was cold even for early January but Alan's arm was warm around her shoulders.

'I'll be gone this time tomorrow,' he said regretfully. 'I wish it could have been longer.'

'Me too,' Lillian said. 'We've hardly had any time at all to get to know each other.'

His arms tightened around her. 'We've got the rest of our lives for that,' he said, his lips against her ear. 'Anyway, I feel as if I've always known you. The minute I saw you I felt we'd met somewhere before.'

Lillian laughed. 'Maybe we knew each other in a previous life.'

He laughed down at her. 'Yes. I bet you were an Egyptian princess and I was a slave in your court. We were destined never to be together.'

'Oh! That's sad.'

'Terrible,' he said, warming to the subject. 'I bet we were discovered and I was put to some horrible death just for loving you.'

Lillian shivered. '*Don't*! Don't talk like that. We're together now and there's no reason we can't be.' But even as she said it she thought of Laura and all the obstacles she was bound to put in their way.

'I've been thinking,' Alan said. 'I don't know what university will accept me yet – if any. But if it's miles away from here will you come with me?' Lillian hesitated and he went on quickly. 'Oh, I'm not asking you to live with me over the brush, as they say up north. We'll get married.'

'What would we live on?'

'I'll have my grant – if they give me one, that is. And I could get a job in the evenings – in a pub or something. It'd be better than being apart. Maybe you could get a job too.'

Silently Lillian wondered who would give her a job. She'd never had one outside of the home. She was useless as a wage earner. 'I don't know.' She glanced at him sideways. 'And then there's Mummy.'

His jaw dropped momentarily but he quickly hid his dismay. 'Well, that's not a problem,' he said without conviction. 'We'll take her too if you like.'

She turned and smiled wistfully up at him. 'It wouldn't work, would it? I think we're going to have to wait until you get your degree.'

'But that takes three years.' He stopped walking and turned her to face him. 'I love you so much, Lillian,' he said. 'I don't think I can wait that long. Maybe I should give up the idea of going to university and join Dad in the business after all.'

'*No*! You mustn't make that kind of sacrifice just for me.' The rest of her sentence was lost in his kiss.

'The only sacrifice I'm not prepared to make is losing you,' he said softly.

Alan's mother had put on a special high tea for the four of them. There was a cheerful fire burning, making the neat little living room cosy and welcoming and Lillian's nervousness soon vanished as she joined the Blakely family round the table. She found she was able to relax and enjoy herself. Alan's father, who asked her to call him Bill, was jovial and good-natured. His mother was a small, slender woman who clearly adored her only son. She made Lillian feel welcome, urging her to a second slice of the cake that she had made specially. As they washed up together after tea Lillian said,

'Thank you so much for inviting me to tea today, Mrs Blakely. I've enjoyed it so much. We've only spoken on the phone before so it was nice to meet you.'

'Yes. It's good to meet you too.' The older woman smiled. 'Please call me June.' She looked up. 'Alan adores you, Lillian,' she said. 'He says the thought of you brought him safely through his ordeal and I'm sure he's right.' She paused. 'I do hope you feel as deeply for him.'

Lillian knew that Alan's mother was asking her not to hurt her son and the look on the older woman's face tugged at her heart strings. 'Oh, I do, Mrs Blakely – er – June,' she said. 'I know we haven't known each other very long but somehow it doesn't seem to matter. As for me, I love him very much.'

At their next Friday afternoon tea session Hazel and Lillian were both full of news. They hadn't met since before Christmas and had a lot of catching up to do. Hazel's engagement to Peter was apparent by her ring, which Lillian spotted almost at once. Her eyes lit up.

'Oh! Is that what I think it is?'

Hazel blushed. 'Yes. Peter asked me on Christmas Day.'

'Congratulations! I'm so happy for you both,' Lillian said. 'It's a gorgeous ring. I hope you'll think of me for bridesmaid when the time comes. I've never been a bridesmaid.'

Hazel laughed. 'Naturally. We've no immediate plans though. Peter has to pass his exam first and then get a job. It could be anywhere in the country.'

'I hope you don't go too far away,' Lillian said. 'I really don't know what I'd do without you now.'

Hazel shook her head. 'Surely now that Alan is safe he'll be home for good soon and he'll be whisking you off to the altar himself.'

'He came home on leave for Christmas actually,' Lillian told her. 'He dropped in on me on Christmas morning. Talk about a shock!'

Hazel laughed. 'A nice one, though.'

'Oh yes, a lovely one. We saw quite a bit of each other while he was at home and he took me to meet his parents. He said he wanted us to make the most of his leave.'

'And did you?'

'Did we?'

'Make the most of it?'

Lillian blushed and sighed. 'Oh, Hazel, it was so romantic.' She looked up, her cheeks pink. 'He says he loves me. It's hard to believe after such a short acquaintance but he says he knows and he's sure and – and . . .'

'And you?'

Lillian nodded. 'I feel the same. But I'm so afraid that it's too much too soon. After the horror of what he's been through and me thinking he was dead all those weeks. Maybe we're both getting carried away.'

Hazel was smiling. 'Sometimes it's nice to be carried away.'

'Oh, Hazel, I want so much for it to be real,' she said. 'I want it to last – to be for ever, but I still can't quite let myself believe it.'

'What about your mother?'

The smiled vanished from Lillian's face. 'Oh.' She sighed. 'She's been impossible, Hazel. She's so nasty about Alan and his family. To hear her talk you'd think they were peasants and we were landed gentry or something. She behaves as though we're living in the Middle Ages. I've always known she's snobbish but I wouldn't have believed she could be this bad. I'm determined though. I'm not going to let her spoil it for me, but I have to admit that it does make it difficult for me to keep seeing Alan. It does take the shine off.'

'I'm sorry to hear that.'

'Well, never mind,' Lillian said resolutely. 'I've quite made up my mind not to let her ruin things for me. Anyway, enough of that.' She looked at her friend. 'Any more news?'

'Poor little Ruby has been in hospital. She caught a cold at

Christmas and it turned to pneumonia.'

'Oh no! Poor Ruby.'

'She's gone away to a convalescent home now. I do wish we could get her away from those awful Joneses,' Hazel said. 'If only her mother would turn up and take her home.'

Lillian shook her head, 'Hardly likely now, is it?'

Hazel went to collect Ruby on the day she was discharged from the convalescent home. She took the bus out to Kimbourne where the Hope Grange Convalescent Home stood on the cliff overlooking the sea. Ruby looked so much better than when she had left hospital. She had put on weight and there was colour in her cheeks. Hazel saw that with care and attention Ruby could blossom into a very pretty girl. The matron spoke to Hazel as they waited for her to collect her things.

'Ruby is a sweet child,' she said. 'I gather that life hasn't been easy for her. Do you know her foster family?'

'Yes. It's the family she was billeted on soon after her evacuation,' Hazel said. 'Unfortunately her mother seems to have disappeared and Ruby has had no alternative but to stay with the Joneses; something which they clearly resent. She works for them in their greengrocery shop in return for her room and a pittance. I strongly suspect that they exploit her.'

'Well, she should be on light duties for at least two weeks,' Matron told her. 'Perhaps you'll make that clear to them.'

'I will.' Hazel smiled grimly at the prospect. 'But I'm afraid the advice will probably fall on deaf ears.'

Ruby was quiet on the way back to Valemouth on the bus. Hazel tried hard to cheer her up. 'We'll keep in touch, Ruby,' she said. 'You must come and see me every week. We could have tea every Sunday if you like.'

Ruby was staring at Hazel's left hand as it lay in her lap. 'Are you engaged?' she asked.

Hazel looked down at her ring. 'Yes.'

'So you'll be getting married,' Ruby said. 'Perhaps you'll go away to live. Anyway, you'll want to see your chap on Sundays.'

'He's not here, Ruby,' Hazel told her. 'He's away in London, taking another teaching qualification so I don't see him very much. Anyway, I know he'd enjoy seeing you as much as I do.'

Ruby turned her large brown eyes on Hazel. 'I know you mean to be kind,' she said. 'But I'd rather you didn't make promises to me. I know you mean it now, but some time soon you might not be able to do those things.'

'Oh, Ruby.' Hazel took the girl's hand and held it tightly. 'I know how badly you've been let down. I'll make you one promise and that is that I'm going to do everything I can to get you away from the Joneses and into a nicer job somewhere.'

Ruby smiled but she looked unconvinced. 'Thank you,' she said softly.

Myrtle did not look pleased to see Ruby and even less delighted to see Hazel. But at least Edgar thanked her for bringing Ruby home.

'We couldn't go, see,' he said. 'Couldn't leave the shop.'

'Got the business to think of,' Myrtle echoed defensively.

'Quite.' Hazel handed Edgar the carrier bag containing Ruby's pathetically meagre belongings. 'The matron of the home told me to tell you she is to be on light duties for a couple of weeks,' she said.

Myrtle sniffed. 'Not that she's ever on anything else.'

'*Very* light,' Hazel repeated. 'And short hours. She should get plenty of sleep and good food to eat.' She looked from one to the other. 'Unless you want her to be ill again and I'm sure you don't want that.'

'*That* we don't,' Myrtle said. 'Cost us a fortune she 'as, what with the doctor's bill and everything.'

Laura continued to be difficult about Lillian's relationship with Alan, even after he had returned from his leave. She took to her bed again, blaming Lillian, saying that the shock of her daughter's outrageous behaviour had made her ill. When Lillian took her meals up she barely spoke and if she did it was to make some caustic comment or complain about something.

'You don't know what you're doing to me,' she said one morning when Lillian took her coffee. She had changed tack – switched from the autocratic parent to the vulnerable victim. 'I was feeling so much better until you were stupid enough to let that awful man turn your head.'

'You've no right to say he's awful when you don't even know him, Mummy.'

'You're right. I don't know him and I have no wish to. I know his sort though.'

Lillian looked at her mother. 'What does that mean?'

Laura shrugged. 'No doubt you'll find out – to your cost,' she said with a smug little smile.

'That's as maybe,' Lillian had no wish to pursue the subject further. 'Anyway, I don't really see that my seeing him should make any difference to you.'

'Not make any difference to me!' Laura hoisted herself further up in the bed. 'Having to watch my only daughter making a fool of herself? Having to lie here helplessly while you throw yourself away on some – some ignorant wastrel!'

'Mummy, to begin with you are not helpless and never have been,' Lillian said. 'And secondly, Alan is neither ignorant nor a wastrel.'

'I daresay he thinks you have money,' Laura said. 'He looks at this house and he thinks he's in for a cushy life.'

'I've told you: Alan is going to university, but even if he wasn't his father has a very good business which Alan could take over if he wished.'

'Do you really want to marry a *plumber*?' Laura spat out the word as though it had a disgusting taste.

'There is no prospect of marriage at the moment,' Lillian said quietly.

'And I sincerely hope there never will be!' Laura said. 'I'd rather see you in your *coffin* than married to such a person.'

'*Oh!*' Lillian stepped back in horror, the colour draining from her face. 'How dare you say that to me!' she said. 'That's a really cruel, evil thing to say and I – I'll never forgive you for saying it.' As she turned and left the room Laura called after her,

'*Lillian*! All right – I shouldn't have said it. But you drove me to it. It's your own fault. What you're doing is enough to try the patience of a saint!'

As Lillian sobbed at the kitchen table Jean did her best to comfort her. 'She's a lonely old woman, Lillian,' she said. 'She's probably terrified that you might marry Alan and leave her. She's frightened of being left alone.'

'So why is she doing her best to drive me away?' Lillian said, drying her eyes. 'I don't know how much more of it I can take.

Honestly, Jean, there are times when I almost hate her.'

Jean put her arms round her. 'You don't mean that. Let me have a word with her. Maybe I can make her see your side of things.'

But the following morning something happened to put all thoughts of Laura's aversion to Alan out of their minds. An official-looking letter arrived for Jean by the first post. She opened it to find that the house in Woolwich where she and the children had lived had been demolished in a direct hit by a V2.

'We're homeless,' Jean said in a stunned voice as she looked up from the letter. She passed it to Lillian across the breakfast table. 'My poor Dave. Not only a prisoner of war but nowhere to come home to now either.'

'Oh, Jean, I'm so sorry,' Lillian said. 'What will you do – will you go up to London – see if there's anything you can salvage?'

Jean shook her head. 'It's not worth the rail fare. A direct hit means there won't be anything left. I've got no relatives up there any more. There's nothing to go back for now.'

The two girls sat in silence for a moment, then Lillian said, 'Why don't you stay here?'

'Here? I couldn't live in your house for ever,' Jean said. ''Specially not when my Dave comes home. I need to make a new home for him.'

'Yes – yes, of course you do.' There was a moment's silence, then Lillian said, 'I'm really sorry about your home, Jean. It's awful for you, but I can't help feeling pleased that you're staying on in Valemouth. It will be lovely.'

Jean hugged her. 'I've been so lucky, being billeted on you. The kids love it here. The sea air is so good for them. I've never seen them look so well, and Jim loves his school. Maybe I'll look round for a little place for us to rent. I'll have to find a job too. Something part time maybe.'

'What about Dave's work?'

'Dave's an electrician. They're always wanted. I don't think he'll have any trouble finding a job. And I'm sure he won't complain about living near the sea.'

Hazel was preparing to leave for home on Friday afternoon when the door of her classroom opened and Miss Jenkins, the head-mistress's secretary looked in.

'Oh, Miss Dean, so glad I've caught you. Mrs Hardy would like a word with you before you go home.'

Hazel paused in the act of putting on her coat. 'Oh – all right. I'll be along right away.' She took off her coat again and hung it up. What could Mrs Hardy have to say to her she wondered. She followed Miss Jenkins along the corridor and was ushered into the headmistress's office.

'Ah, Miss Dean.' Mrs Hardy looked up from behind her desk. She had come out of retirement soon after the outbreak of war to replace Mr James, the headmaster who had joined up. She peered at Hazel over the tops of her spectacles. 'Please have a seat,' she said. 'I have something I wish to say to you.'

Hazel sat down. 'I hope there is nothing wrong,' she began. The older woman shook her head.

'Not at all, Miss Dean. Not at all.' She took off the spectacles and laid them carefully on the desk in front of her, then patted her tightly permed grey hair. 'It's this way, Dennis Briarly whose class you have been teaching will shortly be rejoining us. I hear from his wife that he is to be invalided out of the army following a wound he received during the Normandy landing.' She pursed her lips. 'It was promised to Mr Briarly when he went off to the war that his job would be kept open for him.'

Hazel frowned. 'I wasn't told that when I was appointed,' she said.

Mrs Hardy looked up sharply. 'No. As you know I took over from Mr James when he joined the RAF. It was he who made this arrangement with Mr Briarly and I was not aware of it at the time of your appointment.'

'I see.' Hazel thought this highly unlikely. 'So am I to understand that you are asking for my resignation?'

Mrs Hardy cleared her throat. 'I couldn't help noticing, as have other members of staff that since Christmas you have been sporting a rather splendid engagement ring,' she said. 'And so of course clearly you are shortly to marry.'

'I don't quite see . . .'

'It has always been the policy of this school not to employ married women and so of course your position would shortly become untenable anyway.'

'My fiancé and I have no plans to marry at the moment and in any case—'

'I myself am here only as only a temporary measure,' Mrs Hardy interrupted. 'As soon as Mr James returns I too will be relinquishing my position.'

Hazel was tempted to point out that there was quite a difference in their ages but she restrained herself.

Mrs Hardy picked up the spectacles and began to fiddle with them. 'And of course Mr Briarly has a young family which makes his need greater than yours.'

'I see. So – when do you want me to leave?'

'As soon as it is convenient to you,' Mrs Hardy said rather too quickly. 'We have no wish to cause you any hardship of course. But all things being equal perhaps the end of this term – Easter?'

'Easter? But that is only five weeks away,' Hazel reminded her.

'Quite.'

Hazel was about to point out that her contract stated that a term's notice on either side was customary but the look on Mrs Hardy's face told her she'd be wasting her time. She stood up. 'I'll see to it that my letter is on your desk by Monday morning.'

Mrs Hardy slipped on her spectacles again and made a note on a pad. 'Thank you so much, Miss Dean,' she said with a thin smile. As Hazel opened the door she added. 'I'm sure that the governors will appreciate your co-operation.'

By the time Hazel arrived at her rendezvous with Lillian she was almost twenty minutes late. Lillian was already there.

'Hello, I was just wondering if anything had happened,' Lillian looked up and noticed Hazel's strained face. 'Oh dear! It *has*, hasn't it? Sit down and tell me.'

Hazel slid into the chair opposite. 'Putting it plainly, I've got the sack,' she said numbly.

Lillian stared at her. 'The sack? You can't have.'

Hazel recounted the interview with Mrs Hardy. 'I'm still in shock,' she said. 'After Easter I'll be unemployed. She gave me no leeway at all. She even had the cheek to point out that as I was engaged I'd soon be asked to leave anyway. It's the school's policy not to employ married women. She said she'd noticed I was sporting an engagement ring – *sporting*! She made it sound as though I was flashing it around like a neon light!'

Lillian shook her head. 'I'd have thought that the war would have abolished archaic rules like that,' she said. 'Think of the married women serving their country and the ones doing men's work all through the war.'

'They'll probably find themselves on the scrapheap too, once the men come home,' Hazel said. 'I'll just have to start looking round for another job.' She took a grateful sip of the tea Lillian had poured for her. 'I shan't be sorry to say goodbye to all those bored fourteen-year-olds though.'

CHAPTER ELEVEN

After quite a long search Jean found a ground floor flat to let two streets away from The Laurels and by the end of March she was preparing to move. Laura was devastated.

'This house is going to seem quite empty without them,' she complained one sunny Saturday morning as Lillian helped her back to bed after her bath. 'Jean has been like another daughter to me and as for little Jim . . .'

Lillian sighed. She'd heard it all before. 'They're not going far and you still have me,' she reminded her mother. 'Jean has promised to bring the children to see you every week.' She was tempted to remind Laura about the fuss she had made when she knew she was required to take in evacuees.

'She tells me she's going to get a job,' Laura said. 'I think it's appalling. What about those poor children?'

'Jim is at school and Katie will be going to a nursery,' Lillian explained. 'Jean has found a cleaning job with a nice family. It's only for a couple of hours in the mornings and they are happy for her to take baby Patsy along with her.'

Laura was shaking her head. 'It would never have done in my day,' she said. 'A mother's place is in the home with her children.'

'That's all very well for those who can afford it,' Lillian said, her patience wearing thin. 'Anyway, it's really none of our business, is it?' She tucked in Laura's covers. 'Do you want your coffee now?'

'No. I don't feel like coffee this morning,' Laura said petulantly. She eyed her daughter. 'I take it you are still corresponding with that man.'

Lillian looked at her. 'If you mean Alan, yes, he writes. He tells me he won't be required to sign on to another ship since his ordeal.

He's to have on-shore duties.'

Laura sniffed and turned her head away. 'I'm not interested.'

'Then why did you ask?'

'Because I can't believe that you're being so stubborn about maintaining the association.'

'It's not an *association*. Alan and I love each other,' Lillian said.

'What on earth are you saying, girl?' Laura looked scandalized. 'It is extremely immodest to make statements like that. In any case you can't possibly know your own mind. You hardly know the man.'

'You brought the subject up,' Lillian reminded her. 'It's a lovely day, quite warm and springlike outside. Don't you think it would be nice to come downstairs for a while?'

'You're changing the subject.'

'Because there's nothing more to be said. Now, do you want to come downstairs?'

'I'll think about it.'

'Well ring your bell if you want me to help you.'

In the kitchen she told Jean about the conversation. 'She's never going to accept Alan,' she said. 'I don't know what will happen. When he comes out of the Navy I expect he'll go off to university and meet someone else.' She sat down at the table dejectedly.

'Of course he won't.' Jean put a mug of coffee in front of her. 'Something will turn up, you'll see,' she said. 'Would you like me to take your mum's coffee up?'

'She doesn't want any this morning.'

'She doesn't have many visitors, does she?' Jean remarked.

'Only Doctor Frazer,' Lillian said.

Jean looked thoughtful. 'I know what he looks like,' she said. 'But when you were out yesterday afternoon another man called. Your mum dressed and came downstairs after you went out and she saw this man in the drawing-room.'

Lillian frowned. 'She didn't say anything to me. What was he like?'

'Tall and thin,' Jean said, her brow furrowed. 'Bald with glasses; about fifty. Dressed quite formally, like a solicitor perhaps.'

'Sounds like Mr Wilmot, the bank manager.' Lillian shrugged, wondering why Laura hadn't mentioned the visit. 'I suggested she might like to come downstairs and get some fresh air this morning.'

'And will she?'

Lillian sighed. 'She's thinking about it.'

Jim looked up from the book he was colouring with his sister at the other end of the table. 'I want Granny Upstairs to come down and play with us,' he said.

'Maybe she will – a little later,' Lillian said.

Jim got down from the table. 'I'm going up to get her,' he announced.

Peter spent Easter weekend with Hazel at Broadway Lane. It was to be the last time he would get away now until after his exam. He had only managed a couple of weekends away from London since Christmas as he had been augmenting his grant by playing in concerts at weekends. It was something the college encouraged as it gave the students experience.

As he and Hazel breakfasted in the kitchen Hazel was complaining that she still had no new job to go to.

'I've filled in lots of applications but it doesn't look promising,' she said. 'A lot of the male teachers who went into the services will be coming home soon. They're bound to get priority.'

Peter looked thoughtful. 'You could do some freelance work,' he suggested.

'Such as?' Hazel looked up.

'Cramming for matric; coaching for entrance exams; remedial.'

'All that would be for private education,' Hazel said. 'I had hoped to help poor kids who don't get a chance under the present system.'

'You could always apply to teach evening classes?' Peter said. 'A lot of young people who had to leave school at fourteen go to night school and get some further education.'

'Not that many,' Hazel said. 'If only the government would raise the school leaving age.'

'It has to come,' Peter said. 'Fifteen or even older; with some proper educational qualification for them to leave with in line with the School Certificate.'

Hazel sighed. 'If only.' She looked at him. 'You'll soon be looking for a job too. That could be anywhere in the country. Is it really worth me looking for local work at all at the moment? I'll want to move with you.'

'I've been meaning to talk to you about that,' Peter leaned forward and she saw from the sparkle in his eyes that something had happened to interest him.

'Plans have been passed for a new college to be built on the outskirts of Valemouth,' he told her. 'It's to be a college for the performing arts and that of course includes music.'

'How exciting. But surely that's away in the future?'

'The new building, yes,' Peter said. 'But they're anxious to have a college ready as soon as possible so that they can take some students who'll be coming out of the services, so they're going to adapt an old house that used to be a private school: Greymoor Manor out at Ringworth.'

'I know it.'

'And . . .' He was grinning now. 'They have been interviewing since last month and have already appointed a full staff.'

For a moment she didn't take in the implications of what he was saying then light began to dawn. 'Peter! Are you saying that they've – they've actually—'

'Offered me a job? Yes; head of the music department. I start at the beginning of the next school term in September – on condition that I pass my exam of course, but I was offered the job largely on account of my teaching experience.'

'And of course you'll pass. Oh, you clever thing!' Hazel jumped up from the table and threw her arms around him.

'Steady on. You've got marmalade on your chin!' He laughed and kissed her. 'Mmm, delicious.' He pulled her on to his lap.

'This means we can stay on here in this house,' she said 'And that I can go ahead and look for a permanent job.'

'Certainly does. I can't have an idle wife sitting at home eating her head off doing nothing. You'll have to earn your keep, my girl. Which reminds me . . .' He took her face between his hands. 'Hadn't we better start rustling up a local vicar or something – arranging a wedding? I reckon the end of May would be about right; don't you?'

Lillian was passing through the hall when the telephone rang. She stopped and picked up the receiver.

'Hello, Lillian Mason here.'

'Lillian, this is June Blakely.' Alan's mother sounded upset, there was a break in her voice and Lillian could almost hear her trembling.

'June! Are you all right? It – it's not Alan?'

'No. Alan is fine. Lillian, can you come round and see me please?'

'Of course – when?'

'Well now – if possible.'

Lillian bit her lip. 'Now? I don't know.'

'I wouldn't ask you to drop everything only it is rather urgent. It's not something I want to talk about on the telephone.'

Clearly something was wrong and Lillian wanted very much to know what. 'I'll come,' she said. 'I'll just get my coat and I'll be with you shortly.'

In the kitchen she told Jean she had to slip out for a while.

'Alan's mother wants to see me,' she said. 'I would have suggested going later but it seems urgent.'

Through the window she could see Jim and Katie kicking a ball round the lawn, watched by Laura who sat swathed in shawls on the paved terrace outside the dining room window. Jean saw her looking.

'Don't worry about her,' she said. 'I'm keeping an eye on the three of them. Patsy is having her morning nap. When she wakes up I'll get them all some lunch. Just take your time.'

Lillian left the house, happy in the knowledge that Jean was holding the fort. She seemed to have a calming influence on Laura. *I just wish I had,* Lillian told herself as she waited for the bus.

June opened the door to Lillian so quickly that it was almost as though she'd been waiting impatiently on the other side for her arrival.

'Come through. I'm on my own,' she said. 'Bill went off early with some pals to an away match.'

Lillian followed her through to the living room. On the table lay an opened envelope and a folded sheet of paper. June picked up the notepaper and handed it to Lillian.

'You'd better read it,' she advised.

As Lillian read her eyes grew wider and wider. The letter was from her mother. Basically it accused Alan of avarice and greed.

Your son and my daughter cannot possibly have anything in common, she wrote. *Lillian has been very carefully brought up and*

educated. She has led a sheltered life and is therefore vulnerable to the wiles of scheming men. As she can hardly be described as a pretty girl there can be only one reason for the unseemly haste of this courtship but I can assure you that I will move heaven and earth before I allow my daughter to be duped into such an unsuitable alliance. No doubt when your son learns that no monetary gain is to be had he will turn his attentions elsewhere; something for which I shall be extremely grateful. Believe me, no good can come of this liaison.
Yours, Laura Mason

'Oh no!' Lillian looked up at June, her eyes full of tears. 'I – I can't believe she would stoop so low,' she said. 'I'm so sorry.' She dropped the letter on to the table as though it was burning her fingers. 'Please – I'm sure you must know that I was completely unaware . . .'

June wasn't listening. Her hands clenched and unclenched at her sides as she said, her voice shaking with emotion, 'Bill and I have always worked hard. I helped him to build up the business and when we saw that Alan was bright we sacrificed so much to send him to the grammar school. We've always had such high hopes for him; I always wanted him to go to university and Bill agrees with me now.' She spread her hands. 'Why else do you think we still live in this house when we could have moved to a bigger house in a better area? Alan has been worth all of it. He's made us so proud. He's the best son any parents could wish for and reading those words – having him spoken of like that,' she pointed to the letter. 'For anyone to accuse my Alan of being after a girl for her money . . .'

'Please, Mrs Blakely – June; please don't show the letter to Alan or – or to your husband. Can't we keep it to ourselves?'

June shook her head. 'Don't you think Alan deserves to be warned – to know what kind of family he is thinking of marrying into?' she said. 'It makes me feel sick inside just *thinking* about what she says. What kind of woman is your mother, Lillian, to say such cruel and unjustified things when she hasn't even met him?'

'She – she's not well,' Lillian said. 'Ever since my father died she's hardly been out of bed. I think she's just afraid – afraid of being left alone.'

June was staring at her. 'Are you saying that if you and Alan married she'd have to live with you?' The look of horror on her face said it all.

'*No!*' Knowing she'd said the wrong thing, Lillian cast around in vain for some way to put things right. 'I – I'm sure that we could—'

'I think you had better think again,' June said. 'Do you think I want to see my boy saddled with a mother-in-law like that? No marriage could survive that kind of malice.'

'I love Alan,' Lillian said, tears running down her cheeks. 'I'll go home and talk to her – make her apologize. I'm sure she didn't mean it. Sometimes she gets a little carried away. Sometimes . . .'

'If you really love Alan you'll be prepared to make a sacrifice.'

An icy chill clutched Lillian's heart. The silence that hung between the two women was like a brittle thread. Lillian opened her mouth to speak but her throat was too tight for words. 'Sac – sacrifice?' She managed to whisper at last.

'Yes.'

Lillian swallowed hard. 'You mean – you want me to give Alan up?'

'If you really love him you'll realize it's for his sake.'

'But – but he loves me too. What about his sacrifice?'

'Lillian – can I ask you something?'

'Of course.'

'If you had to choose between Alan and your mother who would you choose?'

Lillian stared at her. 'Well, Alan of course, but surely it would never come to that?'

'How old is she?'

'Sixty-six.'

'You do realize that she could be around for another twenty years.'

Lillian let out her breath on a sigh. Her shoulders slumped. She felt defeated.

'Can you really see yourself having a successful marriage living with your mother?' June went on, her voice gentler now. 'Can you imagine trying to bring up a family in that situation? One thing I can guarantee, Lillian. If she's like this now, she certainly won't improve with age.'

'What shall I do?' Lillian tried hard to keep the tears at bay. She knew in her heart that what June was saying was true. Laura would never let her go. She knew only too well what her mother was capable of, and she would never accept Alan as a son-in-law.

'Write him a letter,' June said. 'Just explain the situation. Tell him you are releasing him because it isn't fair to expect him to agree to impossible conditions.'

'I . . . I'll do it tonight,' Lillian said.

'No, Lillian.' June went to the sideboard drawer and took out a pad and envelopes. 'Do it now.'

Lillian looked up at her. 'Now? But . . .'

'I'm sorry dear, but if you have time to think about it I'm afraid you won't be able to bring yourself to do it.'

'You don't trust me?'

'I'm sorry, but not on this occasion.' June went to the door. 'I'll leave you to do it on your own. I'm not going to stand over you.'

'I suppose you want to read it when I've finished,' Lillian could not keep the bitterness out of her voice.

'No. It's private; between you and Alan,' June said. 'But if you don't mind I'd be grateful if you'd let me post it.'

'On one condition,' Lillian said. 'I'll make sure Alan won't want to see me again but I don't want him to see that letter.'

'How can I be sure?'

'I'll let you read my letter if in return you tear that one from my mother up in front of me.'

June considered for a second. 'All right,' she said at last.

'You'll promise me that no one will ever know?'

'I promise.'

Lillian let the tears flow as she travelled home on the bus. The other passengers eyed her, some with concern; others with open curiosity. No one spoke to her, except the conductor as she was getting off at her stop.

'Cheer up love. It might never 'appen,' he said, giving her shoulder a pat.

The house was quiet when she let herself in. Jean had left a note on the kitchen table.

Gone round to the flat to measure up for curtains. Your mum's gone back to bed. Back soon. Jean.

Lillian took off her coat and went slowly up the stairs. Outside Laura's door she straightened her shoulders and took a deep breath. She opened the door and walked straight in.

Laura was sitting up in bed reading. She looked up in surprise at her daughter's unheralded appearance. 'Really, Lillian! Have you never heard of knocking? I might have been asleep.'

'Why did you do it?' Lillian demanded.

'Why did I do what?' Laura took off her reading glasses and looked at her daughter.

'Why did you write that deeply offensive letter to Mrs Blakely?'

Laura shrugged. 'Oh that. Someone had to act.' She put down her book. 'I know you have very little experience of the world, Lillian, but you were making a complete fool of yourself, throwing yourself at that man. Clearly he was out for all he could get. Someone had to put a stop to it – to save you from yourself.'

'The Blakelys are decent, respectable people,' Lillian said. 'Alan is their son. They're proud of him. The letter you wrote was downright insulting.'

'If the cap fits, as they say.' Laura was unrepentant. 'They know now that even if my idiot of a daughter is prepared to be taken in by a confidence trickster I refuse to have the wool pulled over *my* eyes.' She peered at Lillian. 'Is that where you've been – round to their house?'

'At Mrs Blakely's request, yes. She rang me. She was extremely upset.'

'Good! That means that my message went home,' Laura said.

'No doubt you'll be happy to know that I have written to Alan, telling him I shall not be seeing him again.'

'Very sensible.' Laura put on her glasses and picked up her book again.

'You're not getting it, are you?' Lillian said between clenched teeth. 'You have ruined everything between me and the man I love and you have insulted three innocent hard-working people.'

'Really, Lillian, don't be so melodramatic.'

'If you think I can stay here with you when I know what you are capable of then you are mistaken.'

'What on earth are you talking about?'

'I'm leaving,' Lillian said. 'I've put up with you all these years. I sacrificed my education and most of my youth just to be ordered about by you as though I were the lowliest of servants, but now you've gone too far. I'm not prepared to let you ruin my life any longer. I shall be packing my bags and leaving as soon as possible.'

Laura snorted. '*Huh*! Fine words! And where do you think you're going? What will you do for a living? You're not fit for anything, Lillian, which is why I've put up with you all these years. No one in their right mind would employ you and you've nowhere to live and no money. So stop your childish tantrums and calm down. By writing that letter I was protecting you. I've done you a favour.'

'I mean it. I'm leaving,' Lillian said. 'You had better believe me because I'm deadly serious. This time you've gone too far.'

Laura's face changed. Something about the tone of Lillian's voice and the determined set of her jaw told her that the girl meant what she was saying. 'You'd walk out on your home and your mother just because of some spotty-faced sailor who flattered you and softened you up with a tissue of lies?'

'Put it any way you like. It comes to the same thing,' Lillian said. 'I've had enough. I want – no, I need to live my own life and I intend to. As for being unemployable, I can do what I do here. I can clean and cook. I can wait on people. I might even find some appreciation, which is more than I get here.'

'All this just because I got you out of an impossible alliance! Is this all the thanks I get? Have you given a thought to how *I* shall manage?' The harshness in Laura's voice was turning into a whine.

'You'll still have Hilda,' Lillian said. 'And you are perfectly capable of taking care of yourself. You always have been. You've never really needed a daughter – or a carer; you just needed a victim – someone to bully. And as for *thanking* you! Do you really think I'm that naïve? You did what you did out of pure spite.' Without waiting for a denial Lillian walked out of the room, closing the door firmly behind her.

Jean returned from her new flat to find Lillian sitting at the kitchen table, a stunned expression on her face and a cooling cup of tea in front of her. The children ran to their toy box in the corner and began to look for their favourites.

'We've been to our new flat,' Jim said. 'There's no upstairs an' Katie'n me are having a bed each.'

Jean was looking with concern at Lillian's distraught face. 'Get what you want to play with, love, and take Katie upstairs,' she said.

'Can we go and see Granny Upstairs?'

Lillian looked up. 'Not now, Jim. She's having a sleep.'

'Oh, OK.'

When the children had gone Jean sat down opposite Lillian. 'What's happened?'

When Lillian told her Jean shook her head. 'Blimey! I never thought she'd go that far,' she said.

'It won't work this time,' Lillian told her. 'I've told her I'm leaving. I mean it too. I'll wait until you and the children have moved out of course. I don't want to involve you.'

'But how will you manage?'

'I'll ask Hazel to put me up till I find somewhere permanent and I'll get a job,' Lillian said. 'I can do anything – cleaning – anything. I don't care. Just to get away from here. I can't take any more, Jean.'

The other girl reached across and touched her hand. 'I can't say I blame you love,' she said softly. 'But what about your mum? Will she be all right?'

'There's nothing really wrong with her,' Lillian said. 'She's perfectly capable of looking after herself, and she'll still have Hilda.'

'Well, if you say so.'

The following Friday afternoon Hazel and Lillian were in totally opposite moods when they met at the Bay Tree Café. Hazel had applied for a job teaching history and English at evening classes at the local technical college. She had heard that morning that she was to go for an interview the coming Wednesday.

'It's only for three evenings a week, but it's better than nothing,' she said. 'And Peter has already been appointed as head of the music department at the new college that's opening at Greymoor Manor.'

Lillian had been putting on a brave front and trying hard to show enthusiasm for her friend's good fortune but Hazel knew her well enough to see when there was something wrong. She leaned forward.

'Lillian – what's wrong?' she asked. 'Here's me going on and on about my own plans and there's obviously something troubling you. There's nothing wrong between you and Alan, I hope?'

Lillian shook her head. 'There is no "me and Alan",' she said.

'Not any more.'

At Hazel's gentle prompting she recounted the story – Laura's letter and the meeting between herself and June Blakely – the resulting row she had had with her mother. 'I've told her I'm leaving,' she said. 'Jean and the children move out at the end of next week and I'll go after that.' She looked up at her friend. 'I've got the most enormous favour to ask of you.'

'You'd like to come and stay with me for a while, is that it?'

Lillian nodded. 'I know it's an imposition and please say no if it's inconvenient. I know Peter comes some weekends.'

Hazel was shaking her head. 'He doesn't get away very often, especially just now with exams so close, and anyway there are plenty of rooms,' she said. 'You're more than welcome to come and stay for as long as you want. But I'm sure all this will blow over. Alan will write and tell you not to be silly and you'll be back together in no time. Maybe this is just the scare your mother needed to make her appreciate you.'

'Alan won't write,' Lillian said. 'I'd be very surprised if his mother didn't write to him too, advising him that it was for the best.'

'He doesn't sound like the kind of man to be ruled by his mother,' Hazel said.

'You don't know what I put in that letter,' Lillian told her.

'So – are you going to tell me?'

Lillian sighed. 'I couldn't tell him about that awful letter. I said I'd made a mistake – that it had all been too quick – too emotional, and that now that he'd gone I realized that what I felt for him wasn't love at all. I said – I said it had just been one of those wartime romances and couldn't last.' She looked up at Hazel with tear-filled eyes. 'And I asked him not to reply as I would return any letters unopened.'

'Oh, Lillian.' There was a lump in Hazel's throat as she reached across the table to touch her friend's hand. 'But surely if you're leaving your mother it isn't necessary to break with Alan.'

Lillian shook her head. 'You weren't there when I met his mother,' she said. 'It was her idea. I don't think she trusts me any more. She believes that Alan will be hurt if he and I stay together.'

'But if you were to tell her you're leaving home,'

'Leaving doesn't mean I don't have a mother any more,' Lillian said. 'Only that I'm no longer living with her. I have to be realistic, Hazel. I can't abandon her altogether. She could still make trouble between Alan and me.' She shook her head. 'It has to be this way. It hurts but as Mrs Blakely pointed out, if I truly love Alan I have to make this sacrifice.'

CHAPTER TWELVE

'Seems like they're all getting their just deserts,' Hilda said as she took off her coat in the kitchen of The Laurels. 'First Mussolini and his missus, now Hitler's done himself and that Braun woman in.' She sniffed. 'It says in the paper he married her the day before. Huh! Much good it did her in the end. One thing's for sure, the war's all but over now, isn't it?' She stopped, suddenly noticing Lillian's suitcases packed and ready by the back door. 'Oh! You're really going then?'

Lillian nodded. 'Yes, I'm really going, Hilda.'

The daily woman eyed her with a mixture of admiration and regret. 'Well, I won't say I'm surprised,' she said. 'Only that you never did it ages ago. I can't blame you. The only thing is where does it leave me? I mean, I'm no nurse. I'm as good as a chocolate teapot in the sick room and anyway, I only come in for a couple of hours a day.'

'My mother is not ill,' Lillian said. 'Now that she's to be on her own she'll have to get up and wait on herself. She knows that she can't browbeat you or pile on extra work, or you'll leave too. I've warned her of that.'

'Well, I hope I'm flexible,' Hilda said. 'I wouldn't see her stuck for anything.'

'I know you wouldn't,' Lillian said. 'And I'll make sure she's not suffering in any way. I intend to keep a check on her although she doesn't know it.' She took a slip of paper from her handbag and gave it to Hilda. 'This is the address and telephone number of where I'll be staying,' she said. 'So you'll know where I am if you need me. But keep it to yourself.'

'Right-oh.' Hilda slipped the paper into her pocket then took

141

down her overall from its peg behind the door. 'Can I ask you something?'

'Of course.'

'What 'appened to break the camel's back so to speak? I mean, what did she do to make you take such drastic action?'

'Let's just say that she interfered in my life one time too many,' Lillian said.

'Oh – I see.' Hilda took her dusters and her tin of polish and went through to the hall. *No prizes for guessin' it 'ad something to do with a feller?* she muttered under her breath.

Hazel made Lillian comfortable in the spare room and the two of them sat up late talking about their plans for the future. Peter's exam was imminent and Hazel was nervous for him.

'It's vital that he gets this qualification,' she said. 'It's conditional on his getting the job at Greymoor Manor College. It's so perfect for him – for us both. I hope nothing happens to stop him getting it.'

'When will he get his results?' Lillian asked.

'Early August.' Hazel held up crossed fingers.

'I'll have to look for a job myself,' Lillian said. 'I've got the small annuity that my father left me but I really need to get work of some kind to augment it.'

'You've got a good brain, you could do anything,' Hazel said. 'Why don't you sign on for a shorthand and typing course at night school? Secretaries are always in demand.'

'But that wouldn't be until September,' Lillian said. 'I need to earn some money now.'

'Don't worry. We'll think of something,' Hazel assured her.

Next morning the postman brought an exciting letter for Hazel. She tore open the envelope as they sat at the breakfast table and let out a squeak of delight as she read the contents.

'*Ooh*! I've got the job at the tech',' she said. 'Three evenings a week and the money's not bad either – look.' She passed the letter across the table to Lillian who passed it back with a smile.

'So you and Peter will both be set up by the end of the year?'

Hazel looked at her friend. 'There's something I haven't told you,' she said. 'With all the trouble you've had I didn't like to mention it, but you'll have to know now that you're living here.'

Lillian looked worried. 'What is it?'

'Peter and I are to be married on May the twentieth, the week after his exam.'

'Oh!' Lillian looked dismayed. 'Oh, I'm happy for you, of course,' she said quickly. 'But you won't want me living here when you're married. You'll want the place to yourselves.'

'You're not to worry about that,' Hazel assured her. 'We'll be going away for a week's honeymoon anyway, so you'll have the place to yourself.' She smiled. 'And I haven't forgotten about you being bridesmaid either. We've decided on a register-office wedding to save money but I want you as my chief witness and then we'll all go for a nice meal somewhere. I thought I'd invite Ruby to the wedding too.'

'What a nice idea.' Lillian got up to hug her friend. 'That will be lovely. And it means we'll both have to go shopping for outfits, won't we?'

'You bet. Maybe we could make a start this afternoon. It's just what you need to cheer you up.'

But the shopping expedition was fated not to take place that day. Just after twelve o'clock the telephone rang. Hazel answered it.

'It's for you,' she said handing the receiver to Lillian who took it looking mystified.

'Hello, Lillian Mason here.'

'Lillian, it's Hilda. Listen love, I don't want to worry you but your mum's in hospital.'

'Hospital?' Lillian's heart missed a beat. 'What happened?'

'A stroke, they think,' Hilda replied. 'I found her when I got there this morning. She'd fallen down the stairs. I rang for the doctor and he got her straight into hospital.'

'How is she?' Lillian felt for a chair and sat down.

'Well, still unconscious at the moment,' Hilda said. 'I went in with her in the ambulance. I'm ringin' from St Mary's now. The thing is love – they think you should be here.'

'I'll come at once. Thanks for letting me know, Hilda.' Lillian's hands were shaking as she hung up. She turned to Hazel. 'It's Mummy, she's had a stroke. She's in hospital and they think I should be there.' She stood up. 'Hilda found her at the bottom of the stairs. I should never have left her. It's all my fault.'

Hazel went to her and took both her hands. 'You're not to blame yourself,' she said firmly. 'I'm sure it would have happened even if you'd been there.'

'I've got to go to her,' Lillian said shakily.

'Of course. I'll come with you.'

Laura lay in a small side ward at St Mary's. Lillian had a word with the sister before she went in to see her.

'Try not to be alarmed at her appearance,' Sister said. 'The stroke has paralysed her left side which has affected her facial muscles. It seems she also has a fractured hip from her fall.'

'Will she recover?' Lillian asked.

Sister shook her head. 'There's no telling. We shall just have to wait and see.'

Sister went with her to her mother's bedside. 'Talk to her,' she said. 'She's unconscious but she may be able to hear you.'

'It's Lillian. I'm here, Mummy.' Lillian took one of the hands that rested on the cover and found it limp and cold. As the sister had warned, Laura's face was grotesquely twisted.

'Mummy, I'm sorry you're ill but I . . .' Lillian pulled up a chair and sat beside the bed, stroking Laura's hand gently. 'Perhaps tomorrow you'll be better.'

Lillian found it hard to believe that the unfamiliar face on the pillow was that of her mother. She looked so different. She swallowed hard. It was so hard to know what to say to someone so unresponsive. 'I'm sorry I left.' she said. After a few more minutes when her mother showed no sign of responding Lillian tiptoed out into the corridor where Hazel was waiting for her.

'How is she?' she asked, getting to her feet.

'Still unconscious. I think I should leave her for now. Maybe by tomorrow she'll have woken up.'

It was five o'clock the following morning when Hazel's telephone rang. Lillian wakened and heard the mumble of Hazel's voice as she answered it downstairs. A moment later she tapped on the door.

'Lillian – are you awake? It's the hospital. They want to speak to you.'

Lillian ran down the stairs and picked up the receiver from the hall table. 'Hello. Lillian Mason here.'

'Miss Mason, this is Sister Harrison, from St Mary's Hospital. I thought I should let you know that your mother regained consciousness briefly but her condition has deteriorated. It's touch and go, I'm afraid, and I think you should come now if you want to see her.'

Hazel was looking at Lillian as she put down the receiver. 'It doesn't sound good,' Lillian said. 'They think I should go at once.'

'I'll get dressed and come with you,' Hazel said. 'We'll get a taxi.'

As they got out of the taxi at the hospital the sun was shining out of a clear blue sky. It promised to be a beautiful spring morning, but Lillian hardly noticed.

It was dim in the little side ward where Laura lay. Lillian crept up to the bed.

'Mummy – it's Lillian.'

Laura's eyes were closed and she was as unresponsive as before. Lillian took her hand. 'I'm sorry,' she said. 'I shouldn't have left you. If I'd been there . . .'

A nurse hovered in the doorway and Lillian turned to look at her. 'I don't think she can hear me. Is she. . . ?'

The nurse came over and picked up Laura's wrist, taking her pulse. She looked at Lillian. 'I'm afraid it's just a matter of time,' she said softly. 'I'll get you a comfortable chair. Stay as long as you like.'

Lillian had hardly slept at all the previous night and the warmth and the dim light in the room made her feel drowsy. Her eyelids were drooping when something suddenly made her alert. She looked at Laura. There was something about her mother's face, a sudden stillness that made her fear the worst. She got up and went to call a nurse.

Afterwards Lillian remembered little of that day, even the fact that later the news broke that the Germans had surrendered and the war was over. Somehow the celebrations passed her by. Hazel helped her through it all; the visit to the registrar – to the under-taker's; in the afternoon to Laura's solicitor where she discovered that Laura had not made a will.

'I think she was planning to,' Mr Brent said. 'She had an appointment with me for later this week, but your father's will is quite clear,' he went on. 'He left everything apart from your small annuity, to your mother but in the event of her death it was to pass to you – the whole estate; house and moneys.' He smiled at her. 'You have no need to worry.'

The funeral took place a week later on a rainy Friday afternoon. There were few people there but Lillian was touched to see Ruby standing in the churchyard at a respectful distance. She caught the girl up after the internment.

'Thank you for coming, Ruby,' she said. 'I appreciate it. It was very thoughtful of you.'

'Hazel – Miss Dean told me.' Ruby said. 'I was sorry to hear about your mum.'

'How are you?' Lillian asked. 'Quite recovered from your illness, I hope?'

Ruby shrugged. 'I'm OK, I s'pose,' she said. 'Still with the Joneses, worse luck.' She was looking towards the small procession winding its way towards the waiting cars. 'I mustn't keep you.'

'Come back to the house for a cup of tea,' Lillian invited, but Ruby shook her head.

'Thanks, but I better not,' she said. 'There was enough fuss about me having an hour off for the funeral. We're always busy of a Friday afternoon.'

'Well, I hope I'll see you again soon.'

'Yes, me too.'

Back at The Laurels Hazel and Hilda served the tea and previously cut sandwiches. Doctor Frazer was there with Mr Brent, the solicitor. Mr Wilmot the bank manager sidled up to Lillian carrying a cup of tea and trying to balance a small triangular ham sandwich on his saucer.

'Miss Mason, perhaps this isn't the appropriate time or place to arrange it but I would be grateful if you could come into the bank first thing on Monday morning. There are urgent matters to discuss.'

'Of course, Mr Wilmot. I'll be there.'

Hilda, wearing an apron over her best black dress looked round conspiratorially and produced an envelope out of her apron pocket.

'Your mum wrote you this letter,' she said. 'She guessed I'd know where you were and she asked me to give it to you. I should've given it to you before but what with everything that happened it slipped my mind' She shook her head. 'Little did she know that she'd be gone by the time you got it, God rest 'er.'

'Thank you, Hilda.' Lillian pushed the envelope into her pocket, deciding to read it later.

Jean laid a hand on her arm. 'I'll have to go in a minute – the kids you know. A neighbour's watching Katie and Patsy for me and

Jim'll be out of school soon. I'm so sorry it happened like this love,' she said. 'She drove you to leaving, though, and you really mustn't feel bad about it.'

Lillian nodded. 'Thank you.'

'My Jim was real upset when I broke it to him,' Jean went on. 'He was ever so fond of her, you know.' She smiled. 'Funny, they seemed to bring out the best in one another.' She looked at Lillian's pale face. 'What will you do now, love? You're surely not planning to live in this great house by yourself, are you? And what about Alan? I don't mean to sound callous but now that there's no – no obstacle in your way . . .'

Lillian was shaking her head. 'I don't know,' she said. 'It's all been so sudden. I haven't had time to think about the future.' She forced a smile. 'I daresay you'll have your husband home soon now.'

Jean shook her head. 'Not till the Japs have given in,' she said. 'The war with Japan is still going on, more's the pity.' She sighed. 'Sometimes I wonder if we'll ever see him again.'

Later when everyone had gone Hazel urged her to go home with her and stay on for a while at Broadway Lane. 'You're in no state to move back in here yet,' she said. 'Surely there's no rush?'

'I don't know,' Lillian told her. 'Mummy always handled all the finances. She kept everything like that very close to her chest. Mr Wilmot wants to see me first thing Monday morning. He says it's urgent. There might be bills outstanding for all I know. I'll have to see if I can find the key to her desk.'

Hazel laid a hand on her arm. 'But not now, love. I think you've had enough for one day. Come home with me.'

The girls spent a quiet evening and by ten o'clock they were both yawning. Upstairs in her room Lillian told herself how lucky she was to have a friend like Hazel. She could never have got through the past days without her. Taking off her dress she heard something rustle in the pocket and remembered the letter. She took it out, smoothed out the creases and laid it on the bedside table. Now would be a good time to read it, she told herself. It would help to draw a line under what had been a traumatic day.

When she was in bed she put her thumb under the flap of the envelope and drew out the letter, seeing at once that it was written in Laura's spidery handwriting. She began to read:

Lillian

No doubt by the time you read this you will already be regretting your hasty decision to leave the comfort of your home, but I am writing to tell you that on no conditions at all will I ever allow you to enter this house again.

For the past twenty-seven years you have called yourself my daughter. The fact is you have never been my daughter. Alfred and I adopted you as a baby. Alfred's sister, Marion lost her head – (and some say her mind too) when she ran away with a man who had promised to marry her. Having seduced her he abandoned her and she begged Alfred and me to adopt the wretched illegitimate child she was carrying to save her from disgrace. I was against the idea from the beginning, but Alfred had a misguided affection for his amoral sister and insisted that we help her, legally adopting you so that you would have his family name – something you do not deserve.

Perhaps now you can see how much you owe me, Lillian, for all the years I have sheltered and protected, fed and clothed you. But you have had all you are going to get. I intend to make a new will cutting you out completely.

For you to abandon your duty at this stage does not surprise me. You are your mother's daughter, feckless and selfish. I hope you will have the fortitude to withstand the degradation that inevitably faces you.

Yours in disgust and disappointment.

Laura Mason

Lillian's hand was shaking as she laid down the letter. She felt stunned. Why had she never been told that she was adopted? So much was now clear; Laura's resentment of her, her cruelty; the many, many unkind things she had said. She had never seen nor heard of her father's sister, Marion – *her mother*, she realized with a sudden pang. Did she look like her, she wondered? Was that why Laura was always trying to undermine her confidence – remarking even in the letter to Alan's mother that she 'wasn't pretty'?

She didn't sleep much that night and the following morning she showed Laura's letter to Hazel, whose eyes grew rounder and rounder as she read it.

'You don't think it could be a spiteful lie, do you?' she said looking up.

Lillian shook her head. 'No. It all fits together now that I think about it. When Daddy was alive she always resented him giving me things – being nice to me. She was obviously eaten up with jealousy and determined to make me pay for poor Marion's downfall.'

Hazel looked thoughtful. 'Well, if, as she says, the adoption was legal you've no worries about your inheritance.'

'Mr Brent said she was to have seen him later this week. I'd better go round to the house and see if I can find the key to her desk. I need to see if she had already written a will. And I need to find my birth certificate.'

'Do you want me to come and help?'

Lillian shook her head. 'No. Thanks for the offer but this is something I have to do on my own.'

The Laurels seemed dark and empty as Lillian let herself in. She shuddered as she stood in the hall, looking at the place at the foot of the stairs where Hilda had found Laura.

Upstairs she was relieved to find that Hilda had stripped Laura's bed and cleaned the room. She searched for the key to Laura's little writing-desk which stood in the corner and eventually she found it, hidden in a vase on the mantelpiece. Having unlocked the drawer, she had difficulty in getting it open, it was stuffed so full of envelopes, many of them unopened. Lillian pulled them out and began to open them one by one. She was shocked to find that most of them were unpaid bills; gas, electricity, rates, the telephone. They must have been on the point of being cut off. Then she found the bank statements – quarterly, three of them – with long columns stamped OD in red ink. Lillian sat back, her heart sinking. Laura had allowed herself to be overdrawn at the bank. She hadn't paid any bills for months. What was going on? She thought of Mr Wilmot's earnest face at the funeral. 'There are urgent matters to discuss,' he had said. Now she realized just how urgent.

In another small drawer she found Laura's marriage certificate, her father's death certificate and – yes – her own birth certificate. It confirmed what Laura had written in the letter. Her mother's name was Marion Elizabeth Mason. The space for the father's name on the certificate was left blank. In the envelope with it was the official record of Lillian's adoption by Laura and Alfred Mason. So – it was all true.

*

At eleven o'clock on Monday morning she was ushered into Mr Wilmot's office. He was a kindly man and had asked his secretary to bring coffee and biscuits for them both.

'It's good to see you, Lillian,' he said. 'I only wish we could be meeting in happier circumstances.'

'Thank you.' Lillian sipped her coffee, wondering where to begin. 'I was going through my mother's papers at the weekend,' she said. 'She always insisted on handling everything herself.'

'Exactly. That is why I asked you to come and see me.' He passed her a plate of biscuits. 'Please, do have one.' When Lillian shook her head he looked uncomfortable. 'If you have been going through her papers you will have discovered that she was rather seriously in debt,' he said quietly.

'I could see she had let things slide.'

Mr Wilmot nodded. 'I'm afraid she had. As you probably know, your father and I were old friends and I felt a certain obligation to him to help her as much as I could. I did warn her that funds were getting dangerously low. I advised her to sell the house and buy something more modest but she was adamant. The Laurels belonged to her parents, you know. She took out a mortgage on it five years ago, but I'm afraid she allowed the repayments to lapse.' He leaned forward, his face grave. 'I kept extending her overdraft until my superiors began to question it. I went to see her only a short time ago in sheer desperation and begged her to declare herself bankrupt, but she was appalled by the idea. I just couldn't make her understand the severity of her situation.'

'So what *is* the situation, Mr Wilmot?'

The bank manager sighed. 'The fact is, Lillian, that if the situation had been allowed to continue The Laurels would soon have become the property of the bank. Not only that, but her creditors are insisting on payment.'

'I see. Is there no money at all?'

'I'm afraid not, unless she had other property or assets she didn't disclose to me.'

'What about the annuity my father left me?'

'She couldn't touch that of course. That money was put in trust for you. It is well invested and is perfectly safe.'

Lillian met his earnest eyes with mounting dread. When it was clear that he was waiting for her reaction she said, 'I suppose the best thing I can do is to sell the house, then?'

'Well, that does appear to be the obvious solution.'

A thought occurred to her. 'It does belong to me, I suppose?'

He nodded. 'Under the terms of your father's will, yes. Mr Brent will have the deeds registered to you under the Land Registry. It will then be yours to do with as you wish.'

'And if I do sell it will I get enough to pay off the creditors as well as what is outstanding on the mortgage?'

Mr Wilmot rubbed a hand across his brow. 'Oh dear, I'm afraid you probably won't. You see, the money your mother owed has been accruing interest at an alarming rate.' He opened a file on the desk in front of him and passed her a sheet of paper. 'This is the present situation. See for yourself.'

The columns of figures on the balance sheet danced under her eyes and Lillian had to force herself to concentrate on them. Clearly Laura had allowed a massive debt to build up. She felt a lump rise in her throat and tears began to prick the corners of her eyes. Mr Wilmot patted her arm.

'Of course, now that the war is over property will be at a premium, so you'd be justified in asking a good price,' he said. 'On the other hand, demobilized servicemen will be looking for smaller, family-size houses.' As Lillian raised despondent eyes to his he quickly refilled her coffee cup. 'However, a property developer might well be interested. A house the size of The Laurels would make several apartments. But even at the best price you can expect I should warn you that you'll be unlikely to come out of it with anything to spare.'

He reached across the desk and patted her hand. 'Put it on the market and let us see. Meantime, leave the creditors to me. I'll do my best to stave them off until the sale goes through.'

Lillian stood up. 'Thank you, Mr Wilmot,' she said. 'Thank you for everything.'

Out in the street everything looked ludicrously normal. The sun was shining and people were going about their daily business. Once again Lillian wondered how everything could look so ordinary when her whole world was falling apart? This was Laura's cruellest blow yet. No wonder she had said that Alan would be disappointed if he was hoping to marry her for her money.

No one would ever want to marry her now, a woman in her late twenties with a mountain of debt round her neck, no home to call her own and no prospect of even earning her own living.

CHAPTER THIRTEEN

When Lillian arrived back at Broadway Lane Hazel was waiting. She opened the door eagerly to Lillian's ring. 'Well – how did it go?' To her dismay Lillian burst into tears.

'Oh, Lillian!' She took her arm. Alarmed by Lillian's white face, she put an arm around her shoulders. She could feel her trembling through the material of her coat. 'Come in and sit down,' she said. 'Let me make you a cup of tea, then you can tell me all about it.'

In the kitchen she pressed her into a chair close to the range. Lillian was still shaking and her hands were icy-cold. Hazel was glad she had decided to light the range this morning. It was almost the end of May and the weather was beginning to warm up but the mornings were still chilly.

She took the kettle that had been simmering at the back of the range and made a pot of tea, watching her friend all the while. Although she was anxious to know what had happened at the bank she decided it was best to let Lillian calm down before she began asking questions. She was clearly in shock. She stirred the pot, then poured a mug of strong tea, sugaring it well.

'Drink it up,' she said as she put it into Lillian's trembling hands. She pulled up a chair opposite and watched as the colour slowly came back into the other girl's cheeks. 'Better?'

Lillian nodded and looked up with brimming eyes. 'Oh, Hazel, I can't tell you how awful things are,' she said, her voice breaking. 'There's no money – none at all. Mummy had let herself get into terrible debt. She even took out a mortgage on The Laurels then defaulted on it. Mr Wilmot says he begged her to declare herself bankrupt but she wouldn't, so now there are all these debts and nothing to pay them with.'

'Oh. I'm so sorry love.' Hazel reached out to grasp her friend's hand. It was far worse than she had imagined. 'Did he advise you what to do?'

'I'll have to sell the house,' Lillian told her. 'There might be enough to pay back the mortgage Mummy took out and some of the creditors – if I'm lucky. If I'm not I don't know what I'll do. I've no home and no way of earning a living, let alone paying off all the debts.'

'Well, you know you can stay here as long as you want,' Hazel said. But Lillian was shaking her head.

'That's wonderfully kind of you, Hazel, but it's not the answer, is it? You and Peter are getting married soon. You won't want me getting in your way. Besides, I've got to learn to stand on my own feet.' She sighed. 'If only I'd been allowed to stay on at school and get some qualifications. Who in their right mind would want to employ me?'

'There are plenty of jobs you could do,' Hazel protested. Lillian looked up at her.

'Oh yes. I could learn to be a waitress,' she said. 'Or serve behind a shop counter.' She gave a dry little laugh. 'Wouldn't Mummy have been proud of me?'

'She was such a snob, Lillian,' said Hazel. 'That is partly the reason she's left this mess behind. It sounds as though she refused to let anyone help her out of it.'

'I'll be in debt for the rest of my life,' Lillian said. 'Now I know what she meant in the letter about having the fortitude to face degradation.'

'Yes, except that I don't think she meant it quite like this.' Hazel looked at Lillian for a moment, then, making up her mind, she went to fetch her coat. 'Come on,' she said firmly. 'You and I are going out to lunch.'

Lillian shook her head. 'No, I couldn't.'

'Yes, you could. And you can,' Hazel insisted. 'This is not the time to sit brooding. Pop upstairs and wash your face – put on a bit of lipstick then we'll go down to the front and have a walk by the sea – blow the cobwebs away. I'm taking you into town to Monty's for a slap-up lunch; my treat. I was going to enquire there about a buffet reception for the wedding anyway.' She gently pulled Lillian to her feet. 'Come on now, Auntie Hazel knows best, after all, we never did get to celebrate VE Day, did we?'

Although it was the last thing that Lillian felt like doing she found that the sunshine and the sea air helped to lift her spirits a little. Most of the beach defences had been cleared away now although the landing-craft traps still stood up out of the water like grim iron fingers pointing at the sky. Some of the concrete gun emplacements were still there too, at the foot of the cliffs, but workmen with pneumatic drills were working away at them. The pier still looked forlorn. It had been blown up at the beginning of the war and the wreckage still stood in the water, a twisted rusting ruin. It would be a while before it could be rebuilt but everything else was being done to make the beach inviting again and there was an air of hope and optimism about the seafront. Already there was a scattering of holiday-makers on the beach, paddling and playing ball.

'Things will soon be back to normal,' Hazel said with a smile. 'Another few months and it will be difficult to remember how bleak it used to be.'

'Except for them.' Lillian was pointing to the once luxurious hotels on the cliff top. Their elegant façades were sadly neglected, the paintwork faded and chipped. Many of the windows were broken and boarded up and the metal-and-glasswork that had once lit up the night sky with coloured neon was rusty – some of the letters missing or hanging crookedly.

'It will be a long time before they'll be open for business again,' Lillian said.

Monty's was one of the town's most popular restaurants. It was always busy but as it was only just after twelve there were still some empty tables. Hazel and Lillian were shown to one near the window overlooking the town's busiest street. Lillian insisted that she wasn't hungry but Hazel ordered for her – locally caught plaice, cooked in the chef's special batter, the recipe of which was a closely guarded secret; and chips; a luxury not often indulged in.

'Don't tell me all that sea air hasn't given you an appetite,' she said.

Lillian managed a smile. 'I'm sorry, Hazel. I told you I wouldn't be very good company,' she said.

'Nevertheless, you have to eat and keep your strength up or

you'll never think of a way out of your troubles.'

'I suppose not,' Lillian conceded.

'Everywhere is beginning to look so much better,' Hazel said, still keeping up her cheerful mood as they waited for their food to arrive. 'It's a pity about the big hotels though. The troops billeted in them have certainly left their mark. Someone who'd seen the inside of the Embassy told me that the soldiers had ripped off most of the doors and the banisters to make fires to keep them warm in the winter. As you say, it'll take a long time to put all the damage right, which is a pity. With so many men coming out of the services over the coming months they're going to want family holidays and . . .' Suddenly she stopped, looking up with an excited light in her eyes.

'Lillian – how many bedrooms are there at The Laurels?'

'Five.' Lillian looked puzzled. 'Why do you ask?'

'Yes, but that's only on the first floor isn't it; what about the second?'

Lillian frowned. 'Well, another five and a tiny boxroom, but those all have sloping ceilings and anyway, apart from the two that Jean and the children had they haven't been used for years. They were once servants' quarters.' She was shaking her head. 'What do the rooms have to do with anything?'

At that moment a waitress brought their food and Hazel stopped talking.

'Well?' Lillian asked at last. 'Are you going to tell me or aren't you?'

'Don't you see? The Laurels would make the perfect private hotel,' Hazel said. 'It has everything – it's only a short walk from the seafront and the town, it's elegant – at least it will be when we've had time to give it some beauty treatment and—'

'Wait a minute!' Lillian was shaking her head. 'I don't know the first thing about running a hotel. Mr Wilmot says that a business-man will probably buy it and turn it into flats.'

'Yes and pay you a fraction of what it's worth. Why not stay in your own home and run your own business?' Hazel popped a fork-ful of fish into her mouth. 'Mmm, this is delicious,' she enthused. 'So *fresh*! I'm definitely going to book here for our reception.' She waved her fork at Lillian. 'Come on now, not another word about anything until you've eaten that up, so get on with it, Lillian Mason.'

Once Lillian began to eat she realized how hungry she was and in no time her plate was empty. Hazel smiled her approval. 'Well done!. Now, what about a pudding?'

They chose ice cream, now being made again after being banned for years. Over coffee Hazel broached the subject again.

'You can do it, Lillian,' she said. 'It's the answer. I bet that if you go to your Mr Wilmot and ask him for some extra time to pay that mortgage he'll agree, especially when he sees your plan.'

'What plan?'

'The one we're going to start making right now.' Hazel beckoned the waitress and asked for the bill and a few minutes later they were out in the street and on their way to The Laurels.

Lillian followed Hazel bemusedly as she walked from room to room. 'Look at the size of this dining room,' she said. 'You could get about twenty people in here.'

'Twenty?'

'Yes, at small tables. There are often auction sales of furniture that was put in storage from the hotels. I've seen them advertised in the local paper. You'd get them really cheap.' She walked through the hall to the drawing room. 'Now this could be the visitors' lounge. And that . . .' She pointed across to the small morning room at the foot of the stairs. 'That could be your own sitting room and office.'

'Well, I suppose . . .' But Hazel was already heading for the kitchen. It was a large room with a dresser stacked with china and crockery. The cupboards beneath were filled with more china, saucepans and other utensils that hadn't been used for years.

'Look at all this,' Hazel said. 'You could cater for an army without buying another thing.'

Lillian nodded. 'I think my grandmother used to give large dinner parties,' she said.

'I'll say she did.' Hazel looked at the large gas cooker and the sturdy boiler that Alan had installed. 'And what could be better than that? Plenty of cooking facilities and hot water. Let's go upstairs.'

All of the rooms were adequately furnished; the first floor rooms were smarter and more comfortable than the second which were more basic. Hazel was undeterred.

'You can charge a bit less for up here,' she said. 'Although I think these sloping ceilings can be very attractive. You can gradually refurbish these rooms and make them almost as good as the ones below.' On the landing she opened the door of the large walk-in airing cupboard and gasped as she looked at the stacked shelves.

'Look at all this linen!' She fingered one of the hemstitched sheets. 'Good quality too. Nothing to buy in this department. Now, what's in here?' She opened the door of the boxroom. Lillian was shaking her head.

'I couldn't possibly let this one,' she said. 'We always referred to it as the attic. It's full of rubbish.'

'Never mind, there are still plenty of rooms.' Hazel came out on to the landing and stood tapping her front teeth with her thumbnail. 'Mmm – it's a pity there's only one bathroom, of course, but when you've made a bit of profit you could have wash-hand basins put in every bedroom. Think of how good that would look in the advertisements.' She looked out of the landing window. 'And just look at that view. You can actually see the sea from up here.' She looked at Lillian whose expression was dubious to the point of incredulity. 'You can *do* it, Lillian. I'm serious. You can!'

'Can I?'

Hazel went to her friend and put her hands on her shoulders. 'You have to love. You have to believe in yourself. Your whole future depends on it.' She put her arms around Lillian's drooping shoulders and gave her a hug. 'I can see that I've overwhelmed you, rattling on like a madwoman. Let's go home now and sleep on it. See how it looks in the morning.'

The moment Hazel opened the door of number four Broadway Lane she heard the telephone ringing. She took two steps into the hall and picked up the receiver.

'Hello.'

'*Hazel*! Where the hell have you been? I've been ringing all afternoon.'

'Peter! Oh, darling, are you all right?'

'Just about. Better now that I know you haven't been kidnapped or run over or something.' There was a pause then he said, 'Well – aren't you going to ask me?'

'Ask you what?'

'Oh dear.' He sighed at the other end. 'What it is to be the centre of your fiancée's universe.'

Suddenly she remembered. '*Oh*! Oh my God, your exam! I'm so sorry darling but a lot's been happening here lately and it slipped my mind.'

'Mmm. It had better be something earth shattering. Still, I'll probably forgive you – in time.'

'So – how did it go?'

'Rather well, I think. I'll be surprised if I don't get a good pass.'

'Should you be counting your chickens?'

'I'm all for counting chickens, which reminds me, I haven't eaten all day. Look, I can't wait till tomorrow to see you so I'm getting on a train this evening.' When she paused he said sharply, 'Well don't fall over yourself with delight! Are you sure it's all right? Only I don't want to put you out.'

Lillian had gone upstairs, making herself discreetly scarce when she realized who was at the other end of the line but Hazel lowered her voice.

'Sorry, darling. Look, of course I can't wait to see you and celebrate the exam being over. There's just one thing: I've got Lillian staying here. Her mother died suddenly. It's a long story and she's having a bit of a crisis. I'll tell you all about it when I see you. You don't mind, do you – her staying here, I mean?'

'Good God, of course I don't mind. Poor Lillian. Why didn't you tell me before?'

'I thought you had enough to think about with your exam looming. So what time will you be here? I'll have a meal ready.'

'Probably about 8.30. I say, does this mean I'm going to have to pretend to suffer from somnambulism?'

Hazel giggled. 'Of course not, silly. Oh darling, I'm so sorry I forgot your special day. It was unforgivable of me. And I can't *wait* to see you – truly.'

'Nor me. I love you.'

'I love you too.'

'See you this evening then. 'Bye.'

When Lillian knew that Peter was on his way home she wanted to go back to The Laurels but Hazel was adamant.

'You'll do nothing of the kind.'

'I feel awful, Hazel. If it wasn't for me you wouldn't have forgotten his exam was today.'

'He's fine about it, I promise. Look, tomorrow the three of us will sit down and talk about what I've suggested. I know Peter will have some useful suggestions to add.' She looked at Lillian. 'Just one thing I want you to know; when Peter is here we – well, we share a room.'

Lillian blushed. 'Well, you are about to be married. Anyway, it's none of my business.'

'Maybe not, but as long as we're sharing the house I thought it only fair to tell you. Peter will be happier that way.'

Lillian put out a hand and touched Hazel's arm. 'I'm so lucky to have a friend like you,' she said. 'Thank you for today – for all your help and suggestions. I don't know what I would have done without you.'

'Don't be silly. I hope we can make it all work for you.'

'Me too, though it all seems a bit like a crazy dream at the moment.' Lillian looked down at her hands. 'I've got a confession to make.'

'What's that?'

'I wish I didn't envy you,' Lillian said quietly. 'Envy is horrible and you deserve so much to be happy.'

'So do you. And you will be someday soon,' Hazel assured her. 'I can feel it in my bones.'

At eight o'clock Lillian announced that she was tired and would go for an early night.

'It's not because of Peter, I hope?'

Lillian smiled. 'You need some time to yourselves and anyway, you've given me a lot to think about today.'

It was almost 9.30 when Hazel heard Peter's step on the path outside. Before he had time to ring the bell she threw open the door and flung herself into his arms.

'Darling! It's so *good* to see you!'

'Wonderful to see you – and to be home.' He looked tired and she drew him inside to the meal she had prepared for him. They talked for a while, about the exam and about their future.

'I'll have to set about organizing some work to tide me over till September,' Peter said. 'I thought I might take on some music students. Would it be OK if I used your gran's piano?'

'Fine, though it might need tuning.' She got up to make coffee but he put out a hand to stop her, pulling her on to his lap.

'Wait a minute. Come here, I want to have you close to me,' he said. 'It's been a hell of a long year.'

She kissed him. 'We'll be married soon.'

'Can't be soon enough for me.'

'There are an awful lot of plans to make,' she told him.

'Plans – what plans?'

'Well, we've booked the register office but there are invitations to send; a reception of some kind to think of; a honeymoon.'

'Can't we just cut straight to the honeymoon?' he asked her with an impish grin. 'Speaking of which, I take it I'm relegated to the spare room.'

'What makes you think that?'

'Well, propriety and all that jazz – Lillian being here.'

'I've told Lillian we'll be sleeping together.'

He stared at her with mock astonishment. 'You fast piece you! What made you think I'd want to sleep with you?'

She laughed as she began to unfasten the buttons of his shirt. 'Do you really want me to answer that?'

He stood up, lifting her in his arms as he did so. 'Yes, but you can do it upstairs.'

'How about the washing up?'

He shouldered the kitchen door open. 'Yeah – how about that?'

Hazel and Peter were awake early next morning and as she lay with her head in the crook of his arm she told him all about Lillian's dilemma. He was sympathetic.

'Poor girl. Old Ma Mason sounds like a real old battle-axe. Fancy the old witch ruining her romance like that.' He looked down at her. 'And you say it turns out she wasn't even Lillian's real mother.'

'No, it seems she was adopted, though it was all in the family, so to speak. It's all legal. Lillian found the papers.'

'And you've suggested that she opens the house as a private hotel?' Peter pursed his lips. 'It's a bit ambitious, and isn't it rather a tall order expecting a girl who's never even handled money to open a business?'

'Maybe, but I wouldn't have suggested it if I hadn't thought her capable of doing it. We were at school together, don't forget. I know she's bright enough to handle it. Besides, Lillian needs this challenge. She needs it to boost her self-esteem. Her mother just about crushed that.'

Peter was frowning. 'That's all very well, but what if it fails? What's she going to feel like then?'

'She won't fail!' Hazel sat up and looked down at him. 'Lillian has experience in running a house, don't forget. She's a good cook too. There's a real gap in the market for this type of small hotel at the moment.' She paused. 'Look, I haven't said anything yet but this is where I come in.'

Peter winced. 'Ouch! Why do I get the feeling I'm not going to like this? You're not thinking of postponing the wedding, are you?'

'No, it's nothing outrageous. I just wanted to talk to you about it first and see what you thought.'

He eyed her suspiciously. 'Go on then – hit me with it.'

'Well, it's the cash thing. I've got a bit of money saved – and we've got this house, already furnished and everything so we don't need much.' She touched his cheek. 'We've got each other too. We're so lucky, Peter. I thought I might make Lillian a small loan. It won't be all that much but it'll help get her started. What do you think?'

He reached out and pulled her down to him again. 'You really are rather a nice person, aren't you, Mrs Grainger-to-be?' He kissed her soundly. 'I think it's a lovely idea.'

'So are you in? Will you help?'

'Me? In what way?'

'With all your worldly wisdom and experience.'

He chuckled. 'Flattery will get you everywhere. OK, I'll do and say what I can, for what it's worth.'

'Did I ever tell you how much I love you, Mr Grainger?' She snuggled against his chest again.

After a moment he looked at his watch and said, 'It's not even six o'clock yet; still the middle of the night really. I think we've talked enough, don't you?'

She laughed and wriggled closer. 'Quite enough.'

He sighed, teasing her with his eyes. 'Mmm – problem is thinking of something else to pass the time.'

When Lillian came downstairs she found Hazel singing in the kitchen as she laid the table for breakfast.

'You sound happy.'

'I am. It's so good to have Peter home for good at last.' Hazel turned to her friend. 'After breakfast we're going to have a council of war, as Peter calls it. He says three heads are better than two, even if they are sheep's heads.'

Lillian smiled. 'I like him already.'

Hazel poured two mugs of tea and passed one to Lillian. 'Well, this is a good chance for you to get to know him. There are only two weeks to the wedding. We're going to have to send out invitations today; not that we're inviting all that many guests.'

'I can help address envelopes.'

'Bless you. We'll get to that later.' Peter appeared in the doorway. Shaved and dressed in a casual open-neck shirt and flannels, he looked handsome and relaxed. 'Do you want the works for breakfast?' Hazel asked him. 'I've been saving some bacon and eggs. I know Mary has been feeding you well. We've been keeping in touch.'

'You mean you've been keeping tabs on me? Outrageous!' Peter took a seat at the table and winked at Lillian. 'I warn you, Lillian, once this woman starts keeping an eye on you you've had it,' he said. 'I bet if I went to the North Pole I'd find some Eskimo following me around taking notes. Your life's not your own!'

Hazel grinned unrepentantly. 'Part of my job description.'

Over breakfast the three of them talked about Hazel's plans for The Laurels but Hazel was dismayed to find that Lillian was still having doubts about the idea.

'Peter and I have been talking,' she said. 'I'd like you to accept a small loan.'

But Lillian was already shaking her head. 'No! I couldn't possibly accept. You can't let me take over your life like that. It might all come to nothing and then—'

'*It won't come to nothing!*' Peter put in sternly. 'Not if you're serious and you put your heart into it. But you've got to accept that you need help from your friends too. Now . . .' He cleared his throat. 'I understand from what Hazel tells me that your solicitor and your bank manager were old friends of your father. Is that right?'

Lillian nodded. 'I think they all belonged to the same club or something.'

'Right, well, that being the case they might feel disposed to offer you some help, especially when they see how much courage and initiative you are displaying.'

'I don't feel very courageous.'

'Right – so this is where you put on a big act. I suggest that you go and see both these men as soon as possible. If you get the chance gently remind them that they were old pals of your dad. We'll work out a plan of your projected earnings that you can take along.'

'How do we do that?'

'Easy. We'll get one of those advertisement magazines and see what similar hotels are charging, then we'll multiply that by the number of rooms you have, plus the number of weeks in the average summer season.'

'That's clever.'

'Just common sense really. Show that to your father's chums and we'll see what happens.'

Lillian's eyes were beginning to shine. 'I've got some savings,' she said. 'I haven't spent much of my annuity and I've been putting it by. Maybe I could offer that as a down payment to start paying back the mortgage.'

'No,' Hazel chipped in. 'You'll need that for the decorating materials and extra furnishings. Take my loan as your down payment. It can all be done properly if you insist and you can pay me back a little at a time.'

There were tears in Lillian's eyes as she looked from one to the other. 'What would I do without you?' she whispered. 'Thank you. Thank you both – *so much*.'

Hazel left Lillian and Peter working out the projected business plan for the bank manager while she went out to buy wedding invitations. On her way home she dropped in at Jones's greengrocer's shop with an invitation for Ruby. She found the girl alone in the shop.

'I haven't seen you for ages, Ruby,' she said. 'I thought we were going to keep in touch.'

Ruby coloured. Pointing to a shelf on the other side of the shop she said. 'They've got a licence to sell tobacco now, and they're getting an ice cream fridge so we're open on Sundays.'

'Are you telling me they expect you to serve in the shop seven days a week?'

Ruby shrugged. 'They say it's just for the summer. Anyway, I don't have much choice.'

'I hope they're paying you more money for doing that.'

'Oh – yes.'

'How much?'

'A sight more than she's worth!' Myrtle, who had been listening on the other side of the door chose that moment to waddle into the shop. She looked Hazel up and down, her lip curling. *'Buyin'*, are you? Or did you just come in to snoop as usual?'

'I came in to buy vegetables and also to give Ruby this invitation.' Hazel pushed the envelope into the girl's hand. 'You can open it now if you like. It's to my wedding.'

'She won't be comin'' Myrtle snapped. 'Not if it's on a Sat'day. We're too busy to spare 'er.'

'As a matter of fact it's on a Monday,' Hazel said triumphantly.

Ruby pushed the invitation into her apron pocket. 'Thank you ever so much, Hazel, but I'm not sure—'

'She's got nothing suitable to wear to a wedding!' Rene had been standing in the doorway obscured by her mother's bulk for several minutes. She stepped aside now, eyeing Ruby with scorn. 'Look at her,' she said. 'Greasy hair, dirty nails. Are you sure you want a *scarecrow* at your wedding, Miss Dean?'

Hazel saw red. 'As a matter of fact I was about to ask Ruby to be my bridesmaid,' she said with a sudden spurt of inspiration. 'So I shall be buying her dress. If you'd like to come round to my house, Ruby, on the Sunday evening before the wedding we'll get you fitted out. You're welcome to stay the night.' She looked at Myrtle. 'I'm quite sure that Ruby is owed enough time off in lieu of all the overtime she's worked,' she said. 'I'll come round to pick her up a week on Sunday at about half past six. Good morning.'

Outside as she walked home she wondered if she had done Ruby any favours by insisting on her coming to the wedding. The expressions on the faces of Myrtle and her obnoxious daughter had been a treat to behold, but knowing that Ruby would pay the price she felt a stab of guilt about her small triumph.

Lillian sat in Mr Wilmot's office, her heart beating wildly as he read through the business plan Peter had helped her draw up. Eventually he looked up at her over the tops of his spectacles.

'Well, it's a very ambitious plan,' he said. 'But in the present climate it is one that could well succeed.' He smiled at her and

Lillian relaxed a little. 'Can you explain to me how you mean to finance it?'

Lillian cleared her throat. 'I have saved some money from the annuity my father left me,' she began, 'and a close friend has suggested arranging a private loan for me. I can offer you some money on account of the back mortgage payments and as you will see, the income from the business should help me provide the remaining repayments.'

He peered again at the figures. 'Indeed – given that you do enough business.'

'I think I will,' she said, trying hard to sound confident. 'I've done some research and I hear that many of the small hotels in Valemouth can hardly keep up with the demand for future bookings.'

'Indeed. Surely there will need to be some modifications to the house. How do you intend to pay for those?'

'Second-hand auction sales and kind friends who are willing to help me with redecoration,' she told him.

He pushed the plan aside and smiled at her. 'And the work of running a hotel. It's bound to be hard. Have you thought of that?'

'I'm used to hard work, Mr Wilmot,' she told him. 'I looked after my mother single-handed apart from a daily help. I can cook and clean and I'm used to waiting on people.'

'Hardly on this scale though. I think you'll need help,' he said. 'That will eat into your profits.'

'I have a friend who has offered help until I am established.'

'You seem to have some very good friends.'

'I have.' Lillian licked her dry lips. 'Just as my father had good friends in you and Mr Brent, something I'm very grateful for.'

He looked slightly taken aback, lowering his eyes for a moment, then he said. 'Perhaps Harold Brent and I should have a meeting with you about this. For you to go ahead The Laurels will have to be registered as a business.' He sighed. 'And then of course – regrettably there is the pressing business of your mother's creditors. You'll be relying heavily on your utility supplies – gas and electricity, water.'

She nodded. 'Is there anything at all you can do to help me there, Mr Wilmot?'

He sighed. 'You seem very serious that you wish to continue with this plan.'

'I am – very serious. Running The Laurels as a business is my only hope of a future home and income.'

He nodded and for a few minutes he was thoughtful, then he said, 'If I remember rightly you father set up the trust fund for your annuity when you left school and it expired on your twenty-fifth birthday. That means that you are now free to withdraw the money as a lump sum if you so wish.' Lillian looked up in surprise.

'I didn't know that. You didn't tell me that before.'

'That was when I was advising you to sell the house,' he said. 'The annuity was then your only source of income. I didn't want you to deprive yourself of that.' Lillian's eyes lit up with hope and he went on quickly. 'Once you have drawn the cash out it's closed, of course.'

'But it does mean that I could pay the bills?'

'It does indeed, with some to spare. I wouldn't suggest this normally but as you are clearly serious about this business project and it is better to start with a clean slate as it were, it could be an option. I suggest that you leave the matter with me and I shall see what can be done.' He got up from behind his desk. 'Leave it with me and I will be in touch within the next few days.'

CHAPTER FOURTEEN

Hazel and Lillian found a pretty dress for Ruby in the teenage department at Bingham's, Valemouth's largest department store. It was in a soft shade of grey with tiny embroidered pink and white flowers. It had a pretty lace-trimmed collar and a full gathered skirt. They also found a pair of white sandals to go with it. The girls provided the clothing-coupons between them as Hazel guessed that Myrtle would be holding Ruby's clothing coupon book and would refuse to give it up without a struggle. Luckily neither of them had used their quota of coupons so they had plenty left for their own outfits.

Hazel chose a delphinium-blue suit, as she said it would be useful to wear afterwards. To team with it she found a white blouse with a froth of lace at the neck, and white shoes.

When it came to Lillian it was more difficult. It was some time since she had bought herself any new clothes and she had no idea what really suited her. In the shop Hazel looked at her friend critically. She was still too thin and the strain of the past weeks had taken their toll. She had little natural colour and her hair was dull and lifeless. She still wore it long and tied back and it badly needed cutting and restyling.

'I'm going to treat you to a hair-do,' she said suddenly. 'Come on.' She took Lillian's arm. 'There's a really good hairdresser in this store.'

As they headed for the lift Lillian was arguing. 'No, Hazel really, you've done so much for me. I can afford to have my hair done, honestly.'

Hazel stopped and looked at her. 'Then why haven't you had it done before?' she asked bluntly. 'OK, if you won't let me treat you to that will you let me buy you some make-up? All you ever use is a bit of lipstick and I have to remind you to use that!'

Now Lillian was laughing in spite of herself. 'OK then. You win. You really are getting very bossy, Hazel. I'm beginning to feel quite sorry for Peter.'

Lillian sat in the hairdresser's chair and watched as her long hair was cut off. She saw with dismay the tresses falling to the floor, apprehensive about whether she would like the finished result. But with the weight gone and her hair shampooed and conditioned she saw with surprise that the natural curl she had almost forgotten about had sprung back, framing her face softly and enhancing her large dark eyes. The cut was short but not severe with a little half fringe to soften the line of her deep forehead. Her spirits began to lift.

When Hazel saw her she beamed with delight. 'You look an absolute knock-out! I knew you would. Now we'll go and chose that dress for you.'

The dress they chose was a deep rose-pink with a heart-shaped neckline and a flared skirt that flattered her tiny waist. Once it was paid for and wrapped the girls went to the store café for a cup of tea.

'I'll have to leave you to make your own way home,' Hazel told her over their second cup. 'I have to meet Peter to make the final arrangements with the registrar at four o'clock. But I got you this.' She handed Lillian a bag with the store's logo on the front.

Lillian peered into the bag and flushed with pleasure. Inside was foundation cream, powder and rouge and a new lipstick in a soft shade of pink. She stared at her friend. 'How did you manage to get these? Cosmetics are in really short supply.'

Hazel winked. 'I know the girl on the make-up counter,' she confided. 'She's an ex-pupil.'

'It's all so lovely. Thank you so much.'

'Well, quite apart from the wedding, you're going to have to be smart for your new job,' Hazel said. She looked at her watch. 'I'm sorry, love, I'll have to go.' She got up and gathered up her shopping. 'You'll be OK?'

'Fine. I can't wait to get home and try on my dress again.'

Lillian travelled down in the lift and out into the May sunshine. Over the past couple of weeks they had achieved so much. After Mr

Wilmot had confirmed that opening The Laurels as a business could be a viable proposition he had given her the name and address of another client of the bank who had run a successful small hotel for many years, suggesting that she might be willing to advise Lillian. She had called on Mrs Jayson at Ocean Lodge on the East Cliff and the lady had been friendly and helpful, showing her how to keep the books and manage the emergency ration coupons; how to organize the catering so as to avoid waste and how to handle the day-to-day running of a private hotel efficiently. She had invited Lillian to work along with her for a few hours each week so as to get into the feel of running a hotel. When she left Mrs Jayson had even offered to recommend guests she was unable to accommodate.

Back at The Laurels she and Hazel, helped by Peter, had painted most of the bedrooms, working most days from early morning till dusk. True, they had colour-washed over existing wallpaper in most cases, but the rooms looked fresher and brighter, and as Peter pointed out, there would be a few quiet months during the winter when serious decorating could be done. Lillian had attended an auction sale and bought six small tables with matching chairs for the dining room and two extra single beds as two of the large rooms on the first floor were to be turned into family rooms. She had also bought a large refrigerator which Hazel assured her she would need. With the help of Hilda, who was as excited about Lillian's plan as she was herself, the whole house had been given a thorough spring clean.

It was only when Lillian had first seen the advertisement that Peter had inserted for her in one of the national holiday magazines that she realized that her plan was no longer a dream, but actually turning into reality.

The Laurels Private Hotel
64 Marlborough Road
Lillian Mason, proprietor
Comfortable homely atmosphere
Dinner, bed and breakfast
Four minutes' walk from the beach and shops.

Her tummy had turned somersaults as she read and reread it. Now it was real and true. Now it was all up to her. She *had* to make it work. Since then, on Mrs Jayson's advice, she had looked into suppliers for food – meat, vegetables, bakery and fish and found several local wholesalers who were willing to sell to her on special terms, and last week she had received her first two bookings. She was on her way.

As she walked along the street a bright display of flowers in a florist's shop caught her eye and she stopped to look. The profusion of brilliant colour delighted her, but after a moment's gazing at the multitude of exotic flowers she realized that a person standing behind her was looking – not at the flowers but at her reflection. She returned his gaze and her heart lurched. The face reflected in the shop window smiled tentatively.

'Hello, Lilly.'

Disbelievingly she turned and found herself looking into Alan's hesitant face. '*Alan!*' She searched for some appropriate words but found herself tongue-tied.

'I wasn't sure it was you at first,' he said. 'You've had your hair cut. It suits you.'

'It – it's for the wedding.'

His face dropped. 'Wedding?'

'My friend, Hazel, is getting married next Monday.'

'Oh – I see.' He looked relieved.

'It's good to see you, Alan,' she said. 'Are you home on leave?'

'Not exactly,' he said. 'I'm getting my ticket in a few weeks' time. Turns out my little boating holiday did no favours to my inside – gastric ulcer.' He pulled a face. 'Not much use to His Majesty's Senior Service any more.'

'Oh, Alan. That's so unfair.'

'Not when you think of what happened to the other poor devils.' He shrugged. 'I'll be glad to get out, if I'm honest. The local quack reckons that with an operation and the proper diet I'll be as right as rain in no time.'

There was a small silence, then Lillian said. 'I hope you get on all right. Will you let me know?'

'Of course I will – if you want me to.'

'W-well, I suppose I'd better go.'

He caught at her sleeve. 'Lilly – please – can we go somewhere and talk?'

Her heart leapt, longing for the chance to be with him for just a few more minutes. 'Well, all right.' She nodded towards the botanical gardens across the road. 'It's not too busy over there at this time of day.'

They walked side by side along a path bordered by colourful displays of tulips and wallflowers till they found a bench. Alan led her towards it.

'I got home a couple of days ago,' he told her. 'I went round to your house but there was no one there.'

She nodded. 'I've been staying with Hazel. My mother died.'

'I know. Mum told me. She saw it in the paper.' There was a pause and he tentatively took her hand. 'She feels really bad, Lilly. She told me about the letter – the one your mother wrote.'

Lillian looked at him sharply. 'She promised she wouldn't. The letter I wrote – it was part of a bargain we made.'

'I know.' He squeezed her hand. 'She told me everything. Mum is so sorry, Lilly. She realizes now that what she made you do was wrong. It wasn't fair – to either of us. None of it was your fault.' She was silent and he reached out to cup her chin, turning her face towards his. 'Can you imagine what it did to me when I got your letter?'

She swallowed hard at the lump in her throat. 'Can you imagine how much it hurt me to have to write it? But your mother was adamant. She was very angry. She didn't want me to be part of your life any more.'

'But now everything's changed,' he said.

'Because my mother has died?' She shook her head. 'I'm not so sure. Perhaps she thinks I might take after her – share her snobbish ideals.'

'She doesn't. Will you come with me to see her?'

She shook her head. 'I could never understand why she couldn't see that I was just a pawn in all of it,' she told him. 'And anyway, there's another reason now why she wouldn't want you to involve yourself in my life.'

He frowned, 'Which is?'

'After my mother wrote that letter I walked out – left her. And she died a few days later, so now I have the guilt of that on my conscience. But what is worse, she died leaving huge debts which I am now liable for. And by the way, it turns out that she wasn't my mother after all. I was adopted.'

The shock was clear on Alan's face then he reached for her other hand and held them both tightly. 'Oh, *Lilly*! My poor love. To think I wasn't there when you needed me. But I am now and I'm going to help as much as I can to try and make it all up to you. I . . .' She was shaking her head as she disengaged her hands.

'No, Alan. You have your own life to sort out; your health and your future plans. I'm not going to drag you down with my problems.'

'You wouldn't! I love you, Lilly. I always have, ever since that first day. University isn't an option this year – maybe it never will be now. Dad has been marvellous; he's paying for my operation and he says I can work with him again when I'm fit enough, up until I'm ready to decide what I want to do.'

'That's good. They think the world of you, Alan, but I still think they won't want me in your life.'

His mouth took on a stubborn set. 'If you think I'm letting you go now that I've found you again you've got another think coming! I don't care what you say, Lilly, I want you. I think you're wrong about Mum and Dad but even if you're not it doesn't make any difference.' He looked at her. 'Unless – unless you meant what you said in that letter – that you made a mistake – you don't really love me at all?'

The lump in her throat almost choked her and the tears she had held back began to overflow, trickling down her cheeks. 'Of *course* I still love you, Alan,' she whispered. 'I never stopped. I only wanted to set you free.'

He shook her gently and his voice was rough as he said, 'Don't you know that when you love someone you can never be free, you silly girl?' He pulled her close and kissed her. Lillian closed her eyes and relaxed against him, letting the kiss drown her senses like the yearning dreams she'd believed would never come true. The kiss lasted a long time but when their lips parted they were both trembling and they clung to each other, oblivious of the amused glances of passers-by enjoying the sunshine.

Alan held her away from him and looked into her eyes, 'Will you marry me, Lilly?'

She smiled sadly. 'Oh, Alan – not yet – maybe not for a long time. We both have a lot to get through first.'

'But we can be together?'

'Of course we can. And we will be. After all, there's lots of time and we still have so much to discover about one another. Besides, I haven't told you everything yet.' When he looked apprehensive she laughed. 'Don't worry. It's nothing shocking. I'm about to open The Laurels as a private hotel.'

'You're kidding!' His face broke into a smile. 'What a wonderful idea! Good for you.'

'It's to help pay back all the debts. It was Hazel's idea. It was either that or sell up and as I've never trained for any kind of work I had no idea how I would earn a living. I'm terrified and excited all at the same time. The advert has gone in, the house is all ready and I've even had my first bookings.' She took his face between her hands and kissed him gently. 'So you see what I mean, we both have a few bridges to cross before we'll be ready to marry.'

'Just as long as I know you're mine nothing else matters,' he said.

When Hazel heard about Lillian's meeting with Alan she was delighted. Her first thought was that he must come to the wedding.

'I'll write an invitation for him now and get Peter to take it round this evening,' she said. 'It's going to make my day perfect having you two together again.'

On Sunday evening Hazel went round to the Joneses to collect Ruby alone. Peter had offered to go with her but Ruby had only met him once and Hazel thought that the girl might be shy and intimidated in his presence. Besides, after much cajoling he had been persuaded to spend Sunday night at a neighbour's house so that the girls could have the house to themselves to prepare for the big day.

When Ruby saw the dress they had chosen for her to wear her cheeks turned pink and her eyes filled with tears.

'Ooh! It's lovely,' she exclaimed. 'But it's too good for me. Rene was right. I look like a scarecrow.'

'No, you do not!' Hazel said firmly. 'Come on now, let's see if it fits. I had to make a guess at your size.' When they slipped the dress over her head it fitted and suited her to perfection, though she was obviously deeply ashamed of the tattered underwear she was wearing. Hazel pretended not to notice.

'Lillian and I are going to give you a makeover,' she explained. Noticing the girl's apprehensive expression she added quickly, 'Oh, don't worry. It's just a nice warm bath with lots of scented bath salts, a shampoo and set for your hair and a manicure. Then tomorrow you can wear a little dash of lipstick with the dress.'

Ruby looked relieved. 'Ooh, it sounds lovely.'

They spent most of the evening on Ruby. While she was in the bath Hazel laid out a set of her own underwear, taking the ragged hand-me-downs away. When Ruby saw the dainty lace-trimmed undies she opened her mouth to say something but Lillian held a finger to her lips and shook her head behind Hazel's back. Ruby got the message. While she sat wapped in an old bathrobe of Hazel's her hair was shampooed and set in rows of tiny pincurls. Lillian found a hairnet and pinned it on for her.

'When we comb it out in the morning I think you'll be surprised,' she said. 'Now, let's have a look at those hands.'

Reluctantly Ruby held out her hands. The soak in the bath had helped to soften the roughness but there was still a dark rim under the nails and the cuticles were torn and ragged. Lillian found her nail file and some cold cream and went to work on them.

'There,' she said at last. 'They'll be as good as new by morning, then we'll put on a coat of clear varnish before you get dressed. I'll ask Hazel to find you an old pair of cotton gloves to wear in bed.'

Lillian was in a deep sleep at six o'clock next morning when she was wakened by Hazel shaking her shoulder.

'Lillian! Wake up. Listen, it's important!'

Lillian rubbed her eyes and sat up. 'What is it? What's the time? Is the house on fire?'

'No. Listen, I woke early and I couldn't get back to sleep so I started thinking. When you open The Laurels you are going to do the cooking and the business side of things, helped a bit by me – yes?'

Lillian frowned. 'Yes. You knew that.'

'And you've got Hilda for the housework, coming in every morning – right?'

'Yes. Hazel, are you crazy? This is your wedding day and all you can think of is who—'

'Shut up and listen.' Hazel put her fingers against Lillian's lips. 'You still haven't got anyone to run errands, do odd jobs and wait at tables.'

'I know. I'll have to advertise eventually. I had thought I might manage without for the time being.'

'Don't you see, you don't *have* to!' Hazel's eyes were shining. 'Wake up, dozy! It's *Ruby* I'm thinking of.'

'Ruby?'

'She could live in. You know that little room at the top of the house – the one you said you couldn't let to anyone. We could do it up for Ruby. It's tiny but we could make it really cosy for her. We could get her a little black dress and frilly apron for wearing in the dining-room. It would look *so* professional. It needn't cost you very much and she'd jump at the chance to escape from the appalling Jones ménage. She'd absolutely *love* it.'

Lillian was smiling now. 'Why didn't I think of that?' She hugged Hazel. 'What would I do without you? You're a genius!'

Hazel breathed on her nails and rubbed them against her shoulder. 'I know. Some of us have got it – others haven't,' she said airily. She looked at Lillian's alarm clock. 'Oh my God! Look at the time! I might be a genius but if I don't start getting ready soon Peter will think he's been jilted!'

The register office ceremony went off well, with Ruby and Lillian looking lovely as bridesmaids with their little posies of flowers. Only a handful of guests attended the buffet reception at Monty's; one or two of Hazel's colleagues from school, Hilda; Jean and the children; two college friends of Peter's, one of whom was his best man. Lastly there was Alan who stuck to Lillian's side like glue.

Hazel looked radiant and Peter was clearly bursting with pride as he stood up to make his speech. There was a ripple of affectionate laughter he spoke the time-honoured words, *my wife and I*, looking down at his bride with so much love in his eyes that Lillian fumbled in her bag for a handkerchief. Alan, who was sitting beside her, silently passed her his own.

'Our turn next,' he whispered. 'By the way, have I told you how beautiful you look?'

'Yes.' She reached for his hand and squeezed it. 'Several times.'

'Mum and Dad want you to come and have a meal with us,' he told her. 'I told them what had happened to you and they wanted me to tell you how sorry they are.' He looked at her. 'They always liked you, you know.'

Lillian smiled. 'Well, we'll see.'

'When am I going to get the chance to look round this new hotel-to-be?' he asked.

'Tomorrow, if you like,' she told him. 'I'll be moving back to The Laurels tonight after Hazel and Peter have gone off on their honeymoon.'

'Why don't I come and help you with your luggage?' he said. 'Then I could see the place at the same time.'

She laughed. 'I don't really need any help, unless you call one suitcase luggage!'

He shook his head, exasperatedly raising his eyes to the ceiling. 'Well, can I come and *not* help then, Miss Independence?'

She laughed. 'Of course you can.'

'We could go for a drink and a bite to eat first if you like,' he said.

She nodded. 'That would be lovely, Alan.' She looked around for Ruby and spotted her talking to Jean. 'I've got someone I need to speak to before she leaves. Will you wait for me?'

He grinned. 'Need you ask?'

On the other side of the room Lillian touched Ruby's arm. 'Have you enjoyed today?'

Ruby sighed. 'Oh yes. It's been lovely. Didn't Hazel look smashing?'

'Yes she did. Ruby, are you still unhappy at the Joneses?'

The girl nodded, her smile vanishing. 'I hate the thought of going back there. If only I had somewhere else to go I'd leave tomorrow.'

'Would you like to come and work for me?'

Ruby's eyes grew round. 'For you? I mean yes, I would. But what as – and where would I live?'

'You could have a room at The Laurels. It's where I live and I'm turning it into a private hotel. The work would be – well a bit of everything really.'

Ruby looked incredulous. 'Oh, Lillian, I don't know what to say. I'd *love* it. But when would it be?'

'Very soon. I think the best thing would be for you to come round to The Laurels and see me. I could show you round and we could talk about it in more detail.'

'When?' Ruby asked breathlessly.

'Tomorrow evening after you close – say half past six? We could have something to eat together.'

'Oh!' Ruby's eyes filled with tears. 'Why are you and Hazel so good to me?'

Lillian smiled. 'I suppose because we're all victims in one way or another,' she said after a moment's thought. 'Of the war; of bad relationships; of just plain bad luck. Maybe a bit of all of that. I've had so much help myself. Now it's my turn to help you.'

There was a stir in the doorway and someone announced that the happy couple's taxi had arrived. They were about to leave. Outside in the sunshine Hazel hugged Lillian hard. 'Thanks for all your help.'

'No, thanks for yours. Have a lovely honeymoon.'

'Have you asked her?' Hazel whispered.

Lillian nodded, reaching for Ruby who was standing nearby and pulling her closer. 'Yes, I have and she says yes,' she told her friend with a smile.

'Wonderful. That's made the day.'

As Hazel climbed into the taxi Peter bent and kissed Lillian's cheek. 'Take care of yourself and try not to get into any mischief while we're away,' he said, Then he glanced at Alan. 'Oh, I don't know though,' he said with a twinkle. He winked at Alan. 'Look after this girl,' he said. 'She deserves the best!'

A moment later they were driving away, the tin can that Jim had surreptitiously tied to the taxi's rear bumper rattling along behind them. Lillian sighed.

'It's all over then,' she said. Alan slipped an arm round her waist.

'No. It's just beginning.'

Alan was impressed by his conducted tour of The Laurels. It ended with the little box room on the second floor. The sloping ceiling came almost down to the floor on two sides and it was stacked with boxes full of discarded articles, miscellaneous pieces of furniture and piles of old newspapers and magazines.

'This is the room Hazel thought we could do up for Ruby,' she said doubtfully. 'Though it doesn't look quite so promising now I look at it again.'

Alan pulled some of the boxes aside. 'I don't know, it could be made into a really nice room with a bit of work,' he said. 'Get rid of all this junk; plasterboard those two walls, a lick of paint and a bit of carpet on the floor and hey presto!' He looked at her. 'When do your first visitors arrive?'

Lillian felt her heart lurch. 'Two weeks on Saturday.'

'Well, looks as though you've got everything else sorted, so why don't I help you fix this room up? Dad's got some materials stashed away at the yard. We'll start first thing tomorrow – right?'

She looked at him in amazement. 'But you're not fit, Alan. What's your mother going to say when she knows you're doing manual work for me?'

He laughed. 'It's only a bit of tummy trouble, not a dicky heart or two broken legs! As long as you keep me supplied with plenty of milky drinks and little tasty snacks I'll be fine.'

'Are you sure?'

'Absolutely. I'm fed up with doing nothing and I certainly can't kick my heels around doing nothing till they haul me in and start carving me up, can I?'

'Don't talk like that!'

He laughed and kissed her. 'When I come out you can spoil me rotten. Till then I'm perfectly capable of being Dan Dan the Handy Man.'

By the time Ruby came round the following evening Lillian and Alan had made a good start on the box room. They had cleared the rubbish, carrying everything down to make a bonfire in the garden. They had swept and thoroughly cleaned the room and Alan already had the two false plasterboard walls in place. Lillian had polished the little dormer window and, hidden away among the boxes she had found a generous length of material, white with little yellow daisies. If she were to borrow Hilda's sewing machine she could make a pair of pretty curtains. It was in this room that she had found the pram and cot that now belonged to baby Patsy; now, also stacked away she found a single bedstead, complete with mattress and a little dressing-table with a rickety leg, which Alan insisted he could fix.

As they were snatching a quick lunch Alan said, 'Pity there's only the one bathroom.'

'That's what Hazel said,' Lillian told him. 'But every room has a wash-stand with a basin and jug.'

'Mmm.' Alan pulled a face. 'A bit old-fashioned nowadays though, isn't it?' Seeing her worried look he added quickly. 'More for you than the visitors. It means you'll have to trail upstairs with cans of hot water every morning.' He drank the last of his milk. 'Tell you what – when the season is over – next winter, Dad and I will update your hot-water system and put washhand basins in each bedroom.'

Lillian shook her head. 'I couldn't possibly afford to spend any money until all the debts have been paid.'

Alan grinned. 'Maybe I could persuade Dad to do it as a wedding present to us.'

Lillian wagged a finger at him. 'That's a long way off and you know it. Anyway, it wouldn't benefit you at all, would it? And once you're fit again you'll be off to university.'

'Maybe I've had second thoughts about that,' he said with a wicked grin. 'Maybe I'd rather be the husband of the proprietor of a private hotel. After all, your mother always said I was after your money, didn't she?'

When Ruby saw the room she was delighted. 'A bedroom all to myself,' she said. 'I've never had a room of my own before. I can hardly believe this is happening to me.'

Lillian was touched. 'It's only a little attic room and I know it doesn't look much yet, but it will be nice and cosy when we've finished and I'll make it pretty for you.' She slipped an arm round Ruby's shoulders. 'It's to be a place just for you, to come and do as you like when you've finished work for the day.'

'It's going to be like heaven, Lillian,' Ruby said, her voice catching with emotion. 'Thank you ever so much. I can't wait to move in.'

CHAPTER FIFTEEN

Ruby finished unpacking her few belongings and sat down on the bed to survey her new surroundings. Her own room; her very own. She could hardly believe her luck. Lillian had made the little room under the eaves so pretty. The walls were painted a sunny shade of lemon. On the bed was a white fringed quilt and there was a real carpet on the floor. Not new of course but clean and soft to her feet. She took off her shoes and revelled in its softness under her toes. At the little dormer window hung the curtains with the tiny yellow daisies that Lillian had made and the dressing-table wore a matching skirt.

To think she would never have to hump sacks of potatoes in from the back yard again or push the handcart all the way back from the auction market in the rain and snow; never have to stand with her feet and hands numb with cold in the draughty shop through the long winter days or lie awake at night unable to sleep for the searing pain of her chilblains. But being free of the Joneses themselves was best of all.

It would be hard to forget the day she'd broken the news that she was about to leave.

'What do you mean, you're givin' me a week's notice?' Myrtle challenged, looking Ruby up and down.

'I – I've got another job.' Ruby hated confrontations; particularly with Myrtle. She had been dreading this one but she knew she had to stand her ground and be firm.

Myrtle was staring at her disbelievingly. 'Another job? What job? You might've asked me before you started applyin'.'

'I didn't apply, I was offered the job,' Ruby said. 'And – and I said yes.'

'Don't believe you,' Rene put in spitefully. 'Who'd offer you a job? You can't do nothing, you're useless, you.'

'And where do you think you're gonna live, pray?' Myrtle demanded, her hands on her hips. 'You needn't think you can stop here and work for someone else my girl!'

'I'm to get a room too,' Ruby told her. 'It goes with the job.'

Myrtle's eyes narrowed. ' 'Ere, what you been up to, young Ruby? Has some feller asked you to be his 'ousekeeper?' She sneered. 'Gonna supply some bloke with *'ome comforts*, are you? Walkin' in your ma's footsteps?'

Ruby coloured. 'I'm going to work for Miss Mason at The Laurels, the hotel she's opening,' she said. 'She asked me at the wedding.'

Rene stepped forward and poked Ruby in the chest. '*You*? In a hotel? I hope she keeps you well out of sight. Put the paying guests right off their grub, you will.' When Ruby failed to retaliate she snorted and turned on her heel. 'Good riddance, I say. It'll be a relief to have you out of the way, messing the place up with your scruffy clothes!'

'I hope you know you have to give me a month's notice,' Myrtle said. Ruby shook her head. Lillian had already warned her that this might happen.

'I don't really have to give you any notice at all,' she said, trying to keep her voice level. 'As you've never paid me a proper wage I'm not really your employee. But I don't want to leave you short-handed.'

'*Short-handed*!' Myrtle gasped and her face turned an alarming shade of purple. 'Well! Of all the bleedin' sauce. You ungrateful little bitch! Me and Edgar have housed, clothed and fed you like one of our own all these years and now you turn round and tell me you're leavin'; walkin' out without so much as a by-yer-leave, never mind a thank-you. Well, you better pack your bags and sling your 'ook right now, my girl, 'cause when my Edgar hears about this I couldn't be responsible for 'is actions. He might well lose his temper and floor you! So the sooner you get out, the better!'

Ruby had been only too glad to leave, hoping as she packed that it would be convenient for Lillian.

As it happened Lillian was delighted to see her. Her first visitors were due at the end of the week and she needed all the help she could get. To Ruby the house looked beautiful, everything shining and smelling of wax polish. There were flowers in vases everywhere and all the rooms were smart and fresh, waiting for their occupants.

Ruby was shown the dining room and taught how to lay the tables – how to fold the napkins and the right way to serve the visitors with their meals. Lillian had written out a list of her duties for each day which she fastened to the wall above her bed so that she would forget nothing. She was introduced to Hilda – Mrs Brown, who was kind and friendly and who promised Lillian that she would keep a motherly eye on Ruby. But when Lillian gave her the little black dress with the frilly muslin apron she was overwhelmed.

'Hilda helped me make it,' Lillian explained. 'We cut up a black silk dress of my mother's and the apron is made out of net curtain material. You don't need coupons for that. It's to wear at mealtimes, when you're waiting at table,' she explained.

Ruby blushed with pleasure. 'You went to all that trouble for me.' She had to keep pinching herself to make sure she wasn't dreaming. 'Oh, Lillian,' she whispered. 'I don't know what to say, I don't really!'

Peter turned the key in the door of the little lakeside cottage and looked at Hazel as he picked up their suitcase.

'Well, it's goodbye to Lake Windermere.'

Hazel nodded and took his arm as they set off up the track. 'And hello to married life,' she said. She looked up at him. 'Thank you, darling for a wonderful honeymoon.'

He bent to kiss her. 'No, thank *you*. Two weeks of sheer heaven. But now it's back to reality – exam results and earning our own living.'

She hugged his arm. 'You're not worried about the exam results, are you?'

He shrugged. 'Not really but you never know with the arts. It's not like maths or English where it's either right or wrong. It all depends on how much you please the examiner.'

'I'm sure the examiner loved what you did,' Hazel assured him.

'Maybe – it's just that the job is conditional on my passing.' He looked at her. 'And now I'm an old married man with a ball and chain.'

She gave him a little push. 'If you call me that again I'll . . .'

He laughed down at her. 'Go on, you'll what?'

'I'll make you cook your own dinners for a month!'

He opened his mouth in mock horror. 'I give in. It's a fair cop, missus. If you are a ball and chain you're made of nine-carat gold.'

'Idiot! I must be at least twenty-two.'

Suddenly the sound of a car's horn made them stop laughing. 'That's the taxi,' Peter said. 'We'd better get a move on.'

The little track leading to the cottage had been too narrow for a taxi to negotiate so the driver had said he would wait for them at the top. They arrived breathless from hurrying, their case was stowed away in the boot and they began their journey to the station and the train for home.

The weather had been perfect for their stay by the lake; long golden summer days with hardly a cloud in the sky. They had wakened each morning to the sound of birdsong and lapping water; picnicked at the lake's edge; sailed in the afternoons and gone for long walks during the warm, mellow evenings, stopping off for a bite to eat and a drink at one of Windermere's hostelries.

One day they had decided on impulse to take the short bus and train trip to Mekeley Moor to visit the school where they had first met. They arrived during the lunch break and in spite of their unheralded appearance they were warmly greeted. Gerald Mayfield looked extremely well and walked with only a slight limp. Anyone who was unaware of his war injury would never guess that he had lost a leg. He immediately invited Peter to look round the school garden, which was his pride and joy. As they walked away Gladys Brompton looked at Hazel.

'Come into the staff room and I'll make you a cup of tea,' she said. As Hazel followed her she noticed that Gladys looked somehow younger. She had changed her hairstyle from the scraped-back bun she had previously worn to a shorter style, curling softly round her face. Hazel was also surprised to see that she was wearing a little make-up – something that softened her rather sharp features enormously.

The staff room looked the same and Hazel took a seat by the window, watching a group of children kicking a ball round the playground. She felt rather awkward and wished she could have gone with Peter and Gerald. Gladys busied herself with the tea making, eventually turning to hand Hazel a mug and the biscuit tin with the faded picture of the king's coronation that she remembered from her own days at the school. She smiled as she took off the lid.

'Nothing much changes, does it?'

'Quite a lot changes as a matter of fact,' Gladys said. 'Miss Jameson has retired and gone to live in Somerset with her widowed cousin. Mr Tebbut finally decided to retire too. We found it almost impossible to find another games and woodwork teacher but we were eventually lucky enough to have found Miss Trent.' Gladys smiled. 'She is remarkably creative and she has managed to get the girls interested in working with wood as well as the boys. This term they've all been making pokerwork letter-racks. And of course when it comes to games she's a lot more athletic than poor Mr Tebbut with his arthritis.'

'She sounds a real find.' Hazel sipped her tea. 'So – you'll be getting ready to wind down for the summer holidays soon,' she remarked, still stunned by the change in Gladys who now, to her surprise turned bright pink.

'Yes,' she said, lowering her eyes. 'Gerald and I are hoping to take advantage of it by taking the honeymoon we didn't have time for when we married a month ago.'

Shocked, Hazel said, 'Oh! Congratulations.' She noticed for the first time that Gladys wore a wedding ring. 'I'm sure you'll both be very happy.'

Gladys nodded, blushing like a young girl. 'Oh, we are.' She paused, turning the gold band slowly on her finger. Then she looked up at Hazel. 'I'm glad you've come today,' she said. 'It gives me an opportunity I thought I might have missed. I owe you an apology.'

'No!' Hazel was surprised and embarrassed. 'Of course you don't.'

'Oh, but I do,' Gladys insisted. 'I behaved appallingly to you – to Gerald too. I have no excuses to offer, except . . .' She glanced at Hazel. 'Except that I've always loved him, as you probably guessed, and I felt – mistakenly – that you were betraying him behind his back. I know better now. Gerald has explained everything.' She stood up and crossed the room to Hazel, holding out her hand. 'Please, Hazel, will you forgive me? Can we be friends?'

'Of course we can.' Deeply touched by the older woman's humility, Hazel stood up and took the hand she offered, then, on impulse she reached out and hugged her. 'I'm so glad that you and Gerald are married, Gladys' she said. 'You're so right for each other and I know you're going to be very happy.'

'I'm happy for you and Peter too,' Gladys said. She laughed shakily. 'Speaking of which, I think it's time we went and rescued him. I know I shouldn't say it, but I'm afraid that Gerald can sometimes get quite boring on the subject of his precious cabbages and beans.'

The first week was over. The Laurels was now officially a hotel and as Lillian waved the last of the week's visitors off she heaved a sigh of relief. Everyone had seemed happy and satisfied with the service she had provided. Hilda had arrived for work the previous Saturday with a flat parcel under her arm.

'Here you are, it's a good-luck present,' she said as she handed it to Lillian. Inside the wrapping was a leather-covered book with Visitors' Book stamped on the front cover in gold lettering. They had placed it on the hall table with a pen and bottle of ink beside it, hoping that the visitors would take the hint and write something in it. After waving off the last of the visitors Lillian rushed back into the hall to see if there was anything written on the pristine first page.

Without exception all of her visitors had written their appreciation.

Lovely holiday – home from home.
Smashing food. Comfy room – what more could we ask?
Can't wait till next year!

Lillian felt herself glow with pleasure. She had tried really hard to make a success of it. Now she knew that she had got it right. Hilda looked over her shoulder.

'Well, well!' she said. 'Not bad eh? But no time to rest on our laurels if you'll pardon the pun, dear. Another lot arriving in a few hours' time. Better get our skates on!' She lowered her voice, glancing round to make sure they were alone. 'And what about our little treasure then? Didn't she do well?'

It was true. Ruby had taken to the work like a duck to water. Nothing was too much trouble. She was cheerful and polite, clean and fresh looking and she had a smile for everyone. Last night when the visitors had paid their bills she had knocked on Lillian's door.

'Lillian, I thought I'd better give you this,' she said holding out a handful of assorted cash.

Lillian looked at her and then at the money. There were several half-crowns and a ten shilling note. 'What is it, Ruby?' she asked.

'The visitors gave it to me,' Ruby said.

'But it's yours. They're tips. You've earned them. The visitors obviously liked you and they wanted to show their appreciation.'

Ruby looked at her, round-eyed. 'You mean I'm to keep it – *all* of it?'

Lillian laughed. 'Of course. Save it up and at the end of the season you can buy yourself something nice.'

Ruby beamed, her cheeks turning pink. 'Thank you, Lillian.'

'Don't thank me. You've earned it.'

Week followed week. The bookings rolled in. Hazel had been right; demobilized servicemen wanted first and foremost to take a holiday with their families, to celebrate and re-establish their family life. The atmosphere was one of relief, joy and hope. The war was all but over; the men were home safe and sound. In spite of the austerity that post-war Britain was beginning to struggle through the feeling was that things were on the way to getting back to normal. Life could begin again.

Saturdays were to become known as 'change-over day.' Before the new visitors arrived there were rooms to clean and beds to change; tables to strip and re-lay with crisp white cloths. There were cruet sets to refill and cutlery to polish. Hilda and Ruby shared these tasks and occasionally Jean would come in and give then a hand with the cleaning. Lillian had the following week's menus to plan; food to order and the laundry to count, list and prepare for collection.

The emergency ration coupons that the visitors handed in had to be checked and the official return form filled in and posted off to the Ministry of Food. To Lillian's surprise Ruby asked if she could do this job. She did it with great efficiency and Lillian also discovered that she had very nice handwriting.

'How would you like to make out the bills?' she asked her. 'I think you'll do it very well.'

Ruby flushed with pleasure. 'I'd love to,' she said. 'And – and . . .' She hesitated and Lillian prompted her.

'Yes, what were you going to say?'

'If you like I could help you with the booking letters,' Ruby offered.

'Thank you, Ruby. We'll give it a try, shall we?'

On Saturday nights they were usually all exhausted. That was when Alan would put in an appearance, whisking Lillian off for a run in the countryside in the van he would borrow from his father, helping her to wind down and prepare for the week to come. It was hard work, but Lillian had never been happier. She loved it more than she could ever have dreamed possible.

It was on one of these Saturday evenings in late July that Alan broke the news that he was about to go into hospital for his operation.

'I had the letter this morning,' he told her. 'Next Wednesday is C-Day for me.'

She looked at him. 'C-Day'

He grinned. 'Carve-up day.' Seeing her shocked expression he laughed. 'It's nothing to worry about. I have it on the best authority that the surgeon used to be a vet and he's done this op at least once before – ten years ago, it's true – and that was on a horse but at least—'

'*Alan*! Please don't joke about it.'

He pulled her close and kissed her. 'It's OK, really love. Joking is the best way to get through it – for me anyway. Seriously, this is routine, you know; an op they do all the time. I'm told that lots of service blokes come down with gastric ulcers. It must be the horrible grub they made us eat.' He looked into her troubled eyes. 'Tell you what, from now on we'll refer to it as my "old war wound" or OWW for short. OK?'

As always he was able to make her laugh, but it didn't stop her from worrying about him. The following Wednesday she was glad she had something to occupy her. As the morning wore on she looked more and more often at the clock, imagining him being wheeled into the operating theatre, put under anaesthetic – then –

and then . . . she refused to let herself think any further than that.

When Hilda and Ruby had helped her to serve the evening meal Hilda looked at her.

'Right, that's it,' she said. 'I'm fed up looking at your miserable face! Off you go now and find out how he is. Ruby and I will finish up here.'

Lillian shook her head. 'He's not allowed visitors this evening.'

'No, but you can go round and see his mum – she must have rung the hospital by now. At least you can get the latest on how he is.' Hilda gave her a shove, pulling at her apron strings. 'Go *on* now. I don't want to see that glum look on your face when I come in tomorrow.'

June Blakely greeted her warmly. 'Lillian. How good of you to come.' She opened the door wide. 'Do come in and have a cup of tea with us, dear.'

In the cosy little living-room the three of them sat round the table where June had just made a pot of tea. She chattered away as she poured.

'I rang just after two o'clock as they said,' she told Lillian. 'They told me that everything had gone well and that there were no complications. No visitors tonight, of course, as he's still groggy from the anaesthetic but normal visiting times tomorrow.' She passed Lillian a cup. 'Bill and I thought that maybe you'd like to go in the afternoon, because of your visitors' evening meal. We can go in the evening. Is that all right?'

'It's very generous of you to let me go first,' Lillian said. 'But I must admit that the evening would be difficult.'

Alan's father looked at his wife across the table before he spoke. 'We've been hoping that maybe we'd see something of you before this,' he said.

Lillian felt her cheeks warm. 'I know. I was just . . .'

'You were afraid I still blamed you for the letter your mother wrote,' June put in. 'I hope we can put all that behind us now. Not just because your mother's gone, God rest her, but because I was very wrong to speak to you as I did. Alan thinks the world of you. We want the best for him and we . . .' She glanced across at her husband who nodded. 'Bill and I happen to think that means you.'

Lillian smiled. 'What a lovely thing to say. Thank you.'

Bill said, 'We think you've been very brave, starting up a business, turning your disaster into something good. We admire your courage. Alan tells us you're making a big success of it.'

'I'm doing my best,' Lillian told him. 'And I'm enjoying it very much.' She moistened her dry lips. 'By the end of the summer season I will have paid off all my mother's debts and even made a profit.'

'Good for you!' June said, then quickly added, 'Not that it would have made any difference to us if you hadn't, of course.'

'It would to me though,' Lillian told her. 'I'd never saddle Alan with debt. Until The Laurels is fully profitable on a permanent basis I won't agree to becoming engaged.'

June reached across the table to pat her hand. 'Well, I'm sure Alan will have something to say about that.'

'Once he's well he'll probably be off to university,' Lillian went on. 'So I'll have plenty of time to prove my worth.'

'What was it that poet chap said about the 'best-laid plans'?' Bill chuckled. 'Just let's wait and see love, shall we? Just let's wait and see.'

Lillian found Alan sitting up in bed looking much brighter than she had expected. She bent and kissed him, putting the flowers and magazines she had brought him on the bedside locker. He looked at her.

'Wot, no grapes?'

She gave his shoulder a gentle push. 'You know perfectly well you're not allowed them.'

He grinned. 'Couldn't resist. So – how are you?'

'No, how are *you*? You're the one who's had the operation.'

'Oh yes, I nearly forgot.' He took her hand and squeezed it. 'Seeing you is the best medicine I could have.'

'How do you feel?' she asked. 'Does it hurt?'

'Only when I laugh!' He chuckled at his own joke and then winced. 'Oooh! I'm not joking either.' He bent closer. 'All these chaps in here have been waiting to get a look at you,' he whispered. 'I've told them all what a smasher my girl is.' He chuckled. 'Look at them all, hiding behind their newspapers, trying to pretend they're not looking at you round the sides!'

'Alan Blakely! I've been worried to death about you and all you can do is makes silly jokes. Now tell me how you really are.'

'The doc tells me I'm lucky,' he told her. 'It wasn't a very big ulcer. It seems that some patients have to have part of their stomach removed but they only had to do a little tailoring job on me.'

'So you'll soon be fit again?'

He nodded. 'Looks like it, as long as I don't go mad on the fish and chips.' Suddenly serious he reached out to touch her cheek. 'What about you love? You look tired. Not overdoing it, are you?'

'I haven't slept very well since I knew you were coming in for this,' she said. 'But now that I've seen you're all right I'll be fine.'

'Want to see my OWW?' he asked, the grin back.

She shook her head. 'No!'

He pulled a face at her. 'Chicken!'

When the bell sounded for the end of visiting time she looked at him with regret. 'I've got to go. The time's gone really quickly. Your mum and dad are coming in this evening.' She made to stand up but he caught at her hand.

'You're not leaving me without a kiss are you? A proper one this time, not just a peck.'

She leaned towards him but his arms closed around her and held her tightly, kissing her hard. 'I love you, my Lilly,' he whispered, his lips close to her ear. 'I can't wait to get out of here.' He looked into her eyes. 'You'll come again tomorrow?'

'Only if you promise to behave yourself,' she said.

'Tell me you love me or I'm not letting you go,' he said.

'Alan! The bell's gone and Sister is staring at us.'

'Say it quick then.'

'All right, I love you.'

'No – like you mean it.'

She leaned close to his ear. 'I love you – very much.'

'That's more like it.' His arms released her. 'See you tomorrow then. Be good till then.'

Lillian walked the length of the ward, her face bright pink as the other patients grinned, one or two winking at her. The one in the end bed even whistled softly as she escaped gratefully through the door.

Much to Alan's disgust he was sent away to a convalescent home in the New Forest to complete his recovery. Lillian could not make the twenty-mile-round bus journey there and back in one day so they did not see one another during his stay there, making do instead with telephone calls, letters and postcards.

On Friday, 10 August Hilda arrived at The Laurels breathless with excitement.

'What about the news then?' she gasped as she took off her coat.

Lillian looked up from cutting bread for toast. 'What news?'

'Haven't you had the wireless on?'

'Not this morning, no.'

'Well,' Hilda was pulling on her overall. 'It's this bomb – this new secret weapon thingummy, atom or something. They've dropped one in Japan and it's flattened a whole city. They reckon the explosion was like a massive great mushroom. Turned everything into vapour, it said on the wireless.' She tied her overall strings with a flourish. 'Them Japs'll have to give in now, won't they?'

Horror-struck, Lillian stared at her. 'What about all the people?' she said. 'It must have killed thousands.'

'I daresay it did,' Hilda said. 'But look what they did to our folks. You won't catch me feelin' sorry for them.'

'Innocent women, children and babies,' Lillian said.

'Like the ones in the Jap prison camps,' Hilda said. '*Our ones!*'

'Oh, I hate war,' Lillian said with a shudder.

Hilda grunted. 'You an' me both!' she said as she stumped off to her duties.

Hilda was right about the Japanese surrender. Four days later the war in the Far East was finally over. The Laurels was full to capacity and there was great excitement as the news broke. Immediately a plan was put into operation for a celebration party. A spokesman came to ask Lillian's permission.

'You're not to provide anything, Miss Mason,' the man said. 'Just glasses and plates and so on. We're all clubbing together and we're going to scout round for drinks and stuff this morning. We want you to be there, of course, and all your friends too. Can't let an occasion like this go without celebration, can we?'

Lillian rang Hazel to invite her and Peter to come and found that Hazel had some excitement of her own to impart.

'Peter heard this morning that he's passed his exam,' she said. 'With distinction. He's gone off to see his new headmaster, but I'm sure he'd love to come, Lillian. We both would.'

'That's wonderful. Give my congratulations to Peter, won't you.'

'I will. How is Alan by the way?'

'He came home from the convalescent home last weekend. He's done very well and the doctor is very pleased with him. Do you think it'll be all right for him to come to this party?'

'Oh yes,' Hazel said. 'After all, it's not every day we can celebrate the end of almost six years of war.'

'I suppose you're right. I'll just have to keep an eye on him. I don't want him eating or drinking anything he shouldn't. I thought I might ask Jean too. She must be relieved. Her Dave will soon be home now.'

'How is Ruby shaping up?' Hazel asked.

'Wonderfully well. She's a real treasure and she looks so much better. You'll hardly recognize her. She's even taken over some of the office work.'

'She always did have very nice handwriting,' Hazel said. 'And she's good with figures.' There was a pause at the other end of the line and Lillian said,

'Hazel – are you still there?'

'Yes, I'm still here. I've just had another one of my brainwaves.'

'Heaven help us!' Lillian laughed. 'What is it this time?'

'Never mind. It's still in the embryo stage. I'll give it some more thought and speak to you about it when I've thought it through.'

The party was an enormous success. Everyone was in high spirits. Somehow or other the visitors had managed to get hold of plenty of drink from somewhere or other and Lillian and Hilda worked hard all afternoon making sandwiches. But, as Hilda remarked later, it wouldn't have mattered if no alcohol had been available because everyone was high on the news that the war was over at last. Jean looked in with Jim and Katie for a couple of hours but she couldn't stay long as a neighbour was keeping an eye on baby Patsy.

'I'm waiting now to hear when I can expect Dave home,' she told Lillian. 'I can't wait for us all to be a family again. The kids hardly know him. Jim remembers him of course, but Katie only really knows him from his photo, and as for little Patsy . . .' She sighed. 'I hope he hasn't changed too much. I hope I haven't.'

Lillian patted her shoulder. 'He'll be fine. You both will. All he'll want is to be with you all again.'

At two in the morning Lillian was still washing up in the kitchen.

The visitors had all gradually drifted off to bed; she'd sent Hilda home and Ruby upstairs to bed just after midnight. Only Alan remained to help with the washing up and refusing to leave until the last glass and dish were put away.

'I don't know what your mother will think of me,' Lillian said, 'Keeping you out till this hour – and you just out of hospital.'

'I'm fine,' he told her. 'I can have a long lie-in tomorrow but you'll have to be up at the crack of dawn getting breakfast for all those people as usual.'

'We've all agreed that breakfast will be at ten tomorrow,' Lillian said. 'So it won't be that bad.'

'Nevertheless, you look exhausted.' Alan put the last plate into the cupboard and took off the striped apron Lillian had made him wear. He looked at her and held out his arms. 'Come here.'

She went gratefully into his arms and laid her head on his shoulder. 'Thanks for helping me,' she said.

'Couldn't let you do it all on your own, silly.' He kissed her forehead and brushed back a stray strand of hair. 'Lilly – once this season's over can't we get married?' he said.

She looked up at him and shook her head. 'Alan, please. You know what we agreed. We both have a long way to go before we can take a huge step like that.'

'I don't see why.' He looked down at her. 'You do love me, don't you?'

'You know I do.'

'And you want to be with me?'

'Of course. But I also want it to be right. I want us to start on the right foot. You've got your education to finish and I have this business to build. By the end of this season I hope to have paid back my mother's debts, but there'll still be the mortgage repayments to meet and there will be months with no visitors at all. With wages and general living it's going to be some time before I can start making a substantial profit.'

'But don't you see? I could help.'

She looked at him. 'How?'

'If I go into partnership with Dad I—'

'No, Alan.' She was shaking her head. 'You can't give up the chance of going to university for me. If you did you'd regret it and I'd feel guilty. I just won't let you do it. We'll get married. I want it as much as you do – but when the time is right; when we're both ready.'

He pushed her down onto a chair and pulled up another one, facing her. 'Lilly, listen. If I go in with Dad we can expand the business. With all the big hotels needing refurbishment there'll be plenty of work. We're even thinking of taking on a couple of electricians too. Dad has always had a reputation for good work and reliability but he's getting on a bit now and he needs—'

'You! He needs you. Oh, *Alan*, that's so selfish!' She was remembering Bill Blakely's words to her when Alan was in hospital and they had spoken about university. *The best-laid plans – just let's wait and see.* He'd had this in mind all along. 'It's emotional blackmail. You can't let your father get in the way of your chance of a university education.'

'He's not! What he's offering me is better, much better.' He reached out and took both her hands. 'Look, if I spend the next three years studying what will I finish up with? A degree and maybe the qualification to do what – teach? Lilly, building up Dad's business I could be earning twice what teachers get – three times – even more. And when Dad retires the business will be mine. Not only that, you and I could be together now. Not years from now.'

She shook her head. 'No!'

He frowned and dropped her hands. 'Why not? What's your objection?'

'I've told you.'

He frowned. 'You don't see yourself being married to a plumber, that's it, isn't it? You want a husband with letters after his name; a bloke who goes to work in a suit, not overalls.'

'You know it's nothing like that. I've never been a snob and I never will be. I just can't bear to see you letting a golden opportunity slip through your fingers.'

'I don't think you quite understand what an opportunity *this* is. Blakely and Son could be the biggest – the best firm in town – maybe even in the county. We'll expand into central heating, electricity, installing bathrooms. The first few years will be hard, I grant you, but once we're established we'll be able to employ others to do the hard work.'

Lillian stood up. 'I can't talk about it any more tonight,' she said.

'But I'm not going to change my mind.'

He stood to face her. 'You're tired,' he said. 'So am I, if I'm honest. We'll talk again.' He kissed her briefly. 'You haven't forgotten that Dad and I are going to put washhand basins in all your bedrooms as soon at the season is over, have you?'

'I don't think so, Alan.' She lifted her chin. 'Not this year. I'll have them put in when I can afford it and not until then.'

He looked at her as though he was seeing her for the first time. 'You know what we agreed,' he said. 'You know that Dad said it was to be his wedding present to us.'

'Yes, and now I can see why,' she snapped. 'Oh, Alan, can't you see when you're being manipulated?'

In his eyes she saw a mixture of hurt and shock. 'My Dad would never try to manipulate me,' he said. 'But if that's how you feel there's nothing more to say.'

'No, because you and your family have already made up your minds, haven't you?' Lillian challenged. 'You fought – almost *died* for your country and now you're letting yourself be twisted round your father's little finger. I'm so disappointed in you, Alan.'

His face was white with anger as he turned and walked out of the kitchen without another word. She made no attempt to follow him but stood motionless as she heard him walk through the silent hall. As the front door closed behind him she sat down suddenly at the kitchen table and laid her head on her folded arms, letting the tears flow.

CHAPTER SIXTEEN

Hazel arrived just after lunch the following day. Not that Lillian had eaten any. It had been 3.30 a.m. when she had eventually dropped into bed, and the sky was already light before she fell into an uneasy sleep. It seemed like no time at all before the alarm clock was shrilling its get-up message and she had to drag herself out of bed to make the visitors' breakfast.

Hazel took one look at the dark-smudged eyes in her friend's pale face and shook her head. 'You look as though you could do with a rest,' she said. 'I'll come back some other time.'

But Lillian reached out to take her hand. 'Please don't go, Hazel. I need someone to talk to.' She opened the door of her sitting-room-cum-office. 'Come in here. We shan't be disturbed. Hilda's gone home for a rest and Ruby's gone into town.'

Sitting opposite Hazel Lillian recounted the disagreement she'd had with Alan in the small hours of that morning. At first Hazel was inclined to brush it aside.

'You were both tired,' she said. 'Yesterday was an emotional day and then there was the euphoria of the party and everything. He'll come round—'

'But I won't,' Lillian interrupted. 'I can't let him do it, Hazel.'

'But surely it's his decision. He's a grown man after all.'

'He's a grown man being manipulated by his father,' Lillian said. 'Just as my mother manipulated me. I'll always regret giving up my education and I believe he will too. And the frightening thing is that he's being made to believe that he's doing it for *me* – so that we can be married.'

Hazel shook her head. 'Oh, surely not.'

'Bill Blakely is so clever. He even suggested that he and Alan should put wash basins in all the bedrooms for me during the off-season as a wedding present.'

'So. . . ?'

'Can't you see the thinking behind it? I'd be in his debt – under an obligation.'

'I'm sure the thought never entered his head.'

'I'm sure it *did*.'

'So what are you saying? That you turned the offer down?'

'Of course I did! I told Alan that they could do the job when I find I can afford to pay for it and not until then.'

'Ouch!' Hazel winced. 'He won't have liked that.'

'No. But I didn't like being accused of being a snob – of not wanting to be married to a plumber. I can't believe that Alan really thinks I'm as shallow as that!'

Hazel sighed. 'Oh dear. So how were things left between you?'

'He walked out. He looked furious.' Unable to control her feelings any longer Lillian choked on the words. 'He's gone, Hazel,' she said, covering her face with her hands.

Instantly Hazel was at her side. 'Oh love, don't. He'll be back.'

'He won't. You didn't see the way he looked at me. I – I told him his father was using emotional blackmail.'

'That wasn't very nice.'

'It *isn't* very nice. No one knows it better than I do. I've suffered it first hand!'

'Lillian, Alan is only considering doing this because he loves you so much and he wants to build a good life for you both. Being apart for the best part of three years is no picnic, believe me. Peter was only away for one year and that was bad enough.'

'I know. Do you think I wouldn't have missed him?' Lillian said. 'But I was prepared to make that sacrifice. I wanted us both to have proved ourselves before we took that final step.'

'Maybe Alan doesn't think you have anything to prove except your love for each other,' Hazel said gently. She took a handkerchief from her handbag and dabbed at Lillian's cheeks. 'Come on, love, try to see it Alan's way. After all, it is a good opportunity. Blakely's have always had a first-class reputation. I know Gran wouldn't have anyone else for her plumbing jobs.' She bent forward to look into Lillian's eyes. 'You wouldn't really risk losing him on a point of principle, would you?'

Lillian sniffed back the last of her tears. 'It's not just that. I'm so afraid it will drive a wedge between us. If it doesn't work out or if Alan later regrets missing university it'll be my fault because he'll have made the sacrifice so that he could marry me. On the other hand, if he turns his father's offer down and goes to university his parents will say that I've driven him away from them. I can't win, can I?'

'I think it's something the four of you should get round a table and discuss,' Hazel said. 'A lot of what you're saying is hearsay. Perhaps you should hear the question from all sides.'

Lillian heaved a sigh. 'There's no point now, anyway, is there? I've sent him away. It's over.' She stood up, silencing Hazel's protests with a wave of her hand. 'That's enough about me,' she said with mock brightness. 'Come through to the kitchen and we'll make some tea. You came round to tell me about this idea you've had and here I am boring you with my problems.'

With some misgivings Hazel followed her friend through to the kitchen. She knew Lillian well enough by now to know when a subject was well and truly closed. There would be no point in trying to open the question again today.

As they waited for the kettle to boil Lillian said, 'So what was your idea; it was about Ruby, wasn't it?'

'Oh that. Yes. It's simple really. You said she was writing letters for you – making out the bills and so on and I thought, why not get her to enrol at night school for a secretarial course?'

Lillian looked doubtful. 'But that would involve typing and shorthand and so on, wouldn't it? I haven't even got a typewriter.'

'Then you should get one,' Hazel said. 'You could pick up a good second-hand one. You should get some proper stationery too. It needn't cost that much and it would look so professional. Can't you just see it with *The Laurels* in lovely dark-green flowing script on the letterheads? Ruby could take over all your admin work.'

'I'd have to pay her extra,' Lillian said thoughtfully. 'I'm not being mean and of course she's worth it, but I'm still having to watch the pennies. That means doing as much of the work myself as I can.'

'It needn't be much,' Hazel said. 'Take her off some of her other jobs to lessen the load. She loves being here and she adores you. I know she'll be happy with whatever you can afford until you're on your feet.'

Lillian brightened. 'I'll see what she thinks, shall I?'

'OK, but don't wait too long. Enrolment nights are next week and the term begins the week after that.'

When Hazel had gone Lillian set about preparing vegetables for the evening meal, glad to have something to take her mind off her problem. She had told Hilda to take the rest of the day off. Last night's late revels had taken their toll of the older woman and she had looked washed out this morning. She had just finished peeling the potatoes when she heard Ruby come back from her trip to the shops. A moment later the girl appeared in the kitchen doorway.

'Can I help?'

Lillian looked up. 'You can start stringing those beans for me if you . . .' She stopped in mid-sentence as she caught sight of the girl's white face. 'Ruby! Are you all right?'

Ruby looked at her for a moment, her eyes huge with distress, then, to Lillian's dismay a large tear escaped and ran down her cheek, followed by another, which she hastily brushed away with her fingers. Lillian quickly dried her hands and pulled a chair out from the table.

'Sit down. You look as if you've seen a ghost. I'll put the kettle on for a cup of tea.' Waiting for the kettle to boil, she sat down and looked at Ruby. 'What's wrong?' she asked, handing her a clean hanky. 'Please – dry those tears and tell me.'

Ruby dabbed her eyes and sniffed. 'I was on my way back from the shops and I passed the Alhambra. There was a queue for the first house.' She glanced up at Lillian. '*Brief Encounter* is on.'

'I know.' Lillian took her hand and found it icy cold. 'Go on, what happened?'

Ruby swallowed hard. 'I – I saw Mum,' she said.

Lillian frowned. 'You mean – someone who looked like her?'

'No! It was Mum. She was in the queue. She was with this American soldier – holding on to his arm and laughing. I know it was her. I'd know her anywhere.'

'Did you speak to her?'

'Yes. I went up to her,' Ruby said, her voice husky. 'I said, "Hello, Mum" and I touched her arm.'

Lillian waited for the inevitable. It came with fresh tears from Ruby.

'She just stared at me,' she said, trying to force the words past the knot in her throat. 'She shook my hand off and said I'd made a mistake.'

Lillian squeezed the cold little hand in both of hers. 'You have to remember that you were just a little girl when she last saw you, Ruby,' she said gently. 'You're a young woman now. It's hardly surprising that she didn't recognize you.'

'I said who I was, though,' Ruby said. 'I said, "Mum – it's me, Ruby". But she just went red and pushed me away. She said, "Look, I've got no idea who you are or what you want, but you've made a mistake. Now clear off before I call a policeman".'

'And you're still sure it was her?'

Ruby nodded miserably. 'I even recognized her voice,' she said. 'I should know by now that she doesn't want me any more, shouldn't I, after all the letters she never answered? But I kept telling myself that maybe she'd moved – got bombed out – lost the address. I even used to have this dream where she was looking for me. Sometimes I even thought she must have been killed in the blitz.' She swallowed hard. 'Even that was better than believing she didn't want me.' She looked up at Lillian with brimming eyes. 'But now I can't pretend any more, can I?'

Lillian's heart ached for the girl. She pushed a cup of tea towards her. 'Drink that up while it's hot. I've put plenty of sugar in it for the shock. Listen, Ruby, I'm going to tell you a secret. My mother – at least the person I used to call mother was really just the woman who adopted me. My real mother gave me away when I was a baby, so you see I know how it feels not to be wanted.'

Ruby looked up at her. 'Honest?'

'Yes, honestly. But it's something you have to learn to live with. It doesn't mean you're worthless. It doesn't make you any worse or any better than anyone else. The problem is all with the person who's rejected you. You have to tell yourself that you are a worthwhile person – make the best of yourself – be your own person in this world, Ruby, and believe me you're doing all those things. You're doing really well.'

'Do you mean that?'

'I certainly do. You're invaluable to me here at The Laurels. I don't know what I'd do without you. And there's something else. Hazel has been here this afternoon and she has suggested that you might like to go to night school at the college where she's going to be teaching and take a secretarial course so that you can be my secretary and handle all the administrative work. How does that appeal to you?'

Ruby's face lit up. 'Oh! Do you really think I could do it?'

'Do it? Of course you can do it, Ruby. You can do anything you put your mind to. Hazel was your teacher and she always said you were bright and that you deserved a better chance in life.' She smiled. 'So you like the idea?'

'Yes, very much. What do I have to do?'

'Well, Hazel said that the enrolment nights are next week. Perhaps you should go round and see her. She'll give you all the details.' She glanced up at the kitchen clock. 'And now we'd better get on or there'll be no dinner served at The Laurels this evening!'

Hazel was upset at the news of Lillian and Alan's falling out. She told Peter about it when he came back from seeing his new head-master.

'Do you think I should go round and see him?' she asked. 'Try to smooth things over.'

Peter shook his head. 'I wouldn't,' he said. 'In my experience trying to put things right between friends who have had a row only makes things worse.'

'But I can't just do nothing. You should have seen her. She's so miserable. And I wouldn't mind betting that Alan is too.'

'In that case it'll sort itself out,' Peter told her. 'One of them is bound to give in. Take my advice and let sleeping dogs lie.'

But Hazel wasn't so sure. Something in the way that Lillian had spoken made her sure that she would not change her mind. Perhaps Alan would change his, she told herself. But a few days later she spotted an advertisement in the local paper. It was a large, half-page spread and read:

Blakely & Son
Valemouth's Premier Plumbers and Heating Engineers
William Blakely is proud to announce that his son,
Alan, will shortly be joining the firm
following his demobilization from the Royal Navy

Hazel closed the paper with a sigh. So Alan had made his decision. He wasn't budging either, and he certainly hadn't wasted any time. She wondered what Lillian's reaction to the advertisement would be.

On the following Saturday two of the couples who were leaving The Laurels early asked to see Lillian. Ruby came through to the kitchen to fetch her.

'We couldn't leave without saying goodbye and thank you, Miss Mason,' said one of the men holding out his hand. 'It's been such a memorable holiday. We've made so many friends and we've appreciated so much all that you've done to make us comfortable.'

Lillian felt her cheeks warm. 'It's good of you to say so,' she said. 'But it's what I'm here for.'

The man's wife gave him a nudge. 'What Tom is trying to ask is, are you going to open for Christmas?' she said. 'Because we – all of us who've been here this week, would like to book – that is *if* you're opening and *if* you've any vacancies. It's been so memorable, what with the VJ party and everything.'

The request took Lillian's breath away. 'Well – I hadn't really given any thought to it,' she said. She looked at the four hopeful faces. 'But I can hardly turn down a full house of bookings, can I?'

'Then it's on – we can all come back here for Christmas?'

Lillian laughed. 'If that's what you really want, yes.'

One of the men opened the dining room door where the others were still at breakfast. 'It's all arranged,' he announced. 'The Laurels is open for Christmas and we're all coming back – right?'

Lillian heard the whoop of enthusiastic assent go up and for the first time since she had opened she knew for sure that her venture was a success. By the time all the visitors had departed her book was full of provisional bookings for the Christmas break and she had promised to write to everyone with the cost of the stay when she had worked it out.

Hilda seemed as pleased as she was. 'Well! That's what I call a result!' she beamed as she started up the stairs to begin changing beds, her arms full of fresh linen. 'And here was me thinkin' I'd have to spend Christmas on me own.'

Later that evening, when the Saturday rush was over Lillian was sitting with her feet up in her sitting room, listening to the wireless.

Ruby had gone up to bed early with a new magazine and the work was finished for the day. Normally it was the time of the week that Lillian loved best; shaking off the busiest day of the week and looking forward to Alan's arrival and a pleasant evening to spend together. Now everything was different. Like Hazel, she had seen the advertisement in the local paper. It had pierced her to the heart that he had taken so little time to let her go. It felt like the ultimate betrayal.

Suddenly the telephone rang, interrupting *Saturday Night Theatre*, to which she was only half-listening. She turned down the volume and picked up the receiver, her heart bumping at the thought that it might be Alan. Her voice shook slightly with apprehension as she said, 'Hello. The Laurels. Lillian Mason speaking.'

'Oh – hello.' To her disappointment the voice at the other end of the line was female and had a cockney twang.

'Can I help you?' Lillian asked.

'It's – I'm Mavis Sears,' the voice said. 'Ruby's mother.'

Lillian was shocked and angry and she made up her mind instantly that she would not allow Ruby to be upset again. 'I see. If you want to speak to Ruby I'm afraid—'

'*No, I don't*! Look, I'm sorry but it's really you I want to talk to. Could we meet somewhere – without Ruby knowing, I mean?'

Lillian was stunned by the woman's colossal cheek. 'I don't see what business you can possibly have with me,' she said.

'*Please*, it's really important,' the woman said.

'If you're thinking of coming here—'

'No! Not somewhere where Ruby might see me.'

'What is all this about?' Lillian asked, suspiciously.

At the other end of the line the woman hesitated. 'I – I'll explain, but I'd rather talk – face to face.'

In spite of herself Lillian was beginning to be curious. 'I'm very busy. When?'

'Now.'

'*Now*? I can't possibly arrange to come out and meet you at such short notice.'

'But I'm already almost there,' the voice interrupted. 'I'm at the end of your road, Marlborough Drive, isn't it? I'm in a phone box. There's a pub on the opposite corner. It's called The King's Head. Can you meet me there, in the lounge bar in about ten minutes?'

Lillian was stunned by the woman's audacity. At the beginning of the conversation she'd made up her mind that nothing would persuade her to speak to the woman who was heartless enough to abandon her own daughter, but now something in the voice on the end of the line intrigued her. She sounded breathless, anxious – desperate almost. 'How did you find out where Ruby was working?' she asked.

'I promise I'll explain. Please, will you come?'

'Well, all right then,' Lillian said. 'Ten minutes.'

She spotted Mavis Sears at once. She was just as she had pictured her, bottle-blonde and brassy, wearing too much make-up to conceal the fact that she wasn't as young as she would like people to think. She wore a very short black skirt and a red blouse and she was sitting at a table in the corner where she could keep an eye on the doorway. As soon as she saw Lillian pause and look round she beckoned her over.

'I'm Mavis,' she said, half rising. 'Pleased to meet you, I'm sure. Can I get you a drink?'

Lillian shook her head. 'No thank you.' She slid into the seat opposite. 'I've had a very busy day, as I told you, so I'd be grateful if you'd say what you have to say as quickly as possible. First of all, though, I'd like to know how you found out where Ruby was working.'

Mavis licked her lips. 'I went to the last address I had from her.'

'Ah yes, all the letters she wrote – that you failed to answer. So you went to the Joneses?'

'Yes. They gave me your address.' She glanced at Lillian and took a sip from the glass on the table in front of her. 'Did she tell you she saw me the other day in the queue for the pictures?'

Lillian nodded. 'She was deeply humiliated by your refusal to acknowledge her.'

'I know and I'm sorry but I couldn't, you see. It was a shock and I panicked. I was with Jesse, my – my fiancé. We've been on holiday here and he – he—'

'He doesn't know you have a daughter,' Lillian finished for her. 'So what on earth made you come here for a holiday?'

'Jesse booked it as a surprise. And to be honest I'd forgotten she was here. It was a miracle I still had one of her letters at the bottom of my handbag.'

'Yes, wasn't it?' Lillian smiled ruefully and Mavis flushed.

'It's all right for you,' she snapped, 'lookin' down your nose – judging me. I don't s'pose *you*'ve ever known a minute's trouble in your life – never been up to your neck in debt and wonderin' where the next penny was comin' from. You want to have had my life – up the duff at sixteen, chucked out by your dad and then dumped by the father – strugglin' to bring up a kid on your own. At least I had her. I didn't get rid of her like a good many did.'

'None of that is any of my business,' Lillian said. 'And I'm not judging you. All I care about is Ruby. She's had a very hard time with people who exploited her. She was even very ill with pneumonia at one stage. But now she's working for me and she's doing well.' She leaned forward. 'Ruby has been through the kind of unhappiness that no child should have to suffer. There have been times when she needed you so badly – needed someone to love and care for her and you let her down. I hope you can live with that.'

'I couldn't have her back,' Mavis said. 'It wasn't safe for one thing – bombs droppin' every night. You don't know what it was like down them shelters. Kids caught things – got ill.'

'You don't have to make excuses to me,' Lillian said. 'Why are you here? What do you really want?'

Mavis took out a packet of American cigarettes and carefully lit one. Blowing out a cloud of smoke she looked at Lillian through it. 'I'm gettin' married,' she said. 'Goin' to live in the States. It's a big chance for me. The first real bit of luck I've ever had. It'll be a brand new start. Someone like you can't imagine what that means.'

'And Ruby doesn't have a part to play in this new start?'

'Jesse don't know I've got a kid. I can't tell him now. It could ruin everything.' She tapped the ash from her cigarette, pausing thoughtfully. 'I couldn't believe how Rube had grown,' she said.

'It's what children do,' Lillian said. 'After all, it's been six years.'

'I wouldn't've known her if she hadn't come up to me,' Mavis went on. 'If she'd been with me from the start it'd be different. Jesse would've known, but now . . .'

'He'll find out how old you are,' Lillian pointed out.

'It's not that.' Mavis drew hard on her cigarette. 'Jesse's family are religious you see; his dad's a preacher. If they knew . . .'

'I can imagine.' Lillian looked at her. 'So – what's the purpose of this meeting? What do you want me to do?'

Mavis sighed and ground out the remains of her cigarette in the ashtray. 'I know you think I'm trash,' she said. 'You think I've been a cow to Rube and I don't give a damn about her. I s'pose I can't blame you. But I didn't want to go away without lettin' her know that I did think about her – I did care. And I'm sorry about the other day.'

Lillian wanted to say that she had a funny way of showing it but she bit the remark back. 'So – you want me to say, what – that I've seen you? That you're off to the other side of the world? You want me to say goodbye for you? All the things you should be saying to her yourself.'

'I've left it too long,' Mavis said. 'We don't know each other no more. She's better off without me. I always was a rotten mum and I don't suppose I'd have got any better, but I didn't want to go away with her rememberin' how I was that day in the pictures queue – makin' out I didn't know 'er.' She gave Lillian a bitter little half-smile. 'I'm ashamed of that.' She sighed. 'For what it's worth I reckon she's fallen on her feet with you. You'll put her on the right path – see she grows up straight. I didn't go a bundle on them Jones lot.' She opened her handbag and rummaged in it, coming up with a small silver locket and chain. 'I want you to give her this,' she said. 'Her dad give it me when we was courtin' – when I thought everything in the garden was rosy. It's all I've had to remember him by – not that he was worth it, but Rube don't know that, does she?' She passed it across the table to Lillian. 'There's a picture inside of her when she was a baby. Tell her – tell her it's best she forgets me.' She got to her feet and gathered up her bag and jacket. 'Thanks for comin' and hearin' me out, Miss Mason. Goodbye.' She held out her hand. Lillian briefly touched the scarlet-tipped fingers and before she could say anything more Mavis Sears was walking away.

The enrolment evening at college was busy but Hazel was pleased to spot Ruby queuing up to sign on for one of the secretarial courses. During a break she managed to struggle across the hall to have a word with her.

'Lillian managed to persuade you to enrol then, Ruby?'

The girl smiled. 'Yes. I'm really looking forward to it. And I've met Irene again. Remember, Irene Thomas? She was in your class at school the same year as me.' She pointed across to where a girl with auburn hair was just signing in. 'She's going to be on the same course as me. Isn't that nice?'

Hazel remembered that the two girls had been friends at school. 'Oh, Ruby, how nice for you,' she said. 'You'll have someone to compare notes with. Good for you.'

She could hardly believe the change in Ruby Sears in the few months she had been with Lillian at The Laurels. She had gone from an emaciated little waif with sad blue eyes in a pale face to a bright-eyed young girl with colour in her rounded cheeks and a burgeoning figure. She realized with delight that Ruby was blossoming into a very pretty girl. As they talked she noticed that Ruby was wearing the little silver locket that had belonged to her mother. Lillian had told her about her extraordinary meeting with Mavis Sears and how the news of it and the gift of the locket had put Ruby's mind at rest about the relationship. The girl would probably never see her mother again, but now at least she knew that her mother had at least felt something for her.

The following week both Hazel and Peter began their new jobs. The first few days were hectic. Hazel hadn't been able to wait for Peter to get home on his first day to tell her how everything had gone. On three evenings a week they only had time to share their evening meal before Hazel had to rush off to take her evening class. The winter promised to be busy, but they were happy, both working in jobs they enjoyed. They realized that they were lucky.

Hazel kept in touch with Lillian, going round to The Laurels for coffee or tea at least twice a week. But she was dismayed to find that the rift between Lillian and Alan was still unresolved.

'Don't you miss him?' she couldn't help asking over coffee one morning.

Lillian shrugged. 'I don't let myself think about him,' she said.

'I don't think I quite believe that.'

'What point is there in dwelling on what's past?'

Hazel felt her hands itch to shake her friend. 'It needn't *be* past,' she said. 'One of you has to make the first move. Why not you?'

'Alan knows how I feel,' Lillian said as she piled used cups on to a tray. 'He's made his choice and it's not the best one as far as I'm concerned.'

'He's working for his father, it's true,' Hazel said. 'But no one could put the blame on you, now, could they? Seeing that you've turned him away.'

Lillian looked puzzled. 'What do you mean?'

'He's made the choice for himself, without any reason other than that it's what he wants to do,' Hazel pointed out. 'That being the case no one can say he did it for you.'

Lillian slowly took this in. 'I suppose you're right,' she said at last. 'Not that it makes any difference now anyway.'

'But you still love him. You know you do.'

Lillian shook her head. 'I'll get over it. He obviously has.'

But in spite of her protests she did miss Alan, lying awake many a night, unable to sleep for regrets, wishing she hadn't been quite so uncompromising, wondering if there was the slightest chance that they would ever get back together again.

As winter set in she began to make plans for the Christmas break. She had visited the butcher and persuaded him to put her name on his 'poultry list'. She had shopped around for what few luxuries there were to be found and she had enquired at the Pier Pavilion Theatre as to the cost of a block booking for the pantomime on Boxing Day. Then she had sat down to work out the menus and the final cost of the three day break, doing her best to be fair whilst still making herself a profit. All of her mother's debts had now been settled and she had been able to have stationery printed and to buy a second-hand typewriter. She worked out that with the profit she would make at Christmas she might even be able to pay back Hazel's loan.

Already enquiries were coming for next summer's holidays and Ruby, keen to try out the new skills she was learning, had typed the replies on the newly acquired typewriter, using the letterheads Lillian had had printed which had *The Laurels* logo in emerald-green in the top right hand corner. Over the following weeks all of the visitors who had asked to come for Christmas had accepted Lillian's terms and sent deposits. They were all set for The Laurels first Christmas.

During the second week in November, while Lillian was shopping for Christmas decorations in Bingham's, she ran into June Blakely. She was trying to decide between evergreens and streamers when a voice behind her said,

'Nice to see them in the shops again, isn't it?'

She felt her cheeks grow warm as she turned to see June smiling at her. 'Mrs Blakely! Hello.'

June frowned. 'Oh dear, how formal.' She touched Lillian's arm. 'Come and have a cup of coffee with me, Lillian.'

'I – I haven't really got time,' Lillian stammered.

'Oh, I'm sure you can find time for a quick cup,' June said, steering her firmly towards the lift.

In the restaurant they sat opposite each other at a table by the window. 'How are things?' June asked. 'Is the business doing well?'

'Very well, thank you. Some of my summer visitors have booked for Christmas, which is why I'm buying new decorations,' Lillian told her. 'The old ones were looking rather limp and tired.'

June laughed. 'I know what you mean. Ours are years old, packed carefully away all through the war years.' She looked at Lillian. 'And you – how are you really? You're looking a bit tired too, if you don't mind me saying so.'

Lillian took a sip of her coffee. There was no point in skirting round the subject. They both knew what was uppermost in both their minds. 'Alan will have told you about the row we had,' she said.

'Naturally. You were disappointed that he was giving up his chance of university.'

'Yes.'

'It surely won't surprise you to know that I was too,' June said. 'It's what I'd always wanted for him, but as you know Bill has always been keen for him to join the business. He's worked hard at the business and he's always dreamed that one day he'd pass it on to his son.' She smiled. 'It's a male pride thing. All fathers have it.'

Lillian shrugged, 'It's none of my business.'

'You thought we were putting pressure on him,' June said.

Lillian looked up at Alan's mother and saw the sincerity in her eyes. 'It was just that my mother controlled me all my life,' she said with difficulty. 'She made me miss so much: my education – my teenage years. It hurt me to see it happening to Alan.'

'I can understand that, but I assure you it's quite different in this case.' June smiled. 'Alan is doing so well, working with his father. He's fit and well again after his operation and they both seem so happy building up the business together.'

Lillian swallowed hard. 'I'm glad.'

'But that's not all,' June went on. 'He's studying for a degree in engineering in his spare time. He's doing a correspondence course.'

Lillian felt a huge lump fill her throat. 'Oh! I see. That's good. I'm glad he's happy and doing what he wants.'

'Not quite. I can sense that there's one thing getting in the way of it all,' June said reaching out to touch Lillian's hand. 'And I hardly think I need tell you what that is. He misses you so much. Won't you get in touch with him, Lillian?'

'I haven't heard a word from him since VJ night. I thought – I thought . . .'

'You both *thought* far too much if you ask me. They say pride goes before a fall. Won't you forget your pride for once, dear? You talk about missed opportunities but this is the worst one of all to miss. All Bill and I want is to see the pair of you back together again, so what do you say?' When Lillian looked away she added, 'Did you say you were opening for Christmas?'

'Yes. A three-day break.'

June paused. 'I believe that at one stage that Alan and Bill were going to lay on running hot water in all your bedrooms,' she said.

Lillian bit her lip. 'I can't afford it at the moment.'

June shook her head. 'As I remember that wasn't the deal,' she said. 'What have I just said to you about pride?' She leaned forward. 'They're going through a quiet period at the moment with the run-up to Christmas. Why don't you let them come and do the job for you? There's still time. Just think what a lovely surprise it would be for your visitors. And when you put your advertisement in for next season it would be a wonderful selling point.'

Lillian was smiling in spite of herself. 'Have you ever thought of a career in the diplomatic service, Mrs Blakely?' she asked.

With a wicked twinkle in her eye June took a notebook and pencil from her handbag and pretended to write. 'I'll send our representative round to discuss the matter this evening, Miss Mason,' she said. 'Now let me see – what was your address again?'

When the doorbell rang that evening just after supper Lillian gave a start. Ruby looked at her.

'What is it? What's the matter?'

Lillian moistened her dry lips. 'Nothing. It's just that I think that might be Alan,' she said. 'I saw his mother in town this morning and she said she'd send him round about – about putting in the wash basins.'

'Oh, the wash basins?' Ruby smiled to herself. She was well aware of Lillian's row with Alan and, like everyone else, wished that they would make up. 'Oh. That's nice,' she said. The bell rang out again and she looked at Lillian. 'Well – shall I let him in, then?'

'Wait! I – I don't know.'

'Well, if one of us doesn't soon answer the door he'll go away.' Ruby got up and looked enquiringly at Lillian.

'Oh – all right then.' Lillian sat with clenched hands as Ruby hurried off. After a few minutes she reappeared.

'Someone to see you,' she said. 'I've got some things to do upstairs. I'll see you later.' And before Lillian could protest Ruby had gone and Alan had taken her place. He stood in the kitchen doorway looking awkward.

'Lillian. Hello.' He came forward, holding out his hand. Lillian got to her feet, the thought striking her that shaking hands with Alan was like being introduced to a stranger.

She took his hand. 'How are you?' She tried to remove her hand but he held on to it.

'How do you think?' They looked at each other and he let go of her hand. 'Mum said you had coffee together this morning.'

'Yes. It wasn't arranged. We just ran into each other.'

'I know – she said. She mentioned that you're opening for Christmas.'

She nodded. 'Some of the visitors who were here for the VJ Day celebrations asked if I would.'

'That's good. I hear you're doing well.' He looked towards the table. 'May I sit down?'

'No – I mean, yes, of course,' Lillian stammered. 'But not here – not in the kitchen. Come through.' She led the way through the hall to her sitting room and closed the door, indicating an armchair. 'Please – have a seat.'

He looked at the chair and then at her, then he said, 'Oh, for God's sake, Lilly, I can't do this. I can't be all stiff and formal – not with you. Look, I'm sorry if I didn't come up to your expectations. I didn't mean to ...'

'*Alan!*' she interrupted. 'Don't ever say you didn't come up to my expectations. It wasn't like that.' She bit her lip. 'I – I suppose I was like your parents really. I just wanted what was best for you.'

'And I didn't seem to know what that was?'

She looked at him. 'Of course you did. It's your life. In the end you have to make your own decisions,' she said. 'If you're not happy no one else can be.' She paused. '*Are* you happy?'

'I'm happy at work, yes,' he told her. 'And Mum probably told you I'm studying for an engineering degree. I'm enjoying that too.' He sighed. 'But you know damned well that I'll never be really happy without you in my life. Without you there's a great big empty gap that nothing else can fill, and it gets bigger every day.' When she didn't reply he lifted his shoulders. 'There, I've said it. But if you don't feel the same then there's nothing more to be said.'

His words had filled her heart so full that for a moment she couldn't trust herself to speak, but as he moved towards the door she put out her hands to stop him.

'No, *please*, Alan – don't go.' She touched his arm. 'Of course I feel the same. If you only knew how miserable I've been. There's been plenty of hard work, it's true, but it did nothing to stop the heartache. At the end of each day there was just me – alone with the realization that I'd stupidly sent you away – lost you; that I'd got everything horribly wrong. I don't care what you do as long as you're happy and as long as we can be together.'

For a long moment they looked at each other then he reached out and pulled her into his arms. When they kissed it was as though all the aching sorrow they had both been through dissolved with an almost unbearable bitter-sweetness. Lillian closed her eyes and drank in the feel and the scents of him that she had missed so much; the slight roughness of his cheek against hers; the power of his strong arms holding her. As the kiss ended the weight of sadness and regret lifted like a cloud, making them both feel a little light-headed. He looked deeply into her eyes.

'I love you so much, my Lilly,' he said huskily. 'It's been hell trying to live without you.' He rubbed his cheek against hers and she tightened her arms around him.

'I love you too, darling. Don't let's ever quarrel again.'

Slowly he grinned; the old familiar mischievous grin that she loved so much. 'What, never? Not even for the pleasure of making up?'

'No, not even for that.'

He kissed her again and for some time neither of them spoke, then Alan stirred and said,

'Miss Mason, do you realize that I've been here for almost an hour and neither of us has said a word about those bloody wash basins!'

CHAPTER SEVENTEEN

Peter's first term at Greymoor Manor school had gone well. During the run up to the Christmas holidays he had been busy coaching the choir for the annual carol concert. It had entailed going back into school two or three evenings a week for rehearsals and as these did not always coincide with Hazel's working evenings, it meant that they had not seen much of each other during the pre-Christmas period. Peter had also kept on a few of his more promising private pupils, which took up most of his Saturdays. As the weeks crept up to the end of December Peter was overworked and tired and Hazel found him becoming more and more short-tempered.

'We really need a break,' she said one morning as they found themselves snapping at one another over breakfast. 'I hate this. It isn't like us.'

Peter reached out to take her hand. 'You're right. I'm sorry, darling. We're getting to be like an old married couple and that will never do.'

'Can't you at least give up the private pupils?'

'I promised to see them through their exams,' Peter said. 'I can't let them down.' He kissed the top of her head. 'Never mind, only another week and we'll be breaking up for the holiday. Just think – time for each other, what a luxury. There's nothing to keep us here so what do you say we book up somewhere?'

She looked up at him, her eyes shining. 'Windermere – the cottage?'

He looked sceptical. 'At Christmas? We could find ourselves snowed in up there.'

She slipped her arms round his waist and snuggled close. 'Can you imagine anything nicer? You and me and a roaring log fire? We could close the door on the rest of the world. Why don't we do it?'

He laughed. 'OK, you're on. I'll get on to it later today.' He glanced at the kitchen clock. 'My God! Look at that time. I've got to go. See you later.'

She went with him to the door. 'Don't forget to book the cottage,' she called.

Hazel had promised to go round to The Laurels and when she arrived she found Lillian, Ruby and Hilda busy hanging decorations. She looked around the hall at the holly, its leaves frosted with silver, and at the gold-tipped pine cones which Ruby and Lillian had spent many evenings painting.

'It all looks lovely and festive,' she said. 'So welcoming for your visitors.'

'I think evergreens look nicer than gaudy coloured streamers,' Lillian said, coming down the stepladder. 'But come with me. I've got something even better to show you.' She led the way upstairs and opened the door of the first bedroom they came to. There, in the corner by the window was a gleaming new wash basin with a tiled splashback.

'There's one in every bedroom,' she said proudly. 'Alan and Bill did them all in just under three weeks. I had to have a bigger boiler too, to supply the extra hot water, and I'm paying for that on the "never never" at Bill's suggestion, but they insisted on doing the other work free of charge.'

Hazel smiled. 'It's lovely,' she said. 'And I can't tell you how pleased I am that you and Alan have made up at last.' She looked at Lillian. 'Any talk of wedding bells yet?'

'We've talked about it,' Lillian said. 'And we've decided to wait until Alan's exams are over and he has his degree. I know Bill is longing to retire and hand Blakely's over to Alan. I want to get this business into the black too.'

'How long will all that take?' Hazel asked.

'Not all that long,' Lillian said. 'We've worked out that maybe by this time next year we'll be ready to start making plans.'

Hazel sighed. 'It seems an awful long time to wait when you're in love.'

Lillian sighed. 'I know, but we have to be sensible.'

Hazel pulled a face at her. 'Who needs sensible?' An idea suddenly occurred to her. 'Peter and I are going up to Windermere for Christmas – to the cottage where we spent our honeymoon,' she said. 'Why don't you let me book it for you and Alan for after the holiday? You'll be ready for a break after all the work you've put in for Christmas.'

Lillian looked doubtful. 'Oh – I don't know. I'll have to see what Alan thinks.'

There was a hint of mischief in Hazel's smile as she said, 'It's my guess he'll think it's a wonderful idea.'

Lillian bit her lip. 'All right,' she said after a moment. 'Book it for me. It'll be my Christmas surprise.'

'Good for you!' Hazel looked thoughtful. 'What a long way we've both come since I came back to Valemouth,' she said.

Lillian smiled. 'You're right. By the way, if my calculations are right I'll be able to pay you back the money you lent me after Christmas.'

Hazel shook her head. 'There's no hurry. I don't want you to make yourself short.'

'No. I want to do it,' Lillian insisted. 'I'm gradually paying back all the money I owe so that at the end of next summer season I'll have some real profits to show in the books.'

Most of the Christmas visitors arrived at The Laurels on the afternoon of Christmas Eve. Everyone was in a festive mood and seemed happy to be back, renewing acquaintance with one another. And when Lillian showed them upstairs there were cries of delight at the smart and convenient new additions to their rooms. Christmas dinner was a great success. Lillian and Hilda had done a lot of the cooking in advance and everything went smoothly. In the evening the atmosphere was one of gaiety with everyone ready to make merry. Lillian, Ruby and Hilda were summoned to join the party and when they put in their appearance they received a round of applause.

It was well after midnight when Lillian at last packed Hilda off home and she and Ruby were washing up the last of the glasses in the kitchen. Ruby remarked happily that it was the happiest Christmas she had ever had.

'It's funny,' she said reflectively as she polished a glass. 'If Mum'd had me back I'd never have had a life like this.' She looked at Lillian. 'She must have cared a bit about me though, mustn't she, to come and see you like she did?'

'Of course she did,' Lillian said. 'After all, she was your mother.'

'Funny to think I might never see her again,' Ruby said.

Lillian took a sideways glance at the girl, but to her relief there was no sadness or regret in her eyes. 'I've never actually seen my real mother,' she said.

'Would you like to?' Ruby asked. 'I mean, you must wonder about her – what she looked like, what happened to her.'

Lillian nodded. 'It isn't all that long ago that I was told about her, but I admit that I am curious.' She tipped out the washing-up water and began to dry her hands. 'Still, no point in wondering, is there? As I once said to you, we have to make our own way in the world.'

'I've got so much to be grateful to you for,' Ruby said, reaching up to the cupboard with the last of the glasses. 'My job and my cosy little room here; and now the evening classes. I love it all.' She took off her apron. 'When I've passed the exams I'll be a qualified short-hand typist.'

'So you will,' Lillian said. 'And able to get a better job, have you thought of that?'

Ruby blushed. 'Oh no! I'd never let you down, Lillian. As long as you need me here at The Laurels I'll be here.'

Lillian gave her a hug. 'I know you will. All the same, we'll have to see about giving you a wage rise in the New Year now that you're managing next season's bookings.'

Once in bed with the light out Lillian found herself wide awake in spite of her weariness. It had been a happy and successful day. And there was still Boxing Day to come. The plan was that the visitors were to take an early evening meal before going off to the theatre for an evening at the pantomime. She had invited Jean and the children to join them. Poor Jean was bitterly disappointed that Dave would not be with them for Christmas, but she had recently heard that it was likely he would be home early in the New Year. Alan was to join them too. Lillian was looking forward to seeing him. There had been so little time to be together in the days before Christmas and she had insisted that he spend Christmas Day with his parents, but she had invited him to lunch on Boxing Day and she planned to break her surprise news to him then.

Although she looked forward to the holiday in Windermere with excitement and delight, and although she was sure that Alan would be pleased with the idea too there was still a tiny seed of apprehension at the back of her mind. They had never actually spent any length of time alone together. Suppose they didn't get along; couldn't find anything to talk about? Suppose – her worst fear – suppose she disappointed him?

The following morning when the house was empty of visitors Lillian and Ruby went upstairs to tidy the rooms. Hilda had the day off so that she could visit her own friends. Once they had made beds and dusted Lillian sent Ruby off to Jean's with the children's Christmas presents. She was to spend the rest of the day with them before they all returned to The Laurels to join the others for the trip to the pantomime.

Lillian heaved a sigh of relief. It was nice to have the house to herself for once and she made her way to the kitchen to begin preparing lunch for herself and Alan.

When the doorbell rang at eleven o'clock she stopped in the act of peeling potatoes. They had arranged that Alan should come at 12.30. Surely he couldn't be here already? She dried her hands and went through to the hall to answer the door. To her surprise a woman stood outside.

'Can I help you?' Lillian asked. 'I'm afraid we're fully booked at the moment.'

The woman smiled. She had dark hair and brown eyes and Lillian guessed that she was in her forties. She wore a grey coat with a fur collar and carried a black suede handbag. Her clothes looked expensive and elegant. There was something vaguely familiar about her and Lillian peered at her more closely, wondering if they had met before.

'I'm not looking for somewhere to stay,' the woman said. 'Tell me, would you be Miss Lillian Mason?'

'Yes – er – do I. . . ?'

'No, you don't know me, but I would like to talk to you. May I come in?'

'Of course.' Lillian held the door open. 'Please come through. Can I get you anything – a cup of coffee?'

'Thank you, no.' In the sitting room the woman put down her handbag and took the seat that Lillian indicated. 'I'm taking a risk in coming here today,' she said. 'I may not be welcome. It's just that I was leafing through a magazine at the hairdresser's and I spotted your advertisement. It surprised me slightly. I knew that if Laura and Alfred Mason were still alive this house would not be a private hotel, so I assumed that they were no longer with us.'

At a loss, Lillian nodded. 'That's right.'

'I thought that the house might have been sold,' the woman went on. 'On the other hand I thought there might just be a chance that you might still be here.'

'Me? You said I didn't know you, but you knew my parents?'

'Oh yes.' The woman hesitated. 'It is a good many years since I last saw Alfred. He was my brother. My name is Marion Mason.'

Lillian felt as though something very hard had hit her in the pit of her stomach. She felt for the edge of a chair and sat down on it. 'You – you're Marion,' she said.

The woman looked surprised and concerned. 'You've – heard of me?'

Lillian nodded. 'Just before my – before Laura died she wrote me a letter. We'd quarrelled and I'd left her to stay with a friend. I didn't actually get her letter until after she died. It was sudden, you see.'

'And she said – what?'

'That she wasn't – never had been my mother; that I was adopted. That my birth mother was her husband's sister – Marion.'

For a long moment the two looked at each other, then Marion said, 'And I expect she told you that I was no better than I should be?'

Lillian got up and went to her desk. She took Laura's letter from the back of a drawer where she had put it. She handed it to Marion. 'I don't know why I kept it,' she said. 'It's so full of bitterness. She was a great one for writing letters.'

Marion said nothing. It took her only a minute to read Laura's letter. She sighed and handed it back to Lillian.

'It's a travesty of the truth,' she said. 'I was much younger than Alfred. He was almost grown up when I was born. My mother was an invalid but Alfred adored me – almost brought me up, you could say. Then he married Laura. I was fifteen at the time and when they were first married I lived with them. She resented me from the start. I think she was jealous of the close relationship that my brother and I had.' Marion paused and Lillian could see that the memories were still painful for her. 'I was talented at music,' she went on. 'I played

the piano and I had quite a good singing voice. Alfred decided to
send me away to study. It was my dream, and for once the plan
suited Laura too. She was going to be rid of me. While I was at
college I met Harry. We fell head over heels in love.' She paused,
lowering her eyes. When she looked up again Lillian saw that they
were full of tears. 'You already know that I became pregnant with
Harry's child.' She reached out her hand. 'You, my dear.'

Lillian's heart was thudding in her breast as she took Marion's
hand. 'What happened?' she whispered.

'Harry and I were to be married. We didn't have any money, but
I hoped that Alfred would help me a little. Harry was so thrilled at
the prospect of becoming a father. He had so many plans.' She
stopped speaking and Lillian guessed that something tragic was to
follow.

'Was he – did he. . . ?'

'He was killed,' Marion said. 'One foggy night in London. He
was crossing the street and didn't see or hear the bus. They said
afterwards that he wouldn't have known anything. In just a
moment it was over. Harry was gone and my world was shattered.'

'How terrible for you,' Lillian said, pressing the hand she still
held. 'What did you do?'

'I went to Alfred,' Marion said. 'He was all the family I had. I was
six months pregnant at the time and I had nowhere else to go. Laura
gave me an ultimatum. She said she would bring up my child as
long as she and Alfred were allowed to adopt it legally. But that I
was never to see you or hear anything of you. Neither would you
ever be told about me. Once I had given birth I was to leave and
never come back.'

Lillian shook her head in horror. She had always known that
Laura was capable of vindictive cruelty but this... 'But Alfred was
your brother,' she said. 'Didn't he have any say in the matter?'

'Laura couldn't have children,' Marion told her. 'And being
Laura she blamed Alfred. This was her way of getting the child she
wanted and paying him – and me back at the same time.'

'She wanted a son,' Lillian said. 'She never forgave me for being
a girl.' She looked at Marion. 'So – you never saw your brother
again?'

'Alfred felt very bad about the whole business. He paid for the
rest of my training and he came up to London to meet me in secret

a few times – till Laura found out and made a scene. I've had a good career in music. I was with ENSA through most of the war. I've made a lot of good friends. I can't complain.'

'And you never married?'

Marion shook her head. 'No. There could never be another Harry – not for me. After those first terrible months of heartbreak my life got better – on the surface.' She looked at Lillian. 'But I've never been able to forget Harry or the baby girl I held in my arms for those first brief days; I've never been able to stop myself from wondering what you looked like and what kind of childhood you had with Alfred and Laura. I still feel the guilt of abandonment and the pain of the sacrifice I made. I thought that if I could meet you at last – even if it was just once, I could ask your forgiveness.'

Lillian shook her head. 'There's nothing to forgive,' she said.

'I wish that were true,' Marion said. 'So – Laura never made that new will? At least you got your inheritance.'

'What I inherited was a mortgage and a pile of debts,' Lillian said. 'Which is why The Laurels is now a private hotel.' She smiled. 'But I'm so glad you came to find me and I hope it won't be just once as you say. I'd like us to get to know one another and be friends.'

Marion's eyes were full of tears as she took both of Lillian's hands and held them tightly. 'I do hope so,' she said. 'It's what I've always dreamed of: to be with my daughter again – Harry's and mine.'

After Marion had left, promising to keep in touch, Lillian went back to her lunch preparations in a daze. It seemed almost surreal that she had actually met her mother after all these years, but knowing the truth about her birth made all the difference. If Marion had not made the effort to come and seek her out she would have gone on believing Laura's twisted version of the story.

Hearing Marion's tragic story suddenly put her own doubts and fears into perspective. Suppose Alan had been killed when his ship sank? He might have died in hospital having surgery. And twice they had almost parted for good – once through her own stupid fault. Just thinking about it made her go cold with fear. Life was so precious, so tenuous. Love and happiness could be snatched away in one fell swoop without warning, as had happened to Marion. She told herself that she should grasp at it while it was there and never stop reminding herself of how lucky she was to have it.

When Alan arrived he found her slightly preoccupied.

'Are you all right?' he asked at last.

She looked at him and once again the tragedy of what Marion had suffered at losing her Harry hit her. A lump came in her throat, she threw her arms round Alan and hugged him close. 'Promise me you won't ever go out in the fog,' she said.

He burst out laughing. 'What on earth are you talking about? Have you been at the cooking sherry?' He held her away from him and saw that her cheeks were wet with tears. His smile faded. 'Lilly – darling – what's the matter?'

'Something happened this morning,' she told him. 'Come and sit down. It's a long story.'

She related Marion's story to him and he listened carefully.

'But now that you've found each other you'll stay in touch?' he said when she'd finished.

'Yes.' She sighed. 'It all seems quite dreamlike. It still hasn't quite sunk in, but at least now I know that I wasn't thoughtlessly given away. I was wanted.'

'You still are and always will be – more than wanted, which reminds me...' He put his hand in his pocket. 'I got you this. I know we've said we'll wait but there's no reason why you can't have an engagement ring, is there?' He brought out a little leather box and opened it to reveal a ring with rubies set in the shape of a heart. Lillian gasped.

'Oh, Alan, it's beautiful.'

'Let's try it on.' He slipped the ring on to her finger, where it fitted perfectly.

Alan grinned. 'There – always was a good guesser. Now, better do this the right way.' He lowered himself on to one knee and looked up at her. 'Will you marry me, my Lilly?'

She laughed. 'Oh, Alan, get up! Of course I'll marry you. You know that.' She took his arm and pulled him up. 'And don't think you're the only one with a surprise. I've got one for you.'

'You have?' He looked round. 'Where is it?'

'A long way off,' she told him. 'In Cumberland. It's a cottage by Lake Windermere and it's ours for four whole days – starting this weekend. We can see the New Year in together.'

He stared at her. 'Are you serious?'

'Never more so.'

He slipped his arms around her waist. 'Just you and me – with no one to chaperon us?' She could see the familiar mischievous grin tugging at the corners of his mouth.

'That's what I said.'

'And aren't you afraid I might forget myself and try to make mad passionate love to you?'

Lillian hid her face against his shoulder so that he could barely hear her next words. 'I'll be seriously disappointed if you don't,' she whispered.